CHRONICLES OF
THE DARK

REALM

VOLUME I

AURON ASTEROTH

CHRONICLES OF THE
DARK REALM

VOLUME I

Editor-In-Chief: Mariel Imperial
Assistant Editor: Thrifty Writings
Layout Designer: Jollie Mar Santos

First Printed: 2023
ISBN: 978-1-7380606-0-3

To those who have a home to call, and to those who might have a connection to their home's indomitable realm, this novel is a commendation to your binding strength, unity, and limitless imagination. May the pages of my book cast the magic of the extraordinary planet and its people, celebrating the tapestry of cultures that come together as one under the maple leaf flag.

Contents

CHAPTER 1

FATE

Angel

"Hey, man, are you ready to go?" I typed on my phone through a cloud of smoke that I waved out of my face before clicking the Send button.

As the sun slowly painted the horizon with its golden hues, I found myself once again waiting outside for Cypher. It seemed like an eternity had passed. I had told him we'd leave at the crack of dawn when we spoke on the phone. But there he was, slumbering peacefully like a baby, oblivious to the person waiting for him. When I looked ahead of me, the sun gave its golden rays, and changed the dark color of the clouds which yielded its darkness to start anew.

My supply of smokes dwindled, which only added to my growing impatience, and my once calm demeanor started to slip away, replaced by a furrowed brow. Frustration welled up inside me, and I impulsively flicked the cigarette, watching it land on the moistened grass in front of Cypher's house. Determined to wake him up with my mighty kick, I finally saw him rushing out the door with all his stuff. All I could do was shake my head and laugh. This wasn't the first, nor the last time he would do this.

As Cypher finally joined me, all flustered and apologetic, I gave him a playful, but heavy pat on the back. "You know, Cypher, you were born to be late," I seriously said, and glared at him. "But I guess that's just part of your annoying charm."

"Sorry, dude," he said while flashing his mischievous grin. "I'll buy the coffee."

Knowing full well I had a full mug and thermos because that was how I roll. We have planned this trip of ours for a while. Camping was our thing, and we made sure to embark on such adventures at least once every month.

The funny thing was we seemed to do it more during the winter months, which might seem crazy to most people. I fell in love with the raw nature of things in the middle of winter. The smell of the wet grass, the whitened green nature, and the cold weather made your mouth breathe smoke. It was so calming and peaceful. Plus, we got a chance to sharpen our survival skills.

I've always enjoyed driving with Cypher. He could keep decent conversation most of the time, considering we were into the same things. We had known each other for almost a decade now. We met at our work, and once we both realized the level of awesomeness that's within us, as Cypher liked to say, we had been best friends ever since.

"Who do you think would win in a fight, Batman or Vader?"

Without skipping a beat, I replied, "Hundred percent, Batman. We all know that you can't beat the goddamn dark knight. He always has a plan ahead of time."

He laughed because he knew that was going to be my answer, that was always my answer.

"Unless it involved some god-like being that can kill him in an instant. That's if, and I mean a big IF, he doesn't have any room to prepare before taking them on," I said with full confidence.

"I can't even fight that logic," he said, while lifting his hands in the air as if surrendering. "You know what would be sweet to see?"

"What's that?"

"Seeing those two together, fighting a fucking hoard of zombies! Now, how friggin' awesome would that be?" He looked at me, grinning.

"You always go to zombies," I laughed. "I should have seen that coming."

As Cypher filled my ears with more of his ideas on how he would survive the inevitable zombie apocalypse, the ride seemed to fly by. Before I knew it, we were in a small town almost half an hour away from our camp. It's called Moondry.

"Hey boys, you're back, huh? Another chilly night in the forest?" A retired cowboy leisurely puffs on a cigar, surrounded by the rustic charm of his modest shop, made us turn our heads. We stopped as we always do, talked to the old guy, and picked up a couple of packs of smokes and our beloved Baileys for our camping coffee.

"Did you hear what that lady inside was saying to the guy over there?" Cypher looked over to the counter where the clerk was talking with a man.

"No?" I looked over in the same direction.

"She was telling him that there have been sightings of this massive animal. They think it is a bear or something. A lot of cows and horses were found butchered all over the land out there." He was telling me this with a big grin on his face.

"I doubt that we have anything to be concerned about, with the number of guns and ammo we bring every time we go on these trips." I raised an eyebrow.

He scowled at me, knowing that I'm telling him to stop being a little bitch.

"I wish I would have brought along my sword, that's all," he said as he laughed with naughtiness.

Cypher had always said that he could take a bear with his sword. I wasn't going to lie. I didn't doubt in my mind that he would make that bear regret his life choices.

He was confident in his skills because he was so good at his sword. But you'll never catch me telling him that, he's already such a modest person. I wouldn't want his head to get big, right?

As we pulled into our camp spot, I saw the view that I have been looking forward to for what seemed like an eternity. I couldn't help but notice the poetic juxtaposition of nature and civilization. The towering pine trees symbolized the wild and untamed beauty of the wilderness, while our well-equipped truck and bags represented the comforts of modern living we brought along on our journey.

It reminded me of the duality between nature and civilization, each with its allure and challenges. I loved seeing the view as we came over the hill. The long rows of pine trees, and mountains that stretch along the western skyline. The sea of thin fog was covering the tips of the pine trees as we made it to the base of the hill.

I rolled the window down and the cold mountain air nipped my skin, greeting me. The open spaces on my head felt cold as the wind went over my head until it whistled inside the truck. But instead of getting mad, I let the breeze be absorbed by my body.

"Man, I love the smell of fresh forest air," Cypher said to me as he always does. He knew that my sense of smell was weakened because of a nose surgery years ago.

"Thanks, man," was all I said with a sarcastic smile as I came to a stop with the truck.

As I stepped out of the vehicle, I was deafened by the lack of sound, which I found very strange. But instead of concerning myself with it, I shrugged it off and opened the back of the truck.

"I'm going to go grab some wood," Cypher said as I pulled out my tent from my bag. It took me a blink of an eye to put my tent up. That was why I always took it with me on our camping adventures. Easy to assemble and less hassle when it came to tidying up.

As I finished, Cypher had come back with enough wood for the night. He started to set up his tent, which was the exact same one as mine. It didn't take him long to assemble it like me. Once he finished, I already got the fire going and the coffee on.

"Life is good," he said to me, snapping his chair out with one arm. He dropped it and took a seat all in one smooth motion. That was pretty slick.

"It most definitely is." I passed him the coffee.

"Do you see the size of that moon poking out of the trees over there?" he said while pointing his finger towards the tree line. "It's enormous!"

I turned my head to check it out. The full moon peeked between the trees, its elegance shining through. And when my eyes saw the endless dark woods, my body shivered. The sound of the branches and leaves brushing at each other as the wind blew, a cold breeze echoed in the campsite.

"Did you notice how eerily quiet it's been out here, like no animals at all?"

"Yeah, I also noticed that. There aren't any cows or whatnot like there usually around here."

I nodded in agreement, looking around. We were in a small open space, and trees were surrounding us. The only light that made it to our eyes and surroundings was the moon and the fire. The flames were being blown by the wind as the air started to get stuffy. The shadows coming from the trees seemed to get bigger as the wind whistled. The space we stayed in started to get uncomfortable because it was small and cramped.

"Maybe they gathered up somewhere and stayed where they couldn't be seen. You know, because of those bear attacks we heard about back in town," I finished as I lit up a cigarette. Cypher soon did the same as we sat there in thought. We watched the remaining light disappear and the moon getting brighter.

I emptied the rest of the coffee into my mug after I topped off Cypher's when he looked over at me.

"Do you think we would get a reward for taking that bear down?"

I laughed at the thought, although it was something dangerous. Taking the bear down would be worth it, but risky. We would gain a new experience that we have never had before. Sure, we have hunted, but never a predator like that. The reward would just be a bonus.

"I feel like there wouldn't be a reward for such a thing. It would be more like questions and hopes that we got the right bear." I laughed as I lit a smoke. "Our best bet, if we did run into it, would be to bury it."

Cypher winced at the thought of digging a big deep hole using only our little camping shovels. I laughed at his expression.

As the fire crackled and flickered, the flames danced like fiery storytellers recounting ancient tales and sharing laughter like sparks leaping into the night sky. We found ourselves captivated by the warmth and the company, losing track of time and becoming one with the magical ambiance.

When the night wore on, we finally decided it was time to bid farewell to the mesmerizing blaze. With a bittersweet reluctance, I threw more wood on the fire, not wanting to let go of its comforting warmth while we slept.

Meanwhile, Cypher gathered our leftover garbage and cooler, deftly tossing them into the back of the truck with a sense of responsibility and care.

As I peered into the dwindling flames, their golden glow cast dancing shadows on my face, and I felt a certain sense of melancholy, knowing that the night's enchantment was ending. But suddenly, the tranquil night was interrupted by a loud, powerful howl that echoed through the trees, penetrating our eardrums from all angles. It was as if the wilderness itself vocalized its grandeur and untamed spirit.

In that moment, our eyes met, and we shared a mix of awe and trepidation. The forest seemed to come alive with unseen forces, as if nature itself acknowledged our presence and asserted its dominion over the night. It was a moment of deep connection, reminding us that we were merely visitors in this majestic realm.

"Wolf?" Cypher walked up beside me with a puzzled look on his face holding his rifle at the ready.

"Must be. It sounds close," I shrugged and started walking towards the tents as I slowly let my hand off my side where I kept my Suzy.

"Maybe, those wolves will keep that bear busy all night." Cypher laughed as he headed towards a tree where he rested his rifle down while he did his business before making his way to his tent to settle in.

I woke up to a loud rustling outside of my tent. With an eclectic sound of metal scratching, I could tell it was coming from the back of the truck. I remembered that we packed everything away back into the cooler. So, unless this animal had an incredible sense of smell, I doubted that it would know something was in there.

My hands searched for my weapon while my eyes were fixated on the outside of my tent. When I felt the long cold metallic frame of my one and only Susan, I looked at the shadows reflecting across my tent as most of it was just dancing leaves. When I saw the passing of a quick shadow, I immediately tensed up on my rifle.

I started undoing the zipper of my tent and noticed that Cypher did the same thing. We immediately locked eyes and nodded as if we both understood each other's minds. We moved slower than the hour hand of a clock as we moved towards the sound, trying to keep the noise to a minimum.

Luckily, whatever that creature in the truck was, it gave no reaction. Much of the sound Cypher and I produced was covered nicely by the sound of the whistling wind and the moving leaves and branches.

I stopped in my tracks while aiming at the darkness. I glanced at Cypher as I didn't hear any of his careful steps anymore. Nervous that something might have happened to him, I turned my head to search for him. There, near the first tree, just a few inches away from his tent, he picked up his weapon. He grinned at me as he checked his bullets before moving towards me.

I shook my head at him, as he was pointing his rifle in front of his body. Even though we couldn't see the shadow clearer, we were both in a defensive stance. Turning back towards where I had aimed previously, I caught Cypher flipping me off.

Cypher and I started to stroll toward the truck with deadly determination. As we got closer, I saw a passing silhouette. The dying radiance from the firepit didn't help to guide us to see what it was. Though my mind was already convinced that it was no bear. I had never seen a silhouette of a bear that looked like that. I looked over towards Cypher as he mouthed at me.

"That's no bear."

In the darkness of the dense forest, our campsite seemed eerily isolated. The crackles of the campfire provided the only source of light and warmth. It cast dancing shadows on the trees around us.

We noticed while the noise had stopped. We turned our backs towards the direction of the creature. My heart started to beat loudly and faster, and I felt a rush of adrenaline surge through my veins. My eyes strained to get a clearer look, hoping it wasn't a bear, but my mind couldn't shake the feeling of impending danger.

I always prided myself on keeping my composure calm in most situations, but my body knew that this situation was very different from any other event in my whole life, and my heart let me know this. Fear coiled in the pit of my stomach, and my hands trembled ever so slightly as I gripped my weapon tighter.

Perpetuity passed while we stared, our senses on high alert. The atmosphere grew tense, and every rustle of leaves amplified our unease. The silhouette of the creature remained shrouded in darkness, leaving us guessing its intentions.

Then, suddenly, it leaped from the top of the truck and landed gracefully on the forest floor. The impact had so much force that it produced a vigorous wind, knocking both Cypher and me down on our asses.

We groaned in pain, but the sight of the creature's swift movement jolted us back into action.

With the adrenaline that coursed through our veins, we steadied our weapons and took aim at the potential threat. The air filled with tension as we unleashed a barrage of bullets towards the shadowy figure. The sounds of gunshots reverberated through the forest, echoed in the distance, but the creature seemed unaffected, almost ethereal.

The bullets either hit the ground, sending sprays of dirt and debris into the air, or simply vanished into the darkness, as if the creature was beyond our reach. It moved with an otherworldly grace, elusive and enigmatic.

As fear and confusion mixed with determination, we knew that this encounter was far from over. The forest felt like an ancient, mysterious entity, holding secrets beyond our comprehension. With our hearts pounding and senses heightened, we braced ourselves for whatever might come next, knowing that our survival depended on unraveling the mystery that lurked in the shadows.

We had no time to get back to our feet as it approached us in a quick motion. Both of us backed our bodies up while still sitting our asses on the rough ground. I looked over to see Cypher fighting a jam in his rifle.

I raised my gun, and before I could pull the lever back, my whole body froze. A low, sinister growl came from the beast that quickly haunted me to the core. Before I could even act, a searing hot pain enveloped my calf.

"Oh fuck! Fuck!" I was pulled with ferocity right under the beast. I couldn't help but struggle to free my leg and screamed for help.

"Hey! Hold on! I'm coming!" Cypher's voice rang out, desperate and determined.

I only stopped moving and breathing when I felt his hot, putrid breath right on my face. The body of this creature was enormous. It immediately covered my whole body and overshadowed the spaces on both sides.

The moon's bright rays illuminated the top of the creature's head. The creature's face was dark, and only its mildly glowing yellow eyes were enough for me to think that my time was ending.

Its growl pierced my every nerve and muscle. I gulped down the lump of scared emotions as I moved my hand slowly towards my sheath as the creature's face moved closer to mine; I swiftly plunged my knife hilt deep into its leg. A light flashed through my eyes as memories of my life flew through my mind. My death was my last thought.

I was pulled out of my head by my hand ripping free of the hilt as the creature reared back in pain, I caught a glimpse through the splinters of wood in slow motion as a massive log made its way across the beast's head for what seemed like the second time. My eyes searched wildly around the creature's enormous body when I caught a glimpse of Cypher between the splinters.

His concerned face directed towards me. We were both breathing heavily. He stretched out his hand to help me, but before he could reach my hand, the beast lashed out and struck him faster than I'd seen anything move.

"Watch out, Cypher!" I yelled; my heart pounded in my chest.

I heard a loud bang as his back hit the tree unbelievably hard. My eyes started to get blurry as my breathing became shallow. A cold feeling rushed all over my body. My heart sank with the thought that my friend had just been killed.

"Cypher!" I tried to scream as I saw my best friend's lifeless body. He fell to the ground, only a faint whisper escaped my lips.

"Cypher, please be okay," I pleaded, pain induced tears welled up in my eyes.

I moved an inch to rush over to him, but a deafening roar made my body freeze up like a stone. It brought my mind back to the life-or-death situation I was in right now. Its focus was on me once again. Its eyes started to glow brighter as I saw its mouth drooling. I tried to roll my body toward my weapon while trying to get a distance from the pursuing Goliath.

"Come on, think! You can do this!" I encouraged myself, my heart racing.

Time crawled as the tower of fur approached me to claim my life. The wind was so strong that it carried an ember from the smoldering fire to the pine branches that lined the forest floor, it ignited a fallen pine branch near me. I quickly grabbed the branch and swung in front of me to try to chase away the approaching shadow.

As I kept on swinging the branch, the pine needles blazed brilliantly and with too much intensity. The once small ember had grown and now the whole forest floor that surrounded us had ignited. The surging flames brought tremendous heat and light skyward.

The light got brighter and blinded my eyes, leaving only the heat which felt like it had burned my lungs. My eyes cleared just as I got a glimpse of what I could only describe as a giant gorilla with massive canine features. The beast's howl intensified before it took off into the darkest part of the night.

My eyes couldn't believe what I had just seen. I've encountered many different animals, but this one was probably the scariest and largest I've ever witnessed. Afraid that the beast would come back, I didn't move an inch. Even my breath stopped while searching the dark forest where the beast had gone.

A couple of seconds passed by, and nothing but the sound of the dancing branches and leaves could be heard at the campsite. I laid my head back, not minding the small stones poking my back. The adrenaline that surfaced through my body had died, and the pain from being dragged came back. My eyes blended with the night sky as darkness started to envelop my vision.

When I blinked my eyes, my feet started to walk down an old dirt path. Surrounded by tall yellowish grasses, this place seemed awfully familiar to me. My hands spread out automatically, feeling the corn plants on each side as my body passed them.

My head looked up, and a new feeling spread like wildfire in my body. The sky was as if the entire galaxy was lined up to plaster each planet like a portrait. Each star got brighter as I gazed over them.

I closed my eyes and took a deep breath. My face could feel the wind blowing freshly and making the corn plants dance along. When my eyes opened, the sky was normal again.

The corn that was surrounding me was now gone. There was nothing but a white empty endless field.

Putting my feet in motion to go further down the path, my vision noticed that there was a large silo a meter away from me. My body didn't stop walking.

As my vision got clearer, I could see a large shadowy shape standing on top of the object. My feet stopped when two big yellow glowing diamonds appeared where the eyes should be.

My body stood there frozen. Stunned by what I was seeing. The shadow grew larger while it rose onto the silo, then it jumped from the top and hit the ground.

My eyes blinked at the impact. The familiar emotion surged all over my body while my feet were running through the corn maze. I could hear something substantial behind me. It shredded the field as it got closer and closer. But my body never stopped to look back. I ran as fast as I could.

After a few seconds, I could see my truck off onto the horizon. The odd thing was it never seemed to get any closer. I tried to run faster, but something had grabbed hold of my leg.

My feet tripped and fell into my truck door. I heard my keys fall under the truck. My body dropped down, and I started to search for them. The grip on my leg was pulling me out under the truck.

When it succeeded, a giant shadow covered my line of vision. It felt like those bright eyes were sucking my very soul. I could feel its hot breath.

Its mouth was opened wide, and a roar that pierced my mind started flowing into me filling my eyes with its shadow. Just before the darkness consumed my soul, the glowing bite marks on my leg started to sting.

My eyes felt heavy as a light flashed on and off in front. Everything was so bumpy and stifling. I had no idea what was going on around me. My body was too tired and feeling numb for so many reasons. I heard a muffled voice that sounded miles away ringing in my head.

"Are you alright?" Was that the words it said?

The low, worried tone was very familiar. And the face of my best friend popped into my head. Sounded a lot like Cypher, but I was unsure.

When my eyes opened, the feeling of being lifted into the sky made my vision spiral. This feeling, am I in the truck? Trying to move my eyes around, but everything around me was foggy.

"Angel? Are you awake now? Are you all right, man?" The words were clearer this time.

I shook my head, and when my eyes got a steady look, we were now racing down the road. I looked to my side and saw Cypher driving the car with a deep frown on his forehead. His right hand was on the wheel, and his left hand was directed at me.

"What . . . what happened?" I incoherently asked as several events played in my mind.

"You've lost a lot of blood, man. Put your hands on your leg and keep the pressure on your wound."

I looked down at my leg, his hand was pressing the blood-soaked blanket. I was staring at it for a second. When my eyes blinked, certain flashbacks came back to me, including the insufferable pain overflowing from my leg. My heart panicked when Cypher's hand left the blanket, and my blood started to flow like a broken faucet. I immediately pressed my hands down onto the blanket on top of my leg.

"What the fuck was that thing?" I asked while gritting my teeth in pain and anger.

"I'm not sure. I never really got a good look at it before it knocked the fuck out of me," he replied without looking back at me.

His eyes were focused on driving. Now that my mind remembered a few parts of what happened, I saw blood coming down from his forehead and a few moderately deep cuts on his jaw. I was suddenly pulled towards the window as he made a sharp turn that almost put my head through the glass. Gladly, there was a window to stop my body from being thrown out.

"When I woke up, you were knocked out, surrounded by blood. I had to drag your fat ass into the truck, so just save your strength and keep that pressure on."

I heard a chuckle and laughed a little bit because I was maybe 190 pounds soaking wet. I sprawled over the seat and tried to remember what happened the night before. However, my head was foggy. I was unsure if it was a dog or a bear. But it was clear as crystal that the creature was a monstrous animal.

The sunlight that shined through the truck window warmed my face. I tried concentrating on it. I felt the amount of pain and light-headedness due to all the blood draining out of me. I needed to distract my mind for a second.

I must have dozed off because I was already lying in bed when I opened my eyes. My lips curved upward, thinking that what happened was a dream, but I felt scared when I felt the stingy painful wound on my leg. I looked around and realized it wasn't a hospital. The room was small. Well, a little clinic, perhaps?

I saw Cypher talking to a cop and a person with a lab gown. I looked down at my leg and noticed it had been cleaned and wrapped. It felt a bit uncomfortable, but it was much better than before. I lifted my head as the Doctor came towards me.

"Hi. You can call me Dr. Linux. Your friend over there saved your life."

"And he will never let me live that down," the words escaped under my breath.

"What was that?"

"Oh, nothing. How's my leg, doc?"

She took out her clipboard and flipped a few pages. When she read what she was looking for, she put down the clipboard at my side before answering me.

"Well, besides the 49 stitches and blood loss, it seems you are healing rather fast." She looked down at my leg and examined the bandages.

"How long will I have to be in this bed?" I winced as she touched my cuts.

"I'd say for the day. But you don't seem to be the kind of guy that wants to sit around here all day. So, if you can stand on it with no problem, then I do not see why you couldn't leave anytime you'd like." She looked over towards a cop and Cypher as they walked up.

"If you'll excuse me, I have other patients." She turned to leave.

"Thanks, doc," I said flatly.

I watched the doctor walk past the two and stop and lean into Cypher's ear and whispered something I couldn't hear before she finally departed the room.

"I'm Officer Neil." My attention was pulled toward the officer as he brought out a small notebook and pen from his pocket.

"I would like to ask you a few questions about what happened."

"Didn't Cypher tell you what happened already?"

"Yes. Yes, he did, but we need to get both sides of the story. It's just procedure, especially when someone shows up at a hospital with an unconscious and wounded individual. Plus, your friend over here said that he got incapacitated when he was struck and hit the tree, so we don't quite know what happened after that."

I spent a good part of an hour telling the officer what I recalled that night.

Every time words came out of my mouth to describe what happened; it sent shivers down my spine. Trying to think back on that beast I saw and what exactly it was, this made my leg ache unbearably.

"You ready to get the fuck out of here?" Cypher walked up, passing me a cup of coffee in one of those cheap little Styrofoam white cups he probably got in a vending machine.

"If it means I can get a real cup of coffee, then yes," I said as I took another sip of the cheap brew.

I packed up my things and headed out towards the truck. It was a long uneventful ride as we headed back towards the camp to gather up our gear. We didn't speak much on the trip.

I didn't think Cypher was ready to discuss what happened, or maybe he was still trying to piece it together by himself before blurting out words.

Once we arrived at the camp, we immediately packed our stuff. I stared down at the dried, splashed blood on the ground for a long while. I could still feel the breath of the creature on my face. I couldn't help but shudder.

"I will never, and I mean, never, forget to put our guns in the tents again." Cypher was behind me, trying to pull the jammed shell from his gun.

"I agree with you on that. Listen, I just want to say thanks, man, for what you did."

"What do you mean?" He stopped and looked towards me, confused.

"I saw you attack the creature and take its attention off of me when it took me down, even if it could have killed you."

He started to laugh. "I don't think it was big enough to say thanks, Angel."

"Always so modest." I shook my head.

I threw my last bag into the truck. Kneeling and grabbed some charred dirt off the ground, and watched it fall between my fingers.

"It was pure luck that the fire erupted at that very moment. I can't even imagine what would have happened to us without that fire."

"I don't know, man. I passed out at that point, remember?" Chuckling to me as he rubbed the goose egg on his head.

"Let's just get out of here." I rose and brushed my hands together to get the dust off while heading to the truck.

The ride was quiet, but what were we to talk about anyway? We had narrowly escaped death from some unknown creature. I wanted to get home and jump in my bed. My leg felt as if burning venom was coursing through it. With my palpitating heartbeat, it was a good thing I wasn't driving.

After what felt like forever, I woke up sitting in front of my house. "Sorry, man, I didn't mean to sleep the whole ride."

"It's all right. You need the rest anyway, Grandpa." He smirked with a hint of silliness even though his eyes were tired. "I'm going to head out now. I want to shower so bad, and I still have a bit of a drive to get home. Are you okay being by yourself?"

"What do you think of me? A baby? I'm fine, man. I'm probably going to shower before I sleep for the next few days."

He patted my shoulder while laughing. "All right, man. I'll message you later."

I watched him get inside the truck. He turned on the engine and stuck out his hand in the window to raise his middle finger in the air. I laughed at him and shouted a curse. Shaking my head, I tried to stand up. When I successfully entered my house, a sudden rush of relief and safety spread in my heart.

The shower felt great besides the hot water running down my leg; flashes of that night were raining down on me from every drop of water. I needed sleep. My bed called my name. My eyes grew heavier as I laid my back on the soft mattress. Sleepiness took its grasp and summoned me to darkness.

CHAPTER 2

BEWILDERED

Angel

My eyes opened, and I struggled to focus as my surroundings came into view. The room was dimly lit, with a soft glow emanating from a solitary lamp in the corner. The furniture, mostly old and worn, included a creaky wooden bed, a small nightstand cluttered with medicine bottles, and a dusty chair in the corner. The air felt stale, carrying a faint scent of musty old books and something else that I couldn't quite identify at first.

My eyelids felt heavy as if they wanted to remain closed.

And they did. I closed my eyes once again and was disrupted by the muffled knocking that travelled into my room. The knock continued to grow louder as if encouraging me to wake up.

The first thing I realized the moment my eyes opened, and my vision got clearer was my room and the utter darkness that surrounded me.

I groaned and buried my face in the pillow. As my nose pressed on the pillow, I could swear I smelled something rotting, but only for a split second. I knew that my smell was gone for the most part, but sometimes it sneaked up on me and at the worst of times, I was sure of it considering my luck. I immediately lifted my head and glared at my white pillow. I tried to adjust my sight to the dark as I squinted down toward my discolored sheets.

The sound of relentless knocking snapped me out of my attempt to achieve night vision. Each thump reverberated through the dimly lit room, filling it with a sound of urgency. "I'm coming! Geez. Stop being so impatient," I muttered, my heart already pounding in my chest. "You're going to have to wait for me to limp my ass down there!"

I swung my legs over the edge of my bed, trying to be very careful as I didn't want to feel any hellish pain. Gently resting my hurt leg down to the floor while trying to apply a small amount of pressure. To my surprise, after a second of bracing myself and waiting for the pain to travel from my foot up my whole leg, the nightmarish pain didn't reach my body at all.

My forehead furrowed in confusion. I looked at my supposedly injured leg. It still felt tight, and the bandage was still wrapped around my leg, indicating that I had injured it.

But now it didn't feel like anything, other than . . . normal? I still couldn't believe that there was no pain at all. I tried to bounce my foot on the floor.

I moved the leg where my wound was supposed to be a couple of times before deciding to take it to the next level of this challenge. I clenched my teeth and tried to breathe in and out for a second before standing up. Miraculously, I still felt no pain, stabbing or a mild ache.

A small celebratory smile crept upon my lips. I tried to stomp my feet on the floor and tried jumping multiple times to confirm it once more. As I celebrated my healed leg, the pounding on the door grew louder. The happiness that I could walk again didn't leave me as I walked downstairs.

After a few steps down the stairs, I realized that the loud thumping of my feet was louder than usual. It almost looked like the stairs were bowing down under each step, and the creaking was ultra loud. My train of thought was soon cut off with another set of knocks.

The pounding of whoever that person was, looked like he or she wanted to break my door and receive a foot in their ass. My forehead lines were getting deeper as I took the rest of the steps down when we heard the person starting to yell. It was Cypher.

"Angel?! What the fuck, man? I know that you're in there, Angel. Wake your lazy ass up, dude!"

Of course, it would be Cypher. He would be the only one persistent enough to keep knocking on my door like a maniac, my neighbors must love me, definitely not him though. I shook my head and started to unlock the door. As I turned the knob and pulled, I had to tilt my body to the side quickly as his fist that was about to knock on my door almost landed on my face.

"Hey, Cypher. What a nice greeting for an injured friend, huh?" I said while glaring at his fist.

"Angel! Man! Where the fuck have you been, dude?" he said with a squinted and suspicious stare at me. He put down his hand and I saw him holding a bag in the other hand.

"What the hell are you talking about?" I asked him. I must have had a confused look on my face because he narrowed his eyes at me.

I opened the door wider, signaling him to enter. Cypher came bowling right inside the house. He knew his way to the kitchen without even looking back at me.

I simply shook my head instead of mentioning that he didn't take his shoes off. I still felt drowsy. I didn't have the energy to bring this to his attention, I watched him as he made his way through the batwing doors and towards the table. I closed the door and followed him.

He placed the bag he brought down on the table. He opened his mouth to say something but when he saw me walking towards him, his eyes grew wider in surprise.

"Your leg, dude! I see your leg is doing pretty well," he said.

"Yeah. It's quite strange because I don't seem to feel any pain at all when I put pressure on it. I haven't had the chance yet to look under the bandage though."

"Well, you do heal pretty fast. considering the wound that you have, and it has only been a week. I feel like it should still be pretty tender. We should look at it now," Cypher said with a grin.

"Yeah, that's probably good—" I stopped in the middle of my sentence and looked at him with an unbelievable stare. "Wait, what? A week?"

"Yeah, man. Why are you looking at me as if you didn't know?" He laughed at my reaction as he sat down.

I eyed his expression as if he tried to pull a prank on me. Which he often does so it was a bit hard to take him seriously at the best of times. I sat down in front of him while still eyeing him and waiting for him to burst out laughing.

"Dude, I've been trying to get a hold of you for a week now. I thought that either you have been busy or that you wanted to relax after that day," he said in a serious tone. He grabbed some fries out of the bag he brought. The aroma of freshly cooked burgers and fries wafted from the bag, enticing my senses.

Burgers did sound tempting, and I couldn't help but smile as Cypher popped a fry into his mouth. "Burgers make me feel better," Cypher said between bites.

As he munched the fries, I was only left confused. I looked around to find a calendar and remembered that I didn't have one. When I spotted my phone, I stood up and walked towards the counter. I immediately clicked the lock button and checked the screen. Bewildered, Cypher was right. It's been a whole week and a shit ton of missed calls and messages flashed on my screen.

I walked back over to the table to take a seat, looking crazy at my phone, staring at the date and every message and phone call I missed. As soon as my ass touched the chair, it suddenly shattered! My ass met the floor, and it felt like the whole house trembled with the impact. Cypher, being the bastard that he is, spat out his drink in laughter.

I glared at him and frowned as my ass hurt. "Not funny, dick," I said to him as he stood up while laughing his ass off.

"What the hell happened, man? I thought you weren't eating? Turns out you're pigging out. Haha," he said as he teased and offered his hand to help me at the same time.

I made a face at him first before accepting his hand. When he tried to pull me up, I didn't feel any of his force. I barely even budged. Cypher had a very surprised look on his face before he raised his brows.

"You have been packing on some weight since last time, huh?" he said as he tried to pull me up again.

I saw the muscles on his hand clenched each other. Even the veins on his arm were protruding, indicating that he had to use some serious force to help me up. Unfortunately, my body didn't move an inch.

"Not funny, man. Stop teasing me, and you can pick yourself up now, fat ass." He let go of my hand with a little force and sat back down.

I didn't seem to have any problem at all getting up. I looked over at Cypher, who glared at me and kicked a chair towards me. I sat down with a lot more caution this time, only to hear the wood-cracking noises. Scared that my ass would kiss the floor once again, I stood up and glared at the chair.

"What's going on, man?" Cypher said. "I know you don't weigh more than I do, and I can sit on these chairs fine. Why can't you?" He finished, as he bounced up and down on the chair he sat in.

"I'm not too sure man," I said, full of confusion.

I grabbed the spare metal foldouts I kept in the broom closet. Instead of breaking another chair, this will do even if my ass was uncomfortable.

"So, about your leg . . ." Cypher said to me through his narrowed eyes. ". . . how's it doing?"

I looked at the bag on the table where Cypher kept on getting his fries. While watching him munching, my stomach growled all the sudden with a loud noise as if I hadn't eaten anything for days. I gulped as I realized how dry my throat was.

I reached over the bag and grabbed a burger. That first bite, the taste brought me to heaven. I could have sworn that I'd never had a burger quite like it before. This was the best burger ever!

"Have you taken a look at your leg yet?" Cypher said as he watched me crumple the wrapper and grab another.

I tried answering him while still munching but the words came out garbled. He frowned at me as I grabbed a soda and drank it.

"No. I haven't had the chance yet because you woke me up. Thanks for that by the way," I said with a sarcastic smile.

Cypher shot me the middle finger. I laughed at him as another crumpled wrapper got exchanged for another burger.

"At least I brought you burgers, you ungrateful prick."

"Oh, trust me. I'm very grateful. These things taste amazing! Where did you buy this? Maybe become a regular there," I said with a smile.

I tossed the crumpled wrapper into the garbage can this time as if I was shooting in basketball. I leaned my body over to start rolling up my pant leg where I could now visibly see the bloodstained bandage. I started to unwrap the bandage as Cypher moved his chair to get closer.

He was impatient while staring down at the leg, eating his fries like a child at a movie full of anticipation. We both gasped as the stitches started to come off with the wrap, revealing a light pink scar that looked like it had been healing for an exceedingly long time.

"Uhm, how—how the fuck is this even possible?" Cypher said with clear concern about his features. His eyes travelled up and down to my leg as if looking for a sign that there was still a fresh wound hiding.

"Obviously because I'm a superhuman," was what I said, but on the inside, I freaked out because he wasn't wrong. That was some pretty weird shit.

Cypher laughed. "That is pretty funny, and not surprising coming from you. But in all honesty, dude, what the fuck? What have you been doing for a week? Have you joined a cult or what? Because if you have, you can definitely recruit me."

"The hell, dude?" I frowned at his words as I looked at my scarred leg. "I . . . don't know, man. Luck, I guess?" I said to him with an unsure voice.

"Knowing you, you're probably right," he said as he watched me stand up.

I threw the bandage stained by my blood and another burger wrapper that I ate into the garbage.

"Did you eat all the fucking burgers, you dick?" Cypher was frantic while looking at the bag and wrapper I threw.

"Did I?" I asked with confusion and looked at the wrappers.

"And you didn't even eat your fries! You love fries. Now, I know something is going on. Not fucking cool, man. And here I thought I was the asshole," he finished as he slumped back down into his chair.

I stared down at the fries' box for a second, my thoughts swirling in a whirlwind of confusion. His words struck a nerve, and I could feel the weight of emotions building up inside me. Fear gnawed at the edges of my consciousness as I struggled to come to terms with the changes in my body.

I wasn't used to devouring fries without a second thought, but earlier, even the simplest decisions felt like monumental hurdles. The truth was, I didn't understand what happened to me. It was as if I lost control over my own self, and it terrified me.

I took a deep breath, attempting to hide the internal struggle I faced. The confusion and fear were eating away at me from within, and I couldn't let anyone see the vulnerability that now consumed my being.

"You don't get it," I muttered, my voice betraying the turmoil inside. "It's not about the fries."

His eyes softened, recognizing the pain in my words. "Then what is it about?" he asked gently.

I hesitated, unsure if I could find the right words to convey the emotional storm raging within me. "It's about everything," I finally admitted, my voice trembling. "I don't know who I am anymore. My body feels foreign, like I'm trapped inside a stranger."

"Fuck. I didn't even think about it. My bad, bro," I said as I grabbed a fry out of the box and ate it. I didn't enjoy the taste. Cypher, who watched me like an angry mother, could see that. His face turned to a stunned expression then relaxed.

"Whatever, man. Your greedy fat ass owes me some food. I am hungry," he said in a Southern accent, I laughed a little

"Yeah, yeah. I got some deer in the freezer downstairs. I'll thaw some out and make us some steaks. How's that sound, would that make us square?"

I stood up and froze when I saw the scarred leg taking a lead on my steps. It didn't hurt. My heart should feel at ease and relieved.

I didn't have to worry about missing work, well not any more work anyway, or having a hard time walking down the stairs because of this shit—but my mind said otherwise. It's giving me lots of thoughts that I couldn't even point out what it was. My mind only made stories up to scare me because of what happened the other day . . . rather, than last week.

"Now, that's what I'm talking about! You really know how to tug on the heartstrings. I fucking love steak," Cypher said, fist-pumping the air. He was celebrating as if he won the lottery.

I shook my head at him and laughed at his reaction. I walked towards the door to the basement beside the sink. I turned on the light and took one step onto the stairs.

As soon as my leg pressed against the old wooden stair, I immediately heard the loud creaking. My brain automatically sent red flags throughout my body. It flashed the images of what I did to the chair. My ass suddenly shivered as it remembered the pain from kissing the floor.

Scared that the stairs might break, I turned my back and looked at Cypher. He must have seen the concerned and terrified emotions dripping in my eyes.

He tilted his head as he was sipping on his drink. When he realized what I wanted, he started to laugh at me. He shook his head as he put down his drink on the table. He stood up and walked towards me while patting my shoulder with a smirk.

"Sure, fatty. I'll go down and get the meat. We are going to have a chat about how you managed to gain so much weight and still be so tiny." He shrugged his shoulders, feigning disappointment before heading downstairs.

I watched Cypher's back as he got deeper into my basement. I opened my mouth to tell him to turn left but stopped short because he knew every corner of my house. I shook my head at him and went to the table.

I grabbed my soda and sipped on it when I sat back down. The soda inside my mouth overflowed out my lips as I felt the folding chair creak and start to bend underneath me. My ass immediately got up and I put down my drink on the table. Holy shit! What the hell was wrong with this body?

"This is fucking crazy," I said, full of confusion and uncertainty about what happened. I grabbed the towel hanging from my oven and patted down my chest where the pop spilled. I paced around as I finished cleaning the liquid off, and tossed the towel not thinking about where it might land as my head raced with these recent changes. I stopped and took a deep breath, instead of moping around on the things that weren't in my control, I decided to go out to get a new sturdy chair.

The moment I opened the back door, a beautiful sunset met my gaze and blinded my eyes. I needed to cover my eyes with the back of my hand to get a clearer view. The lines of houses were quiet and gave me a peaceful and calm feeling.

I smiled a bit as I realized I didn't have any memories of going out for a week. When I noticed a small child and my old neighbor standing out on their back deck, most likely watching the sun fall, I waved my hand to say hi. The child waved back at me, but the old man snorted at me. I shook my head and started to stretch my body. I heard some cracking from my bones as if I hadn't done this for a long time.

I went to the garage only a few steps away from my back door. I searched for another chair and my eyes glistened when I saw metal chairs stacked up together. I grabbed one metal full-piece chair I had stored. I coughed when all the dust flew in the air.

I put down the chair and looked for a towel to wipe it. I should have kept the one I tossed, I giggled to myself. When I got back, Cypher had already put the meat in the microwave to defrost it quicker.

"I'm pretty curious as to what's been going on with you, man. You've been M-I-A, dude. I thought about breaking your door down if you hadn't opened it," he said while his back was to me.

"I don't know why you would do that, or even bother knocking if you have the code for the deadbolt." I watched him freeze for a second from my words as I brought the chair through the door.

"Oh, yeah." He returned to what he was doing, hoping I wasn't going to call him out on that one.

He started the countdown in the microwave and walked back over to the table to sit down. I put down the metal chair I got and patted it, testing if it was sturdy enough. After checking it, I went to the counter to get a lighter and an opened pack of smokes.

I lit up a cigarette, and in between the first pull of smoke, a hurtful cough escaped my throat which I'm assuming was from not having one in so long—

but man did it ever feel good.

Cypher laughed. "What now? You can't smoke anymore either? Huh, rookie?"

"I'm not sure, man. It feels like I haven't smoked in a week. My throat is dry," I replied with a raised eyebrow and looked at the smoke in between my fingers full of curiosity.

"Listen, I know you get lucky sometimes with your injuries, but you must admit that there is something fishy going on with this. The fact we haven't even discussed what we experienced out there that caused your wound—the build-up of everything that happened has been eating at me. I don't know what to tell anyone that will ask," he said as he put his smoke out of his pocket.

"I know. I was thinking the same thing. But the truth is I've never felt better. I don't know how to explain it. It's because I've slept for almost a week?" I asked as I only remember sleeping.

"That's pretty fucking weird too. After what happened, everything became weird," he said back to me as he placed the smoke in his mouth and lit it up before continuing. "It's not fair that I still have this fucking goose egg on my head and you're stitched-up leg is all better, like what the fuck?" He pointed his hands down to my leg through a cloud of smoke before settling back in his chair.

We were both quiet for a few minutes staring into the clouds of smoke we were letting out. As we were both reminiscing about what happened that day, a deafening silence pulsated in the kitchen. I tried to puff one more time when a ding from the microwave cut off our silence.

I stood and went over to get the steak out. I prepared the meat when Cypher started to state what he noticed.

"Well, we got attacked by something big. There Is no denying that to be a fact. You slept for like a week. Waking up heavy enough to break all your chairs and potentially ruin your stairs. Lastly, you ate all the fucking burgers! I am supposed to be the asshole." He stopped and took in one more puff before putting his smoke out in the ashtray.

"Look, I'm here for you, dude, and something is going on. And considering I know that you're a lot like me, so going to get checked by a doctor is a no-no— unless you're pretty much dying," he paused.

"What the hell are you doing?" Cypher asked in a high tone as he peered over my shoulder to look at what was going on.

At that moment, I snapped out of it. I looked at Cypher who looked with obvious disgust at me. When he frowned his forehead, I followed his line of vision. Shockingly, I had been licking the plastic package of the meat. But what's even more shocking?

There was no meat in there. The juicy blood of the meat which I let run down my shirt. Cypher walked over to me as I stood there blankly and frozen at what I just did.

"Hey, man. Just what the fuck are you doing?" he asked as he shook my shoulders, trying to snap me out of my trance.

"Are you fucking kidding me?" he said, a little pissed now.

"You ate all the fucking burgers, and now? You ate all the steak, and raw at that! Dude, if you didn't want to share, you could have told me. You didn't have to be such an asshole!"

I wasn't even phased by his rant as the realization hit me. Did I eat the fucking raw steak? My hands trembled as I dropped the bloody plastic down on the floor. The juicy watery blood I hadn't finished licking pooled on the floor. I even stepped back to stop it from touching my feet.

"What the fuck? Did I . . . did I just eat that?" I said while pointing out the package on the floor. "I didn't even realize I was doing that?" I finished staring down at the blood. And even though my brain and heart were grossed at that thought, my stomach said otherwise. I gulped the saliva that started to form inside my mouth.

"Listen, man. Are you sure you are, okay? I think . . . I think there is more going on than we know. Let's figure it out together. I'm going to go get some food because I'm fucking starving. Thanks to you, man. I appreciate it," he paused and glared at me.

"I want you to come by my place tomorrow. We can try and figure this out, okay?" He finished as he patted my back and walked towards the front door.

"Don't tell anyone about this," I said with a shaky voice, not because I didn't trust Cypher, but because I feared what was going on with me.

He shot me the middle finger and grinned at me. "Obviously, man. I'll see you tomorrow. Try not to fall through the floor, and don't break anymore chairs okay, dick? Fucking fat ass," he said with a chuckle. Even though he tried to be funny with his words, his face was trying hard to hide the fact that he was worried and concerned about me.

He went out of the door waving his hand while walking away which turned into a middle finger. I just stared blankly when I heard his truck horn two times. I unconsciously waved back toward his truck.

When he was nowhere near my vision, I shut the door. My feet made their way back to the kitchen. I sat down on the metallic chair and lit up another smoke which wasn't nearly as bad as the first one.

I leaned back and took a long inhale of relief. Being alone now made the whole house covered with silence as it triggered my mind to overthink things. My mind thought about what was going on with my body.

Remembering the vomitous scene I created, my whole body shivered at that. I stared down at the bloody mess on the floor. My stomach started to growl, as my mind fought all my urges to get on all fours and start licking it.

CHAPTER 3
TEST

Cypher

As the sun gently filtered through my window, I woke up the next morning with a heavy feeling pressing upon my chest, a blend of weariness and irritation lingering from the previous day. Despite trying to convince myself it would be a good day, the weight of my emotions seemed to cloud any sense of optimism.

In search of some solace, I decided to step outside my room balcony and inhale the crisp morning air, hoping it would help clear my mind. Yet, as I stood there, taking deep breaths, a surge of anger resurfaced within me, intensifying the heaviness I felt. It was then that I couldn't shake the memory of Angel, my careless friend, devouring not only my burgers but also the prized steak the night before.

I understood he had a lot going on but fuck man, you never fuck with a man's food.

I broke out of my anger for a moment as I took a sip of my morning coffee when I stopped suddenly. All that blood and meat he ate up raw., I shuddered at the thought. I shook my head as it started to pound once again. I winced as I rubbed my hand over the bump on the back of my head.

This feeling of brooding went on as I dwelled on what was happening. I looked down into my cup watching the steam slowly work its way over my lip and into my nose. I took a deep inhale.

I love the smell of hazelnuts. I started to walk over to my shop.

I lived on a large acreage because I hate people. I love how this vast green land gives freedom to my mind and relaxes my heart with the beauty of nature. The numerous lines of trees surrounding the open space where my house and shop were located—the sound of the leaves and branches dancing along with the wind blowing—the magnificent bright line whenever the sun and the moon fight each other—This gave me a feeling that couldn't be exchanged with anything else.

I loved how it gives me privacy and hid me from the reality of this harsh world. I loved how I enjoyed singing at the top of my lungs and not giving a single fuck about neighbors, except for the animals who came over when I had a party all by myself.

I was grateful that I could be myself whenever I wanted to because I was all alone, and no eyes were watching and waiting to judge me. I didn't get many visitors or enjoy having large parties, but I invite most of my closest friends to hang out with me here occasionally.

This land that was given to me by my parents had a very long history of being on this earth. These acres after acres of land had faced many calamities but were still intact and never stopped giving me a peaceful life. I lost count of how big this acreage was because what mattered to me was, I took good care of it and this act in turn took care of my well-being and life.

Angel, out of all my friends, appreciated this place as much as I did. He was born in a small town and moved into the city where he had been for many years, and his reason for staying there despite his love for nature was beyond me. I assumed it had to do with his business since it did need him to be close and always available for sudden calls and emergencies.

I suppose, but fuck what a drag it must be dealing with all those fucking mouth breathers. I couldn't imagine being a man who was required to listen to those kinds of people. No way in hell would I want to deal with that.

But Angel is a lot calmer than I am, I would get into trouble with my mouth or end up hurting someone.

The sound of the singing birds, howling of the dogs—or wolves—the sounds of the frogs, and other animals that kept on echoing on my land let me know that the day would be good. I opened the door of my old shop when I heard the familiar annoying sound of a vehicle heading down my driveway.

I turned my back to look at the driveway where I saw a familiar jeep make its way around the bend a few meters away from me. I couldn't see his face clearly, but I surely could see his grinning teeth looking in my direction. I shook my head as the familiar rusty shitbox was getting nearby.

I put the keys back in my pants and started to walk towards him. A big smile started to form on my lips.

The cheap old jeep I saw driving up rounding my driveway belonged to an old buddy of mine. We liked to call him Ninja. Obviously not his real name, but ever since I met him, we had been calling him Ninja, because he liked to jump around like a little spider monkey and move with full silence like a ninja from one of those Japanese movies.

He was quite impressed with what he does, but we wouldn't tell him that. That old geezer would start a long story about one of the times he did something crazy and almost died.

I started laughing to myself with that thought. I waved to him as he came to a stop, it has been quite some time since he last visited me.

"Well, look at who we have here. What's up, dude?" I started to say even though the truck turned off its engine.

Ninja smiled back at me. He watched me get closer to the driver's seat and wait for him to get out. He took almost ten seconds to get out as he rolled his window up with force.

"My man! Glad to see you again," I said as I gave him a tight handshake and tapped his back. "I see you still haven't upgraded to a better vehicle." He laughed as I patted my hand down onto his hood.

"Shit no, that would cost money. But I did pick up a few things that I think you might be interested in while I was out doing my thing," he said with a gentle smile.

Ninja had always been the guy to run to when looking for stuff, be it an antique or rare item. Just name what you were looking for and he will do his best to find it. He loved to buy and sell all kinds of stuff he discovered.

He doesn't like to miss an opportunity for something that could make him money. But he was a cheap bastard, that's for sure. I suggested to him to open a pawnshop named Free is in the Budget.

"Of course, you did. Why am I not surprised?" I fired back with a teasing tone and smiling face. He tapped my back a bit hard which made the both of us laugh our ass off.

I followed him as we walked to the back of his vehicle. He opened his hatch and boxes of all sizes greeted me. I only watched Ninja's back as he leaned in and started to rummage through his boxes. I pulled out a pack of smokes from my pocket and lit one up while waiting for him.

"What do you have there, huh, Ninja?" I asked as I took a large drag letting a big cloud of smoke out, extending my hand through it to pull out an old wooden baseball bat.

I turned it around in my hand and it looked used and old, but no cracks could be seen on any part of it. I positioned myself as if I was about to hit a pitch and tried hitting the air. It produced a good sound through the air.

"I thought you'd like that," he said with a sense of pride while still pulling stuff out.

"You do know I have like two dozen of these fucking things, right?" I asked as I tested the weight with a swing once again.

"Are you saying you don't want it?" He stopped searching and turned his head toward me with a raised eyebrow.

I looked at him with a smirk and swung the bat up to rest on my shoulder. "Is that even a question? I'll take it."

"Yeah, that's what I thought." He laughed at me as he went back to sorting out his boxes.

"Don't bother going through any of it, man. Simply drop the boxes in the shop, you know I'll take them," I said to him while grinning.

He laughed at my remarks while still busy with his boxes. I walked towards my opened shop. I pointed to a spot using the bat to drop the boxes.

I leaned the bat handle on the wall as I watched Ninja grab a box with overflowing things and drop it where I pointed.

"What do you have planned today?" he asked while still sorting out the boxes.

"Not much. Only waiting for Angel to show up so we can do some work," I replied as I grabbed a few boxes and went to place them in the pile.

"That sounds awesome. It's still pretty crazy what happened to you, guys, out there." His tone went serious as he headed back to his jeep to shut the hatch back up.

I walked to the back door of the shop and opened it. A gentle Breeze started running through my shop. I looked outside the backdoor that led to an open field where I could see the calming view of the trees.

The backside of my shop was used to store all my useless shit. Like Ninja, I loved collecting stuff and you'd be amazed at how fast stuff starts to pile up. But, instead of selling the items, I treated them as if I would have a use for them one day.

Most of my collections were composed of classic cars, antique appliances as well as piles of steel and wood. Or as most people would like to call junk.

"How's he doing? His wound was no joke. It was a good thing that you had your weapons with you. If not . . . well it could have been bad. Hopefully, that animal gets caught soon before someone else gets hurt," he said, snapping me out of my thoughts.

"He is doing good," I said as I shrugged my shoulders.

I turned back around and walked towards Ninja, looking down at the table where my coffee sat no longer steaming. Depression passed through my mind as that seems to happen often, oh well time to make another.

I was about to offer Ninja a coffee when I heard another vehicle making its way to the shop. I didn't know why I had just noticed the sound now when it already pulled up beside the jeep. I must have been lost in my head a few moments ago there.

I tapped the back of Ninja who was lost on his phone, most likely scouring the local marketplaces, he looked up at me and I tilted my head towards Angel who turned off the engine of his truck.

Like yesterday, something felt unusual. I glanced at Ninja who also did the same as me. We locked our eyes as if we had the same thoughts and looked back at Angel's truck.

"I don't remember his truck being that low. Did he change his vehicle, or something is wrong with his shocks?" Ninja asked me with a puzzled look on his face.

"No, he is just a fat ass. I'm joking. I think he said somebody dropped a load into his box a little too aggressively a little while ago and he has yet to get it fixed," I said back laughing but still looking at his truck which looked like it carried an elephant.

The body of the truck almost kissed his tires, I bet every time he hit a bump they rubbed. I gave myself some words of praise for how fast I thought up the excuse.

Angel stepped out of his truck, and to our surprise, the vehicle bounced back a whole 8 inches to its original height. It was a strange and unusual occurrence, leaving both Ninja and me in shock. Ninja looked at me with a curious expression.

Ninja's curiosity got the better of him, and he started asking direct questions about the truck's behavior and Angel's weight.

"How did your truck do that? You don't weigh enough to cause such a bounce!" he inquired with a puzzled look.

"He should probably get that fixed quick. I doubt that's good on the vehicle." One eyebrow raised as he continued.

"Yeah, you try telling him that." I pointed my thumb toward Angel. "The fucker is even cheaper than you are." I forced out a laugh, I dislike lying to my friends.

His forehead was furrowed together as if he wanted to ask a few more questions, but I shook my head to avoid telling him the current situation. I tapped his shoulder and started walking toward Angel.

When I got near him, we made a small fist bump as I tilted my head toward the direction of Ninja who walked behind me. Angel approached Ninja with normal strides, forcing Ninja to stare down at the scarred leg of Angel. I guess it was a little obvious that his injured leg didn't look very injured.

"Hey, Ninja? What's up?" Angel greeted first as he glanced at me secretly with questioning eyes. I shook my head as if signaling to him that the Ninja was unaware of anything.

"Hey, Angel. Long time no see, huh? Your truck seems to be in rough shape, eh?" Ninja said while still trying to take a good look at Angel's leg.

"Sometimes bad shocks can do that," I quickly said as I stepped in between them to block Ninja's glances at Angel's leg. "And don't let the fact he isn't limping fool you. He just likes to play it up like he is a tough guy, you know. Those guys who like to hide their pain," I said without skipping a beat while glaring at Angel. To his benefit, I'm a professional bullshitter and it came out in strides.

Luckily, Ninja didn't know much about vehicles, so he took what I said without any question. The fact that he knew Angel, it made sense to him as to why he wasn't limping. My insides started to relax, relief flooded over me that he didn't keep asking more questions or keep analyzing his leg.

"I didn't know that Ninja would be visiting you, Cypher?" Angel said to the both of us but his eyes were glancing at me.

I looked at Ninja who was now getting one last box out of his truck. "I don't even know if I want to grace you with a greeting. Have you forgotten yesterday, because I sure as fuck didn't, you fat ass. I'm still pretty pissed about my burgers and steak, you dick," I said with a big grin on my face.

Angel raised his eyebrow at me and grinned back. "I knew you would be. Wait here," he said with pride before opening the door of his truck and taking the oh-so-familiar bag out of his truck.

"I brought you a peace offering," he said while offering the bag to me. I whistled as I smelled the aroma coming from within and accepted the bag. "Sorry, dude. I didn't know you were here, or I'd have got you one as well," Angel said to Ninja with an apologetic face.

"No worries, man. I've got to take off anyway. You know I have lots to do!" He said and laughed at us. "By the way, I got this for you but didn't get a chance to get it to you before you, guys, left for your trip." He handed Angel a little box and a puzzled angel opened it up.

Inside was a keychain of a border collie in a sitting-down position. Angel had a dog named Fox Mcleod who had just passed recently, and it hit him hard. Losing a best friend would do that to anyone, and after the experience we had I understood that more than ever.

"I don't know what to say, man, this is awesome." Angel couldn't take his eyes off the keychain as he spoke. "Thank you, Ninja."

"My pleasure, friend. Now I'm outta here!" He smiled widely as he headed towards his jeep.

Angel and I both smiled and waved. We both looked back down at the keychain. Ninja is a good guy and a good friend. I looked back up as Ninja got inside his vehicle. I walked up and tapped the door of his jeep and grinned at him.

"Thanks for the stuff, man," I said with a smile while pointing my thumb back toward my shop.

"No worries, Cypher. Let me know if you have a request. You know this guy could get anything," Ninja proudly said with a wink at me. I laughed at him and stepped back as he turned on his engine.

He made a short salute to Angel who was behind me. "I'm glad you are doing better, man. I'll talk with you, guys, later," he yelled as his jeep started to move.

Angel and I were both watching the vehicle leave. When Ninja was out of sight, I peered down into the bag of burgers Angel gave to me. Memories from yesterday flashed in my mind as I searched for my burgers inside.

"Are you serious, dude?" I said to him with a bit of anger in my voice. Angel looked back up from attaching his new keychain with a puzzled look.

"What?" he asked me while looking at me with innocent eyes which boiled my blood even more.

While glaring at him, I put my hand inside the bag. I started taking out handfuls of empty crumpled wrappers and threw them at the opened window of his car. After two batches of crumpled wrappers, I finally got to the lonely burger buried at the bottom.

"It looks like you had plenty of burgers in here, and you only brought me fucking one of them?" I said as I peeled the burger out of its wrapper and took a big bite while glaring at him.

"You keep this shit up, man, and you're going to end up being fatter than I am in no time. Is that your New Year's Resolution, huh? To get fatter than me?" I finished with a mouth full of burgers. Just three bites and the burger was nowhere to be found now. Angel pulled out his smoke and lit one.

"We both know that will never happen," he said through the cloud of smoke he puffed.

"Besides, you have no idea how hard it was for me to save that one for you. I even slapped my face to remind myself that you'd be pissed, you know," he finished without any regret in his tone and even blamed me!

I gave him a stern look while crumpling the wrapper and throwing it full of force at his chest. His hands automatically moved to catch the wrapper. I snorted at him for catching it and turned my back to him.

"Come with me," I said as I headed towards the shop.

I wasn't going to go into every detail because frankly? That's a shit ton of writing and it already took me a while to remember half of this other shit. I just don't have that kind of patience within me. I was the kind of person to take shortcuts and hate going the long way.

But because of the shit that was happening, I had no choice but to stay up all night. As I went through the process of setting up a mess of tests and such to find out the limits of Angel's newfound condition, my mind was near to the border of exploding. I used all my brain cells for this shit, but I knew it was worth it.

"What are we going to do, man?" Angel asked as he saw me walking to a small table.

I wiped away the stuff that was on top of it. Not minding that it made a mess on my floor, I tilted my head to the other chair.

"We're going to test your conditions, dude. I got tons of lists here that we should do to figure out your situation," I simply said as I shook my fingers in the air.

"And what are we going to do first?" he asked, full of curiosity, as he watched me stretching my arms with a big shit-eating grin.

Naturally, we started with an arm wrestle because that's how we roll. As much as this pained me to say, I didn't win. I was pretty pissed about it but I won't tell him that.

I told him that the sun was in my eyes. I'd rather say that I tripped up my stairs than admit I lost shit. Normally, I was the one who could beat him, but I guess, because he ate dozens of burgers, he had more strength than me. Or at least that was the excuse I had for his new strength.

Time passed by in my shop as we went into a slew of tests. From lifting stuff that weighs twice his body weight without any signs that he had a hard time lifting it at all, which I found impressive. But I still wouldn't tell him that.

Angel came over almost every day for the next two weeks to try out all sorts of things we could think of. As the numbers on the calendar kept on increasing, he also kept on getting stronger. I think I helped him develop more strength with all the tests I threw at him rather than finding answers.

But all I can say was fuck that guy. For years, he and I had discussed what we would do if we had these powers and he lived it now! The fantasy dream that every gamer dreamt of, was his reality now. I was certain I was jealous— scratch that, I know I was a hundred percent jealous.

And of course, I wouldn't tell him that because he would never let me live that down. I hope he never reads this, or else my awesomeness will be gone. Okay, where was I again? Oh yeah!

Last week Angel came over after sending me a text telling me that he needed to talk to me. I hadn't seen him in a few days because he had business to take care of In the city of madness, did I mention that I hate people?

I assumed it was because he managed his own truck company and shit, he showed up at my house looking panicked. This just didn't sit well with me. Angel doesn't panic in any situations where I would be blabbing like a teen girl.

He looked back and forth as he walked towards me. His face looked like he had seen a ghost. 'Till I had seen the holes in his truck.

"What's going on, dude?" I said confusedly as I looked back towards him with a raised eyebrow.

CHAPTER 4

BLOOD

Angel

For weeks, I had been going over to Cypher's house to deal with the aftermath of the strange events that had been unfolding. He said that I should write down stuff that is relevant to what has been happening and keep records of all the changes going on within me.

But in reality, it has been a pain in my ass . . . not the journal, but a large man who happened to be my best friend, Cypher. As much as I found it annoying, I knew it was essential to keep track of my newly found abilities and their impact on my life.

I'd like to clarify what has been on my mind lately, and that my newfound abilities were a gift of sorts. These abilities had manifested after an incident in the woods where I encountered a strange entity. I could lift my truck, which was pretty amazing by the way. I even beat Cypher in arm wrestling which made me proud of myself because I rarely win against his ass.

Also, my sense of hearing has become sharper and more sensitive. Out of all the things that have been going on with me, this one was at the bottom of the incredible and amazing list.

I didn't enjoy hearing multiple sounds at once, and as clear as crystal in my head at that. I disliked all the people's voices that had nothing to do but give some snarky comments about everything, or worse, to other people.

The heightened hearing overwhelmed me in a bustling city, making me hear every annoying sound and snarky comment around me. It became a constant intrusion on my peace and quiet, which was something I valued. I couldn't enjoy a walk without being bombarded by noise pollution.

Even if I didn't want to hear their voices while I walked or passed by, this shitty hearing ability wasn't letting me deal with my business in peace. Who would enjoy an ability like this where you can hear the scornful opinions of others?

I bet normal people wouldn't believe how annoying it was when you live in the city. With all the cars and sirens which are constantly going off and like a broken music player. I was jealous of Cypher's house out in the sticks.

I swore if this noise didn't stop splitting my brain in two, I would be going to go take one of his rooms. Knowing Cypher, he would say no and be an asshole, but I now could muscle my way and get things done. Since I was stronger than he was now, he wouldn't give in easily.

These past couple of weeks have been pretty neat. My leg healed up, and barely had a scar —but I did have this phantom ache going on occasionally. It's hard to explain because there was no real pain.

I could only feel pressure on it which was kind of freaky. I didn't have a choice but to believe it was nothing. Overall, I was glad I didn't have rabies or anything that could cause some serious issues.

I had to call it quits out at the acreage for a bit. I needed to get back to work which I had been neglecting for weeks now. I run a logistics company that I had stepped back from for a while.

I had to make sure I could figure out what was going on before I faced people.

I usually did some long-haul trips for several days or even weeks because I got bored. I used to move appliances at the factory but ever since I got a better contract offer, I was able to generate better money, enough to make a great living. It was a win-win situation where my company didn't usually need me, and I could do work suitable to my liking.

Thinking back on it now, should I get back on the trucks? I could do a better job on those trucks now. I could use my strength to earn more money. And to do that, I would have to face people, right? Fuck that because people suck.

Never mind, the money isn't worth the exchange for my comfort. Unless I gained some sort of Jedi mind trick ability, I could use it to make people blank stare and sign. If not, I would rather stick to what I enjoy. No hassle, no hard feelings.

Days after I was done 'testing', as Cypher likes to call it—more like torture—I attended some meetings trying to play catch up on all I missed. I even went to some of the warehouses to make sure all my trucks and guys were doing well and going smoothly.

At least that's what I would tell Cypher when he called to get me out to his place for more crap. My company was pretty self-sufficient and most of it could be done over the phone.

Usually, I would only get food, my appetite has grown a lot and with my weight change, I felt like I ate for ten. I decided to grab a bite to eat while driving around in my truck. Whenever that happens, my mind would always go into an internal debate on whether I wanted to drive-thru or to sit down somewhere to enjoy the view.

I sat in the parking lot of a warehouse, watching the boys load up. When I noticed an old truck across the street from me with a few big boys. I thought it was odd that they were only sitting there all crammed in like that, but then again people are fucked. I shrugged and didn't think much more of it at first.

"Wait..." Until I realized they were staring at me. I looked around to make sure they were in fact staring at me and not some other vehicle behind me. I didn't see anyone else there besides me, so... "I guess they were staring at me, huh? I wonder what their fucking problem was?" I mumbled under my breath.

I looked at what their group was doing. They all looked like they were discussing something. There was a big guy in there looking as if he wanted to get out and come over, so I drove my truck toward them. I have some pretty dark tint on my truck, so I don't think they knew I saw them.

"Hey?" I waved my hand as I approached them slowly and rolled my window down, they got into defensive mode. The big guy's eyes went wide and reached for the door. Another tapped their buddies' shoulders to get their attention. They were pointing their fingers at my truck which made me feel a bit weird.

When I was only a meter away from them, I was shocked when I saw them taking off like a bat out of hell, driving away as if their lives were at stake!

"What the fuck?" Why would they run off like that if they were looking at me like I owed them something? What the fuck was wrong with these guys?

As I tried to make sense of what had happened, my stomach reminded me of a previous problem - hunger. I decided to satisfy my craving by sitting down inside a cozy diner known for serving rare meat. I doubt a fast-food restaurant would make my burgers rare, anyway.

As I imagined sinking my teeth into that mouthwatering delight, my throat and mouth started to water uncontrollably. I managed to regain my composure and wipe away the drool, grateful that I sat inside my truck and did not stroll around town. A drooling face would undoubtedly attract some odd looks from passersby, and I was relieved Cypher wasn't here to witness this embarrassing moment.

I whistled to some music while thinking of how many orders I would buy for today when I caught a glimpse of that truck with those guys, it was only a couple of cars away from me. I watched them in my rearview mirror. They looked like they were following me, or was it just a coincidence?

Shrugging at the thought of being followed like some celebrity, I parked my truck. I got out and spun the keys on my finger while whistling happily. For some unknown reason, this steak restaurant shined too bright for my eyes.

The sun came from behind and peeked over as if it were saying hello to me. The people who were exiting the restaurant wore smiles on their faces, which only encouraged me to get my ass inside and start eating.

And that's what I did. I entered the restaurant and my stomach clenched hard like I haven't eaten anything in months. I sat down and chose the biggest fucking steak that this restaurant could offer and ordered four of them—extra rare at that.

The waiter who got my order asked me twice to repeat what I had said, but when I said I wanted it extra rare, and to leave all the blood on it. His face got confused.

"Uh, the blood? Sir? On all four of them, sir?"

I looked up at the waiter who eyed me like I was a freak. I nodded at him, and answered, "Yes, four extra rare porterhouse steaks, leave all the blood on the plates," with full of confidence and hunger.

The waiter left me with a puzzled look, but I was too happy to mind. I felt like I could eat a horse. I paused in that thought and started to think about how delicious a horse might be. I shook my head and looked around at all the customers hoping they didn't notice that I drooled on the table, again.

My feet were trembling underneath the table. It looked like I was nervous or something, but my stomach growled inside me and almost forced me to go raid the kitchen to get my order after five minutes of waiting. My hunger got impatient as I could see the other tables eating their steaks full of happiness.

When I saw the waiter come out of the kitchen with a trolley, my mouth went wild with the thought of food. "Finally," I thought to myself, my mouth watering. The waiter stopped the trolley at my side. My mouth and throat couldn't stop drooling and gulping while the waiter slowly opened the tray. I didn't know why he needed to open it slowly, as if wanting to make me attack him.

The feet that I tried to stop making any noise or vibration by thumping nonstop on the floor were getting discontented. I glared at the waiter who prepared my order at my table. At that very moment, my irritation faded.

"Here's your order, sir," the waiter said, placing the four delicious-looking steaks in front of me.

"Thank you," I muttered, barely containing my patience.

The bloody, juicy, reddish steak was in front of me. I was quite impressed with the size of it, and there were four of them. Or maybe it seemed that way since my state was in another level of otherworldly hunger, I was curious as to how long it would take me to eat this all.

I couldn't even wait for the man to place all of them down, my hand immediately grabbed a handful of steak. It was fucking delicious. Words couldn't even begin to describe the flavor that took over my senses.

"These are divine," I said between mouthfuls, feeling the satisfaction wash over me.

The flesh of that first steak melted into my mouth. The spices they put on were just right. Cypher would appreciate this place since he is very particular about his steak.

Everybody seemed to stare when I started to drink the remaining blood juice on the plate. My throat gulped it all as if I drank a soda. I didn't give any mind or care to it.

I put the big plate down on the table as I licked the blood juice that overflowed on my lips. The loud burp from my stomach made a quiet scene, but I ignored the people who were now gossiping about me.

This was why I didn't like this hearing ability. I could hear what those people were saying about me. But none of that mattered since I had three more to enjoy. I'm going to have to place a meat order when I get home, I think.

I leaned back to enjoy my triumph. I picked my teeth that had some threads of meat stuck in between. I rubbed my belly when my eyes glanced at the glass window.

I noticed that fucking truck again, and this time I got pissed. I wasn't a fan of stalkers. Trust me, I learned that the hard way, but I won't get into that right now, fucking pack of smokes.

I decided to do the one thing I knew would solve this issue. I smirked while staring down at each guy in that truck. They were looking at me now, especially that big one. I pulled out my phone from my pocket and messaged Cypher. I typed a message asking if he was home and if we needed to talk.

I waited for a minute before drinking water and leaving a handful of bills on the table. I got up while still eyeing my stalkers. If these guys wanted to follow me, then they could come out to my buddy's place. We could see just how brave they were in the middle of nowhere.

I didn't know why but I got excited, and I wasn't too concerned with Cypher's reaction to this. Fucker was crazier than me, and that's saying something. I entered my truck and turned on the engine.

As I figured, the truck started to follow me. The moment my truck left the parking lot, I could see them in my rearview mirror. Now, I really didn't think that movie applications were accurate to how stupid these people were in thinking that I wouldn't notice.

Oh well, why would I compare that anyway? I shook my head as I reached the town limits. I lost sight of them. I drove for a little while thinking.

Why would those guys be following me? "Do they really think I won't notice?" I chuckled to myself. I started to think about everything going on with me and if that had something to do with it.

I looked at both of my side mirrors when out of nowhere the truck came at me from the side denting my box. Luckily with my superior driving skill, I managed to keep my truck on the road. They drove up beside me. I litany of curses went forth towards them.

I noticed their windows were down and they were yelling at the driver. It was that massive asshole, who ignored them and stared daggers at me.

I kindly shot him the finger and proceeded to accelerate my truck. The fuck? What the fuck is wrong with that guy? Did he just try to kill me? Okay, that was exaggerated, but still, fuck him.

"Alright, that's it!" I muttered to myself, adrenaline pumping through my veins. "If they want to play this game, they'll find out just how brave they are when facing me and Cypher in the middle of nowhere."

He came at my truck again, trying to knock me off the road. My wheels were screeching on the road as I tried to focus my brain on driving straight. But, holy shit, the faces of the guys who were in there with him were pissed at him, I'm assuming for hitting me.

"Fuck you!" I shouted at the top of my lungs when for the third time they tried to hit my truck.

I bit my tongue and smirked at myself. "These motherfuckers need to learn," I said to myself. I watched their moves and waited for the perfect time. When their truck was positioned to hit me, I hit my brakes abruptly. And the moment their vehicle moved to crash into mine, they went skidding into the ditch.

"Whoo!" I screamed when I watched their truck lose control for a minute.

I started to press my brakes to maybe slow down and see what was going on. But then a piece of metal came barreling through my window and whizzed by my fucking head.

"What the fuck?!" I shouted as I bowed my head in a defensive stance, scared that another bullet might come anywhere at any moment.

What the shit are they on now?

"Holy fuck. These people are crazy," I said while my eyes were moving side by side, watching for anything that might come at me.

I started to serpentine on the road. Two more shots hit my box before I turned down an old farm road and flew out of sight. The rest of the drive was uneventful but at the back of my mind, I cursed the hell out of them.

When I pulled into the space in front of Cypher's house, I saw him making his way out of his shop. He looked at his phone. I immediately left my truck and went to him.

My eyes were unfocused while looking at the road I drove down. My heart thumped so loud, and my body was a little shaky. Those bastards might have scared the hell out of me.

"Angel? What the fuck, dude? What's going on?" Cypher asked as he approached me in the middle.

"Get back into your shop and grab your guns. We need to get ready for some company," I said back in haste. He looked at me and with a simple nod, he understood.

He turned back towards his shop without any questions. We both bolted to his shop. He went inside first while I stayed for a minute to search for any signs that those people were getting nearby. When I saw nothing, I immediately followed inside.

I tapped Cypher's back as he loaded his clips in. He handed me a fully loaded long, black, and armored Colt 6920 pivot with two extra clips of 5.56 rounds.

"Are you going to tell me what the fuck is going on?" he asked while picking up his army green service rifle AR-10A2.

I told him about the guys following me, trying to take me off the road that would lead to the bullet holes in my truck. He muttered some curses and even said that he would kill those bastards. I knew this was the right decision to make. I just laughed at him.

We positioned ourselves at the door of his shop where we could both see the road I took. We waited patiently for the truck to make an appearance; time seemingly stood still. Our weapons were against our chest and were ready to point at any signs of our enemy—but it didn't come.

"I don't think they are going to show up. They might feel like there's a monster waiting for them," Cypher said, handing me a smoke. He smirked as if that was true.

Shaking my head at him, I accepted the smoke and lit it up. "They might not know where I am. I did lose them pretty good back there," I said as I remembered my small stance earlier.

Cypher simply nodded as he scanned the perimeter with slow motion. The smoke he puffed out had an effect on his serious but frowned face.

"It was smart of you to bring them out here," he said. "Too bad, they didn't show up. I was looking forward to testing my new gun. fuckers," he finished, looking disappointed as he tapped his rifle.

"You might still get your chance man," I said with a chuckle.

"Why do you think they attacked you? What did you do?"

"I'm not sure, man. People are just simply fucked up," I replied.

"Do you think it has something to do with what has been going on with you? Like the government or something?" he said, full of malice.

"I doubt it, man. No one knew about my hidden gems. Unless their satellite had been watching what we have been doing here which was impossible by the way with all these fucking trees you got. Besides, the government has quite a bit at its disposal. I feel like they wouldn't have much of a challenge if they wanted me so bad," I said while laughing.

We were guessing the reasons when my watch started to beep. It gave both of us a little jump when we heard it. I looked down, pushed the button, and realized that it was already five. I looked back up at the sun starting to hide behind all the trees.

"Oh shit! I must go," I said while putting the gun back in his cabinet.

Cypher insisted I take the gun with me in case, but I declined because I didn't want to explain to a cop why I have a fully loaded semi-automatic assault rifle on my seat and bullet holes in my rear.

Cypher being a worried sick father of mine, he ended up convincing me to take one of his Beretta's instead—a beautiful gun, APX 9mm. He even offered me a silencer which I laughed at. I told him I didn't think that would be necessary.

I made it to my rig in under an hour. While on the way, my mind couldn't stop thinking about that night about a month ago and everything that had happened up to this point. I was only about to turn on my big truck when I jumped a bit from my phone ringing, stupid nerves.

I muttered a curse when I saw who called me. I answered the call immediately. "Sorry, Karen. I'm on my way now."

I hung up and walked fast. I had a quick discussion with Frank in the warehouse about my run tonight, four hours there and another four hours back.

I jumped out and headed back. I hooked up my trailer when my head started to ache. It felt like a nail went to my temple. My whole body got a nasty chill.

My vision has begun to get blurred. My forehead started sweating, and my stomach squirmed in pain. I felt like I was losing consciousness as my body temperature underwent an extreme hot flash.

Not thinking much about it, I tried to lean my back in my seat and drank some water with some painkillers. Thinking that the pain would be gone in an instant, I started my journey once again. I was an hour away out of town when the sun completely disappeared.

I felt significantly worse as time passed by. My vision got worse. My eyes were rolling around like a broken wheel, so I decided to pull over onto the side of the road before something bad happened.

I looked outside of my window and saw endless darkness and space. No lights except for the moon and the post lights on the road. It was fortunate that there were no cars or any vehicles before me.

I sat back, trying to relax my body and my throbbing head. This past month has been taxing on my mind and my body. Between all of Cypher's activities and then the mental overload of dealing with work, I guess this was my consequence for pushing my body to the limits.

When my condition got worse, I decided to light up a smoke to calm my nerves for a little. As I took my first inhale, I immediately got a sharp pain in my head. It felt like a million little pins prick all over my body.

I couldn't concentrate on anything. My mind went blank. I groaned so loud as the pain doubled as the seconds passed by.

I moved my hand to open my door. And because my body felt extra light and weak, I fell out of the truck onto my knees. My skin burned, and my sweat steamed off me. I moved my body from side to side while groaning in pain. It felt like I was on fire!

My heart started to panic as I reached into my pocket. I grabbed my phone and tried to call Cypher. When I went to press the call button, the pain took hold of me again.

I could feel my bones grinding inside my body. My fingers were cracking back and forth as if I was experiencing a seizure. My mouth drooled as the pain became unbearable.

My tears started to form in my eyes as I watched my nails grow longer for an instant. I could feel the bones in my face snapping and moving as if someone was carving my skin with a knife.

And before my mind blacked out, I saw how the bright light from the full moon turned crimson.

CHAPTER 5
CHANGE

Cypher

Getting myself ready to do some needed gun cleaning made my body feel exhausted. I was the worst when it came to stuff like this. Always putting it off 'till the last minute cause I was such a lazy shit.

If I had the choice of not doing anything and only sitting on my ass all day, I do not doubt in my mind that would be exactly how I would handle my day.

Who wouldn't like to procrastinate with this view that I have here? I often hear Angel saying he was jealous of me.

True or not, I would grin at him and state all the things I love about my land. I often teased him about it because he'd often tell me about how lucky I was. I've offered a great many times to have him get a nice trailer and park it out here, but he needed to be close to the city for work, I guess.

I doubted he wanted to be any closer to me anyway after all the ability tests I'd been doing on him over the past few weeks. Laughing to myself at the mess I saw out back from the fun me and Angel have been having, especially me.

I yawned as I moved the chair using my foot while holding my mug and a pack of smokes. I sat my stuff down on the table on the porch and took a seat. I could see rows upon rows of trees enveloped in a soft morning mist and beginning to be touched by the bright light of the rising sun.

It was only five in the morning, so the sun still hid through the shadow of the night. But during this time of year, the sun fought to gain purchase early. I could see some bright yellow much clearer.

The wide, green land, the tall trees surrounding my open fields, the groups of different birds flying above, the sounds of the crickets and singing animals— ah, this was the kind of life I wouldn't want to lose.

As I sit back to enjoy my morning coffee and smoke in front of this beautiful view, my mind is dazed off by Angel. I couldn't stop myself from thinking about all the amazing strength that man had gained over the last month. Though, I admit that I caught myself being a tad jealous.

Of course, I only knew that, and Angel had no idea about it. I mean, who wouldn't feel jealous? We were both there when that monster attacked us, though, I admit that I got knocked out in the middle of the action.

Anyway, his abilities, or what I liked to call powers were something I've dreamt of having ever since I was a little shithead.

I shook my head to stop my mind from thinking about useless things. When my phone rang, I leaned over to check it out and it was an unknown number. I frowned while looking at the number.

I didn't usually answer unknown phone calls unless I expected someone to call after being warned via text. It was ruined by solicitors and the stupid free hotel scams.

Man, how I wish that I would be able to find these people and make their lives miserable like they try to do to me and everyone else. Disturbing my peace and quiet only to scam me. These pieces of shit weren't going to get me.

But why was I getting an off feeling? I looked down at my phone as it rang nonstop, and I raised an eyebrow. I was starting to get a feeling that I should answer this one.

It was as if the numbers on my screen were yelling at me to answer them. I frowned at what my mind was thinking now, so I accepted the call.

"Hello?" I mentally prepared myself for the robot to start speaking.

"Hey, man. It's Angel." Upon hearing that familiar voice, I almost coughed while puffing on my smoke. Angel, huh?

"Listen, man. No questions. Can you meet me at the gas station outside of Phalanx 42?" he asked with urgency.

My forehead frowned as his voice was shaky and felt like something had happened to him. And outside of Phalanx 42? What was he doing there? I shook my head and answered him.

"Of course, I will. It'll take me about an hour to get there. Is it a social call?" I asked as I looked over at my weapon. Which might come in handy again like yesterday.

"No but bring me some clothes. I'll explain once you're here," he finished as I heard the line click.

I stared down at my phone, the wheels turned in my mind. What could be going on with him? Did he get into trouble again like yesterday? No, if that was the case, he would have had me bring some toys. Then what the fuck? I still grabbed guns anyway just in case.

As I pulled up to the station, I could see Angel leaning against the side of the building wrapped in a blanket. I muttered a curse as I saw him like a wet lost puppy. I didn't know if I was supposed to laugh at his situation or be worried. Instead of reacting to him, I looked around the vicinity to search for any signs of action or weird people nearby.

When I didn't notice anything, I pulled my truck up to him. I rolled down the window as I watched him staring off into the distance and didn't seem to notice I was even there. I whistled to get his attention, and it startled him big time.

"You know, man, by the looks of you, I'm going to assume that you either had a good night or a shitty one," I said with a laugh. Though, I was still worried that someone did this to him.

Angel snapped out of it and didn't look amused at my joke. I snorted at his reaction. "Shut up," he said as he stood and walked over. He opened the door, looked in the backseat, and grabbed the bag of clothes.

He then took off the blanket. I was surprised that he was completely naked. No pants, underwear, or anything. I shot my attention elsewhere.

"Are you ok, dude? A little warning next time maybe?" I said as he started to put on the clothes.

"Honestly, man? I'm not entirely sure. I have been trying to think about what happened. All I've come up with so far is that I need a fucking smoke and a fucking shower because I smell fucking horrible like this fucking truck of yours, dude. Do you ever clean this shit?" he asked with an irritating voice.

His nose scrunched from something. He looked at the backseat of my truck and saw some trash I didn't know when and where it came from. He shook his head at me, showing his discontent with what my truck looked like. As he finished putting his shirt on, I handed him a smoke.

"I wasn't going to say anything . . . wait a second, you can smell?!" I asked with a loud tone and my eyes widened at the realization of what he said earlier.

For numerous uncountable times, he's got inside my truck and even driven it. For all the years that we knew each other, Angel has never commented on how smelly my truck was. He commented on how dirty it was, but never, as in not even once, has he said that my truck had an odor.

At first, he looked at me with his eyebrows raised and shot me a glare for taking back the lighter I was supposed to hand to him. He looked at me and I looked back at him as if our eyes were talking to each other. My eyes were giving him a signal about what he said—when he understood and played the scenario back to his mind, his eyes grew wider.

He looked around my truck, trying to find the answer. When I moved my hand in front of my nose as if encouraging him to breathe in, he followed.

"Holy shit?! I can smell?!" Angel shouted vibrantly as his hand froze in the air while still waiting for the lighter.

"Fucking yeah?!" I shouted back as he nodded at me repeatedly like a child given candy. We both laughed as he tried to smell his armpit and cringed.

When he smelled how bad and awful it was, he laughed and cursed me to death. We were laughing our asses like some teens smoking their first joint. The people who passed by in their vehicles were looking at us like we were some kind of crazy guys. We couldn't help it though; we get giggly in stressful situations at the worst of times.

Angel lit up his smoke and took a deep inhale with a sigh of relief. He puffed the smoke as if it made his entire life better. For years of having a weak sense of smell, Angel struggled with it and even took some jabs about it, mainly from me. He couldn't distinguish the smell of poop from the smell of burning food.

And I got it. I got how happy he must be for smelling the inside of my truck. I understood that he must be overwhelmed with emotion about the comeback of his sense of smell. But there was still a big question that must be answered.

"So . . . are you going to tell me what happened?" I said as I lit my smoke.

"I'll tell you what I remember on the way to my truck."

The trip took almost two hours to get to where he left his truck. Throughout our road trip, he told me about his unexplainable experience yesterday. From how he blacked out to the moment he woke up naked in the ditch. Freaking out how he got there, he ran and snatched the first blanket he saw on his way and headed towards the station.

When he got there, the people looked at him confused and concerned. Someone asked him what had happened, but instead of answering, he ran to the washroom. The moment he saw his body in the mirror, he noticed the dried blood all over his mouth.

He looked like someone who attended a face painting event that splashed red paint on his face. He quickly washed it off and that's the time when he called me.

His face frowned. His eyes couldn't focus on one thing, when he described what happened to him, his eyes were staring with emptiness. His legs couldn't stop vibrating on the floor of my truck. It was distracting, but I stopped myself from mentioning it. I had more important things I needed to know.

"Is that all you can remember?" I had a feeling that he had left something out.

How could his smell come back overnight? Why did he have blood on his face? Why did he wake up naked? He didn't answer. He turned his head to the window and stared out into the distance.

Silence filled my truck. Only the sound of my engine and his stomping feet could be heard. I sighed to myself as I didn't want to force him to tell me anything he wasn't ready to tell.

But my freaking mind wasn't shutting up about it. Some nightmarish scenarios played out there. I even shivered as I thought about it. What the hell happened to him?

"We're almost there," he said softly, he whispered into the air.

I followed his finger where he pointed, towards his truck. It sat on the side of the road with the door wide open. I looked at Angel who looked straight at his truck. His feet stopped moving and his body froze as if he remembered something.

I pulled my truck over about a meter away from his rig. We both got out of the vehicle surrounded by silence, neither one of us saying a word. The wind blew on my face.

The air was cold and refreshing as I heard the birds singing nearby. I looked around the vicinity and saw old pine trees lined up along the road. The forest where animal sounds could be heard, where the night was still present inside of it.

Angel immediately walked to his truck and grabbed his phone from the ground. I looked at Angel first and stared at the dark forest. It got creepier as the wind kept on blowing its leaves. It looked like it was getting bigger and nearer so I shook my head immediately and turned my back on it. I followed him while looking at the pile of rags lying on the dusty muddy ground.

I leaned over to grab a piece of something to look at. It was as big as my sleeves. When I got a clear look at them, I realized that they were Angel's clothes that he wore yesterday. I looked at Angel who was busy squirming around inside of his truck.

I looked back at the ground which was full of pieces of cloth. The wind once again blew as the pieces of cloth got carried away along with the dust.

Just . . . what the hell happened here?

I knelt and started examining the pieces. They all looked like they were stretched out 'till they tore off. The threads were loose, and they didn't look like they were cut naturally, it looked like someone stronger than a normal person stretched his clothes off his body.

I saw some red dots and misshapen dried blood staining the clothes. It was very noticeable as it was very red . . . dark red at that.

"Angel, what the hell happened?" I asked with a disturbed voice and troubled expression. I stood up while staring at the red stains. I was confident that this was a piece of clothes that Angel wore yesterday. What I wasn't a hundred percent sure of was if this was a blood stain or something like wine.

My mind still wished for the latter. Even though the stain was redder and thicker than wine, I still hoped it wasn't what I thought of.

My hand dropped the clothes. I rubbed my palms together to take off the rough feeling from the dust. My feet took a step towards Angel who stared down at his phone. He had this blank expression, but at the same time, the glow of his eyes wavered.

He looked nervous but clearly tried hard to hide it from me. I could see his hand tremble as his eyes met mine. I noticed his phone had a black screen.

"Dude," I said with a worried expression.

My hand went to his shoulder. The wind blew so hard. I saw out of the corner of my eye the pieces of clothing were getting carried away from our feet.

The sound from the tree's leaves and branches got louder and clearer. The sun slowly got to its peak. But neither Angel nor I care about our surroundings. There were too many questions that needed to be answered to find a solution— —and Angel was afraid.

He flinched at my hand and pulled away quickly. He reacted as a person that was about to get beaten up. His eyes were unfocused and wavering.

He clenched his teeth as if stopping himself from uttering any word to me. I frowned at him and was about to tap his shoulder once again, but he turned away and walked towards a tree and rested against it breathing so hard.

"Angel, what are you not telling me?" I started to get concerned about his weird reactions, so I asked with a serious face and tone. Every word I uttered had an emphasis on what I felt. And I knew that he felt that.

Angel went into a sudden burst of rage. He screamed at the top of his lungs. It echoed in the quiet surroundings and even reached the deep side of the forest.

The birds flew in the sky in shock at a sudden force that left my friend. His face heated up as the veins on his neck became visible, he screamed and screamed and screamed. His voice got strained and tired after the tenth time, his scream became a high-pitched cry of pain, grief, and anger.

He turned his back to me and punched the tree so hard exploding the trunk into splinters. It sounded like a bomb had exploded. The impact of it traveled deep into the forest. I gritted my teeth as my breathing got heavier. The only thing I could do for my lost friend was to only watch and listen to his agony.

After a few minutes of cursing, screaming, and punching, he got tired. Angel now stood there staring down at his trembling hands, as I slowly walked up towards him. Once I got closer, I looked at his hands which were dripping blood and filled with wooden splinters.

I was about to grab his hands and try to stop the bleeding but froze up at what I saw. The worriedness I held changed into amazement as I watched the little pieces of wood fall out one by one, out of his skin. His wound knitted itself back together. All of it happened in just a matter of seconds.

It left me in awe as I remembered the regenerating skills of the many characters in comic books. It was an amazing thing that happened and to witness but in reality, it made my heart jump towards the first step of being scared.

"I . . . I remember everything . . ." he said, snapping me out of the trance of staring down at his wound that's healing.

"I remember the . . . pain . . . the heat . . . and the change," he said through his deep breaths.

"What do you mean by change?" I asked with confusion.

"Before I blacked out, my body started to change, Cypher. My bones were cracking, and . . . and I got larger and larger. Hair grew all over my body," he held both his arms and squeezed them tightly until I could see how his fingers dug into his skin. "I . . . I got a feeling of . . . of something . . . I felt like I changed into . . . a big . . . big . . . big monster . . ." he finished as he looked up at me with his disturbed face.

I stood there speechless. He looked into my eyes trying to gauge my thoughts. The lights in his eyes were no longer there.

It got darker and deeper as if he got sucked into his darkness. I really didn't know what to say. My mind processed what was going on then I stopped.

He is my best friend and it didn't matter what was going on with him. I would help him with it. I smiled wide.

"A big dog, huh? Like a wolf or a jackal?" I said through my grin. "Dude, if you transformed into any one of them, that would be pretty fucking awesome," I teasingly said and walked towards him. He looked a bit confused as I stood up next to him and patted his shoulder, trying to bring him back from wherever he was.

"And the hand thing? Dude, your hand only healed within seconds. That is so fucking cool," I finished my compliments to him.

My eyes wouldn't leave his hands as it was all recovered now, except for the leftover blood that slowly dried on his hand. A Scar and some pink skins were all that was left of his wound. It was completely freaking healed. Though what I said was pure honesty, Angel still looked at me with unbelievable eyes.

Angel sighed. "I'm not joking, Cypher. This is serious, dude. Don't say that." He glared at me, making me laugh at him as I surrendered my hands in the air.

"Chill, dude. I was only telling you the truth, okay?" I shrugged my shoulders as I smirked at him. "Do you need a hug? I'm a hugger." I opened my arms wide waiting for him to hit me or something.

He frowned at me and pushed my chest to get away from my threat to hug him. I laughed at his funny reactions. But my heart was now at ease seeing how he could finally be getting back to his old self.

"Fuck off, Cypher. I don't want to smell like you," he snorted at me, which made me laugh once again. "Come to think of it. I remembered the thought of a wolf yesterday. The wolf actually makes a lot of sense," he said as I saw a smile across his lips.

"That's what I'm talking about! Being a Debbie downer doesn't suit you at all, dude," I said happily as I put my arm over his shoulder and attempted to pinch his cheek. He pulled back from my pinch and pushed me away from him.

Even though he pushed me with such ease, I still almost tripped because of the force. I glared at him, and he looked at me with an apologetic face, so instead of bucklering over that, we both ended up laughing together.

"Don't worry, dude, we will work through this. It will be an amazing adventure. So, let's go to your place, grab a few things. And I think you should stay out at my place for a bit so we can brainstorm more about what all of this means," I said as I lit two smokes and handed him one. He took it and nodded at the idea.

"It's a good idea. I'll take my truck back to the yard. Go to my place and pack, then I will go to your place tomorrow," he said as he walked over to the pile of shredded clothes. He picked them up and used them to clean the left blood off his hand and then threw them into his truck.

"Ok, that sounds like a plan," I said as I walked over to him.

I grabbed his shoulder with my hands to turn him around and faced me. "You call me if anything happens, okay?" I finished while staring into his eyes.

"Don't worry, I will call you," he assured me with a smile.

I nodded at him when we both understood what we needed to do. I let his shoulders free to get into his truck. After a few minutes, he started down the road.

On the way back, I tried to think about what was going on and what we could do to isolate the situation that Angel was in. Sadly, I couldn't shake the feeling that I shouldn't have left him alone. Let alone let him drive on his own in his current situation.

I made it home still pretty pumped about Angel's predicament. I decided to spend all my time doing research. While checking my phone every twenty seconds in between my reading and writing session. I read everything I could get my hands on about lore and legends.

I printed over 400 pages worth of info from different websites and books from different countries. The last thing I remember was that I was so glad I bought the office-size box of paper from Lapels before my eyes grew heavy.

My phone started to ring, and since I left it beside my head it startled the shit out of me. I picked my head up off the table and groaned at that sudden loud noise. It took me a second to realize that it was Angel who called me before I snapped out of my dazed state quickly and answered the phone.

"Hey, dude. Is everything alright?" I asked in a hurry.

"Yeah, man. I am only calling to let you know that I am going to head out there soon. Do you want to meet me at the diner for some breakfast?" he asked.

I listened to his voice as he spoke. When I confirmed that he was calm and collected right now, I let out a sigh of relief.

"Breakfast sounds awesome. I'll meet you there in an hour," I finished as I hung up the phone.

I looked around at all the papers I had scattered everywhere. When I saw a word that had multiple circle drawings on it, I realized I had an idea to try as an experiment. So, I headed down to my garage and took a knife off my wall. I took a deep breath and started to get ready.

Angel was already there once I arrived. He stood over by his truck having a smoke leaning against it like he was cool or something. I walked over lighting one myself.

"What's up, man? Check this out," I said with a smile as I handed him the knife, I brought with me. He looked at me with a raised eyebrow as he reached out to take the knife from the blade end.

"Ah! What the fuck, Cypher?!" he yelled as he dropped the blade looking down at his hand that was still smoking. "Why did you try and burn me, dude? If you're mad at me, fucking tell me! Don't burn me!" he said angrily, looking at me.

I leaned over and picked the knife up from the blade end like he did to show him that it wasn't hot. "I didn't burn you, asshole. It's silver," I said while smiling. "You are definitely a wolf. A werewolf. Because you were a human first before being a wolf. So, you are a wolf! Congratulations, buddy!"

"I don't think I find this as amusing as you do," he said as he blew onto his hand.

"Perhaps not, but you have to admit that this is pretty sweet. Like, I know it has its downsides but, man, you're a fucking werewolf!" I said in a full excited voice.

At first, Angel frowned at me but after a few of my boasts about it and stating how jealous I was, he couldn't help but smile. "Yes? I suppose if you put it that way. But let's talk inside, I'm fucking starving," he said as he headed to the door.

"You're always fucking hungry, fat ass. But I guess, it's normal so I'm glad for it," I said as I followed him. He just shook his head and laughed at me.

We sat down at the table and ordered some food. I stared at Angel as he made his order which consisted of super rare steaks and a side of more steaks.

"What?" he asked as he noticed me looking at him funny.

"Oh, nothing," I said as I chuckled with a teasing tone. "So, I've been thinking about your condition and I'm assuming that if typical lore holds, then you will only change during a full moon. That's what basically a hundred pages have summarized for me."

"Yeah, that would make sense. Considering it was a full moon the other night," he said and his eyes went darker again.

"So, what if we build you a cage? So, we can watch the change and learn from it. Hopefully, keep you contained from freely roaming around and waking up naked somewhere," I said and smirked at him.

"That could work, but it would have to be one hell of a cage, man. I mean, from what I know about werewolves is that they're pretty powerful. Maybe thrice of my normal power?" he asked, smiling while he bent a butter knife four times, proving his point.

"Fucking show off! I know and I understand that, but we do have a month to prepare for it. The next full moon will happen a month from now," I explained.

I saw the food coming out and heading our way when I noticed a table of men in the back corner booth suddenly all look away when they saw me looking at them except for one. I kept scanning past to make it seem like I didn't notice them, then turned back towards Angel.

"In the back corner there, are they friends of yours? They were watching us," I said. Angel looked up from his food and slightly glanced over towards where I talked about. He suddenly looked back and stopped eating with a serious face.

"Those are the guys that fucking put holes in my truck," Angel said, clearly getting angry.

"How do you want to play this?" I asked while smirking.

My hand reached for the gun holster at my side. I took it off as I reached down, tapping his knee with my spare pistol. Angel smiled and grabbed it, hiding it in his waist. He leaned back and looked back at the men not trying to hide anything.

"Fair enough," I agreed as I turned around and put my fierce gaze on with a grin.

The men at the other table all looked toward us at the same time. We all locked eyes for almost a full minute before one after another they stood up and headed toward the door. The meanest looking one was the last to leave as his buddy grabbed his arm and broke him from his glare. We watched as he headed out of the door getting onto his phone.

"Let's fucking end this," Angel said as he stood and started to follow the men.

"I fully agree," I replied as I stood to follow.

Once we got out, Angel looked at me and nodded toward the back of the diner with hand gestures. He signaled me to flank around to the back the other way from where he was going. I nodded in agreement and turned to head in the other direction from Angel.

I got to the corner, peaked and once I knew it was clear, I proceeded further towards the back. I looked around the last corner and saw nothing but Angel peeking around the corner like me. He nodded at me, and we both left the cover and met in the middle.

"Did you see them?" I whispered as I scanned the area.

"I could've sworn I saw them run into the woods back here, but I'm not one hundred percent sure," he said as he did the same.

"Huh! Pussies," I said while grinning in victory.

I put my gun down but was still in alert mode. "On the bright side, I don't think they know where I live. Let's head back to my place and we'll be extra cautious getting back there. We have a lot of work to do, so let's not waste it on wimps."

Angel nodded in agreement as he handed me a smoke and we both made our way back to the vehicles.

CHAPTER 6
POWER

Cypher

The whole month was a blur. I didn't know if it was just that we were very busy or if we were enjoying what we were doing that made the days pass by so quickly. We didn't go out much unless it was needed. Angel also called in a lot of favors regarding his work, and I didn't have to worry about much to keep our timeline and secrecy.

Luckily for us, I did have a lot of spare metal and electronics laying around. Thanks to Ninja who kept on convincing me to buy his crap. The only problem was cage bars and shackles. Since we still hadn't known how big Angel's wolf transformation was going to be.

Doubling or even tripling the cage's durability would be a good idea so it had to be outsourced. Getting our stuff built to our desired specs took a lot of money to keep people quiet and to keep the transactions a secret from everyone. But luckily for us, we had some friends, and we weren't hurting for cash.

We became all-around workers at my house. We did welding, lifting, cooking, and all. Surprisingly, we hadn't seen or heard anything from the men Angel encountered since we last saw them at the diner.

We didn't have the time to deal with them before the full moon, so keeping their heads down was actually good for us. Not that we're afraid of them, we're only too busy dealing with more important things at the moment.

I gave Angel the printed information I found on websites and books. I told him to read all the 400 pages because first, he should know what he got into. Second, the most important reason, by the way, was because I only wanted him to read and feel the pain, I did read all that stuff.

Angel eliminated the traits he didn't experience, and we kept track of all the traits he has experienced, so far, we found a book entitled The Weirdest Northern. It was a book written by a girl way back in the 1700s, who claimed to be a werewolf too. She stated all the traits, all the weird things that happened to her, and, how she controlled her power.

Angel and I were so amazed at that. We hadn't had any interest in reading a book hundreds of years old. Though we knew a bit of history based on the games we often played, reading a book about the real thing was a different story.

We spent another night full of books related to the Weirdest Northern. There were several books about it, but it wasn't as detailed as the first book, and it appears that they stopped suddenly. I would get into that later perhaps.

We tried following how she controlled her powers. But I guess, like how people were different from each other, werewolves were also different from each other. We tried different things from different resources, but with no luck, we gave up controlling his power. Or we only needed to figure out everything once we saw how he became a wolf.

While waiting for the night of the full moon to arrive, we spent our days and nights experimenting. Mostly, I asked Angel to do something. At first, he would obey me because we were testing his power, but after a test, he would realize that I only messed with him.

He would threaten to punch me, but in the end, we would both laugh. On some nights, we went to the forest near my house to see if he would feel something or a change in his abilities.

His appearance was still like Angel's fat ass, but his ability seemed to be a million times better at night. His sense of hearing was incredible. We tested it by me staying in my shop, while Angel walked into the deep forest.

We used a 25 feet rope to measure the distance he could hear from my house. Amazingly, we used about six tied together lengths of rope until he couldn't hear what I said from inside my shop clearly. Though Angel complained about how he always went back and forth, I only reminded him that it was worth it to figure this shit out.

We also tested his sense of smell. He found anything I hid even if I threw it into something to drown out the smell. His overall biology was impressive, I was envious which I could only admit in my mind, not in front of him.

We tested several of his abilities. Such as his amazing stomach. He could eat five kilos of fresh meat in five minutes, and he was still hungry.

So basically, we spent more money on his food rather than anything. But, when we realized that spending that much money on meat would most likely raise some interest, we thought of another way to solve his bottomless stomach.

I suggested hunting in the forest. We left a few traps in there, which we checked often. We also went out twice a week for some bow hunting, which was super convenient considering Angel's abilities. So, our food problem was solved for the most part for now.

For the next week, we tested Angel's power once again. We used our previous lists of his abilities to see if there was a change or something. Unfortunately, there were no added abilities, but the good news was his power doubled. He could bend a piece of metal using only his thumb and index finger.

The night came quicker than I expected. I could honestly say that I was equally excited and nervous. Excited because I would witness an unimaginable phenomenon that could change what was known about werewolves.

Excited because my dream to finally see a true-to-life breathing form of a werewolf would finally come true. Nervous because of course, we still didn't know what would happen if Angel turned into his werewolf form.

I had several scenarios in my mind. The first scenario was what if the cage wasn't big enough to hold Angel? Even though the cage was big enough to fit two full-sized SUVs in it.

Especially, when we based the size of this cage on the book we had been reading. We also tried to base it around the size of the wolf we met in the forest, from what we could remember anyway.

Would be safe to say that there would be a difference in their size, right?

That thought forced me to do another check of the structure for the ten thousandth time. I tapped a spoon against the steel bars, and when it made a solid sound, I sighed in relief. Those should hold, I hope.

Three thick reinforced concrete walls and hardened steel bars. Two-inch thick steel chains and shackles rigged up to send half a hundred thousand volts worth of electricity to the neck and hands of the wearer.

I suggested starting with two hundred and fifty thousand volts, but Angel convinced me with his troubled face to double it up in case something might go wrong in the middle. I also had a dial pad to adjust and crank it up to a flat million if needed, which wasn't easy to get installed by the way.

I bet it would be a good idea to take this cage outside, but it was very risky. People might see what might be happening on my land. Especially NASA's satellites that might be up above our heads and taking images. If that happened, I bet it would be disastrous for Angel. Even though I was a bit jealous of his power, I didn't want him to get experimented on by others.

Despite my current questions about his condition and all the testing we were doing, Angel seemed quiet. Most of the time, when we were on a break, I'd often see him staring with emptiness and staying quiet. He usually didn't do that unless he was so stressed about his work. But now that he experienced something like this, I couldn't help but understand.

Especially now that it got close to the time, he would first change in front of me. I know he was concerned for my safety. He opened three days ago before D-day about how he was worried about me. He couldn't promise that I would be seeing the light of day the next morning. but we had plans for this.

He overthought things that might happen at night. He was worried and disturbed about my well-being. So instead of assuring him that everything would be fine, I told some jokes to lift his spirits. It was the only thing I was good at. Besides, I wouldn't miss the opportunity to witness something like this.

"Are you ready for tonight, fat ass?" I walked towards him.

Angel stared into the cage. I offered him a mug of coffee I made to calm his nerves and ease mine as well. He shook his head and went back on staring at the cage. His brows were furrowed and almost met in between. His feet were starting to stomp on the ground. I sipped my coffee as I looked in the cage.

"Are you?" he said, turning his head to look at me with concern in his eyes.

I didn't answer him. I only simply sipped on my coffee once again to avoid showing him that I had some concerns. Plus, if I said I was both excited and nervous, he might have felt pressure because of it.

He had been rough on himself trying to control his power to use at this time. He had been going into the deep forest to practice on his own and try to figure out something about his power.

It wasn't an issue, and it didn't bother me that he did it. He knew himself more than anyone else in the world. Maybe he might discover something when I wasn't around.

But his own reason was that he couldn't use his power to its full potential because he was afraid of hurting me without him knowing it.

"I can feel it . . . you know." Angel began opening and closing his hands. His fingers were trembling, but they got reddish when he did the close-open thing. His eyes were staring at his hands' movements. His brows were about to meet in between as his lips were slightly open to release his heavy breaths.

"The power is building fast, Cypher. It was like water . . . that was about to reach the boiling point," he said as his eyes were wavering at his own words.

Watching him making himself more nervous than usual also made me nervous as hell. So, instead of dwelling on the unknown results, I decided to change the tone of the conversation. I reached into my back pocket and pulled out a red ball. I held it out in one hand and bounced it on the floor. I caught it using my other hand and did the bouncing-catching moves for a minute.

"We have taken every precaution we can think of to stop being such a baby. Look, I even got you something. I saw this stocked on my pile of boxes in the garage."

"Seriously, dude?" His eyes were watching the ball bounce up and down. I laughed at him as his face frowned at me, not believing that this was actually working out like that.

"I'm amazed this actually worked. This used to be my father's. It is as old as your ass." I laughed out loud. "I thought we could try a new exercise to get you from disappearing in your head."

"Seriously, what the fuck, Cypher? Besides, this is a serious matter. You might be in danger if—"

"Oh, come on. It's only to try and calm your nerves." I stopped bouncing the ball and threw it toward him. Angel caught it with no problem giving me an annoyed look.

"Just promise me that if this goes south, you'll flip the switch and leave," he said, putting the new ball into his pocket. I frowned at him as he didn't throw it back to me.

"Yeah, yeah. Just how many times would you have to remind me, dude? Don't you worry, you little furry head big guy, I'll make sure I stay safe, you work on clearing your head. Got it?"

I tried to pat him on the head, and he swatted me away. "I'm going to make sure all the cameras are working before the show starts so you can see how brave I am. Can you go check on your leash?"

I smirked at him, and he only snorted at me. I laughed and decided to stand up to do what I said as I walked away. I felt something bounce off my head out of the blue. I flinched at the impact and looked back to see the ball rolling back. I laughed at Angel and shot him the finger.

After our fourth and last check of everything, Angel sat down on the chair inside the cell. I helped him to buckle the chains on his neck and the shackles on his hands. He watched his hands being trapped in with a frightened look on his face.

"Did you make sure you went to pee before the trip?" I teased him. He smiled a bit, making me feel at ease. I tested the restraints and took a step back.

"I'll be fine, dick," Angel said as he leaned back and closed his eyes.

I went back to the upstairs control room. I did a final check on the controlling buttons, the cameras, and the monitors, making sure the film worked and the electrical was good. I looked outside the window and saw that the moon showed through the clouds.

I felt my body get cold from my feet up to the peak of my head. I closed my fists tight, but I guessed, I started to get numb as the show was about to start. If earlier, I could still joke around, now, my mind was blank and various scenarios played inside my head repeatedly.

When the full bright moon showed up its half body, I heard a rattling sound of metal. I looked over Angel in the three monitors with different angles. I focused on the one placed in the top corner of the cage. I saw Angel's chest going up and down as if he had difficulty breathing.

I was about to ask him if he was okay through the telecom we installed but cut off when the laser thermometer I set up made a weird, alarming sound. I looked at it and got amazed at how the red line was about to reach the top of the thermometer. His temperature was so high but weird enough, his vitals were pretty stable considering how his temperature and his breathing, only his heartbeat was a bit rapid.

I looked out the window once again and watched as the tail end of the cloud disappeared and the moon now showing its true form. As soon as the moon became full, I heard the scream from Angel. It wasn't a simple scream of pain, but a scream when you're about to meet the grim reaper. A loud resonating scream almost blew my ears away as it echoed throughout the whole shop.

I turned to look at him quickly on the middle monitor. I was completely speechless at what I witnessed right now. My body stood there stunned as I watched the screen. He screamed with all his might. His mouth was open wide, and saliva drooled down his face.

At first, he tried to remain in the chair, but when his body looked like high voltage was electrifying it, he fell from the chair. His body bounced up and down on the floor before he got onto all fours. His head turned sideways and with force. I was even about to press the button when I saw his head was about to pass his shoulders.

I gulped as if something blocked my airway. Angel's scream, the alarm from the thermometer, and the rattling, screeching sound of the metal cage filled my whole shop. And even though I stayed upstairs, I could feel the vibrations made by his scream through my feet. I was a hundred percent sure; his screams were echoing outside.

I leaned over the monitor to get a closer look. I couldn't look away from the scenes that I had been anticipating seeing in real life that was about to happen right in front of me. I saw Angel's teeth change into something scary.

Long fangs came out of his mouth, ripping his jaw. His nose got bigger and larger until it changed into the nose of a dog. His ears were ripped into two and changed into a new pointed ear.

"Holy . . . mother . . . fuck," I cursed as I watched Angel's head turn into something like a wolf's head.

The fingernails on his hands were starting to elongate one by one and change into something. His fingers grew larger, and the nails kept growing. Unlike anything I'd ever seen.

His entire body started to increase with every breath he took. Hair started covering his whole body. From his face to his toes, hair . . . rather a fur started to coat all the spaces on his body. His back started to twist and stretch, making him longer.

I snapped out of it. That's the only time I could feel my breathing wasn't normal anymore. My heart thumped so loud but got drowned out by the screams of Angel.

I tried to calm myself down as I looked over at his vitals. They were off the charts making the machines keep on producing alarming sounds. I looked back over to the monitor.

Angel took one last glance at the camera as if he knew I was watching him. All I could see was clear concern across his painful face. His bloodshot brown eyes changed to a bright yellow.

It was so clear in my mind. It was as if a yellow liquid had dropped into his eyes and slowly spread all over. Worry crept its way all over my body as I felt something would go wrong. I grabbed the remote. On my trembling knees, I ran down the stairs as fast as I could.

"Angel!" I shouted as soon as I entered.

Not more than a couple of minutes after entering, he stood inside the cage as a large wolf with black and white fur. The cage was barely tall enough to hold the height, but it was wide enough to keep him inside.

Angel let out a ferocious roar deafening me and sending chills down my spine. The wind from the force of his roar almost blew me away. I lifted my hands up and tried to block the air to blow me up. At that second, his roar reminded me of that night from so far ago. The terrifying night we both experienced flashed in my mind like lightning.

I coughed repeatedly when the air became normal again. I tried to catch my breath when my eyes caught Angel's wolf eyes staring at me. He looked at me in silence.

Only his loud breathing could be heard, but more than that, he watched me as if he recognized me. I gulped my heart back down into my chest and mustered up all my courage, I took a step forward. I thought it was going to be fine until he jumped forward suddenly.

The chains that supposedly stopped him from moving any closer to the steel bars suddenly started making the whole building shake violently. The pure rage emitting from him was savage and soul breaking.

I could see in his eyes that all humanity from his former self was gone. This wasn't Angel.

The loud sound of the shackles breaking snapped me out of my thoughts. I shot a glance down at it and saw that he tried to break the other shackle. My mind immediately searched for the dial pad that I held a second ago. My heart raced as I heard a loud snarl from the wolf.

"Shit! Where the fuck—" I was saying out loud as I could hear the metal creaking under the stress. Fortunately, I found the remote. Unfortunately, it had made its way to the front of the cage. I didn't know how it got there, nor had the time to think of it.

I immediately jumped for the remote without any further discussions in my mind. Not even a millisecond, I pushed the button to turn on the voltage. With that shock, Angel lashed out in pure rage. The cage shook and vibrated in a violent way as his beast-looking body tried to break the thick steel bars.

I reached for the remote completely and didn't hesitate once as I heard the shackle starting to give up. I pressed the button and leveled the voltage up to half of its full capacity and straight into my friend. After a second, he howled in rage, lashing out until his last shackle broke, stopping the surge of power I depended on.

I stepped back in time as a giant clawed hand swept out from between the bars to reach me. I leaned back against the wall staring at the creature, slashing and clawing at the bars and walls in frustration trying to get out and probably eat me.

He tried to break the cage for a whole minute, but except for the vibrations and a few large scratches in the walls, I realized the cage was going to hold. He couldn't scratch or even bend a single bar with all the effort he put in.

After a while of watching him try to come at me, I got tired and brazen as I stepped out of reach and watched in amazement. I laughed as I mindlessly pulled out a smoke and lit it staring right into Angel's werewolf eyes, realizing at that moment that I wanted that power too.

CHAPTER 7

THEY'RE HERE

Someone . . .

"I am quite disappointed in you all for losing them," the man said over the phone.

"Sir, we have been searching all over for the last month and they have not turned up anywhere, they just vanished," the big guy replied through gritted teeth. "I have a squad searching the entire city and outskirts turning up nothing."

"You know our rules, either he joins us or he dies. We cannot have strays running around doing as they please. We must not be discovered. It has already been two cycles since he was found, so I am sending Kor to rendezvous with you in the morning. He will be taking command of the mission," the man said calmly.

"I don't think that will be ne—" The big guy was cut off before finishing.

"Soldier, what wasn't necessary were you trying to run the man off the road and shooting at him for getting the best of you." The man's tone grew more aggressive. "You think my men weren't going to report what had happened to me?"

"Sorry, sir." That was all he replied to.

"Kor will be there in the morning, so get your act together because he doesn't take kindly to failure." His tone went back to normal. "You have lost him twice now and I will not lose him again."

"Yes, sir," the big guy replied, looking defeated. "You told us not to intervene while the other humans were around, so we fled and then they lost us. But we will find them again, sir."

"I don't want to hear excuses. I want to see the results. There is only one man. How difficult could it be to track him down? Also, our scouts have picked up some movement in your area from some blood rats. I fear that this little escapade taking this long has led them here. Watch your backs and get the job done," the voice on the phone said.

"Sir," the big guy said as he put his phone back into his pocket and took a deep breath. "Men, move out and keep your eyes peeled and noses up. We might have company."

CHAPTER 8
POWER

Angel

The vibration from my throat tried to escape, but weakness already surfaced all over my body. I felt my eyes twitch although all I could see was darkness. The last thing I remembered was being shackled inside the cage. After a few minutes . . . my mind blocked out once again.

When I opened my eyes at first, I was confused as I was still inside the cage with pieces of broken metal scattered all over the floor. I lifted my hands to see if I had any strength left in me. With utmost determination, I was still able to lift my hands without any problems.

But at the same time, worried that my hands were freed from the shackles. Confused about what was happening, I looked up at Cypher who sat on the floor with his back on the wall.

He read something, but I couldn't quite see what it was. I looked back up to his face and saw him grin at me when our eyes met for an instant. He had a mug with steam coming out of it sitting beside him, while his other hand held a cigarette and puffed on it.

Cypher looked very relaxed while watching me stay inside this cold and big cage. He stood up, rubbing out the head of his smoke in the ashtray beside him, and walked towards me with an unbelievable look on his face.

"Dude! Fuck, you're awake! Finally! You have no idea—"

He started to talk about what he witnessed yesterday but my mind couldn't process any of the words he muttered. He went to the cage's door and searched for something in his pocket. I looked outside of the cage which looked like a storm had landed. Even though we moved most of his things out of his garage, there was still some stuff that was left and now scattered on the floor.

The opened door behind Cypher gave me a hint of what time it was. The bright color of the sun shaded in the dark color of the night. Was it sunrise? Or sunset? But seeing how smoking hot the mug was—which was a coffee for sure—without a doubt, it was a sunrise.

The wind blew from the outside, entered the door, and embraced my body. For a second, I didn't care as Cypher's annoying voice was still ongoing despite not having any words from me. But the next second, I felt how cold it was in this acreage when it was morning.

I shivered when the wind blew once again. I hugged my own body, and that was the moment I remembered how I woke up naked in an unknown place only a few weeks ago. I looked down at my body to confirm it even though I already knew the answer from it.

My eyes shut when I saw Roger out saluting at me. I sighed and glanced at Cypher who didn't give a fuck about my naked body delivering his exaggerated words. I lifted my hand and cut off his blabbering.

"Seriously, dude?" I glared up at him and stood up. "Can you, at least, let me put my clothes on, have a smoke, and some of that delicious-smelling coffee before you start at me? Can you?" I complained with a fierce gaze in his direction.

I moved my hands to emphasize to him my naked body. He followed my hand and almost choked on his own saliva when he saw me naked.

"Don't freakin' laugh. I'm telling you, Cypher," I warned him as I frowned my brows and continued to glare at him. But Cypher, who didn't seem to care, started to laugh at me. I rolled my eyes at him.

"Yeah, yeah. Very fucking funny. Could you please give me my clothing now?" I almost begged as the wind blew once again. which was freaking cold.

"Haha, dude. It must be cold out. Or is it a wolf thing?" he said maliciously. I frowned at him and tried to grab his neck through the steel bars. He immediately stepped back away and laughed at me.

"Okay, okay. Wait, I will open this cage of yours, big dog. Your clothes are beside the chair." Cypher's teasing voice never stopped. I shook my head at his jokes and went out of the cage after he opened it.

I immediately went to my clothes and put them on. I turned back around to see Cypher heading up the stairs, he turned back around and waved me up.

So, once I was done, I made my way up there. It looked like he had been up all night in there, the ashtray overflowed.

His eyes twinkled at something, and I couldn't help but snort at him and step back. He laughed at me, but his face now got a bit serious. That made me wonder . . . what the hell happened yesterday?

Cypher offered me a smoke. A moment ago, he wouldn't shut up and now he went super quiet. I lit up the smoke, puffed on it, and coughed nonchalantly. My throat felt so dry as if I just ate a piece of glass, and there were some stuck in my throat. I coughed multiple times.

Cypher turned his body from me as he went to his sink to do up some more coffee. He was silent and only the ting sound from the spoon and mug could be heard. While he was busy in the sink, I tried to puff some smoke once again, but after coughing again, I gave up on trying it.

Cypher tinged the mug with the spoon to get my attention. I looked at him and saw him walking towards me with a steaming mug in his hand. He gave it to me, and without any further ado, I sipped on it with caution.

The hot liquid immediately gave relief to my throat. I sighed at how delicious the coffee was. I looked back to say something to him, but he was back downstairs looking at the cage in front of him.

I made my way down to join him as he looked at it with a serious look. His blue eyes were given off a glow that I only saw when we were playing a game and he was focused. I sipped on my cup again.

I walked towards the cage to run my fingers across the steel bars. It wasn't bent or anything, but my fingers got a small slice from the prickles sticking out where it looked like something hit them hard. It stung but not enough to make my expression change.

I watched it bleed while sipping on my coffee. I went back to Cypher who had his coffee in his hand. My wound immediately healed and went back to its original state.

"So, the cage had proven its worth, I'd say," I said after inspecting the bars for any bends or signs of breaking. Except for the floor inside the cage that looked like a dog scratched nonstop on it, which was me, by the way.

"That is so cool," he said to me, staring at my hand as I wiped the bit of blood away. "And yes, you did quite a number on the place. I'm thinking of listing all the items you destroyed and billing you for all the repairs. I'd say that you have a bit of an anger problem" he finished with a toothy grin.

I shot him the finger. I looked around his place and saw his antique lamp smashed on the floor, the floor was full of dust, and broken glass for an unknown reason. The more I looked around the more I cringed at what I did, I gulped my saliva and got nervous while looking at Cypher.

He was known to buy old, antique, rare, and limited-edition things that you could only buy at either a cheap cost or at a very expensive one. If I broke the rarest item, he would tell me it was fine, but I would still feel like a bag of dicks. But it didn't make sense since we made sure the cage was empty so why was this stuff broken?

I gave a fake cough. I sipped on my coffee and walked towards the two chairs resting on the walls near the workbench. I sat down and tried to avoid Cypher's teasing eyes. He knew what I thought.

He sat down beside me, putting his mug of coffee on the bench. I shook my head and tried to change the topic. It wasn't like I couldn't pay him or that he needed the money, it was more the point of the matter.

"So, ah, we are going to have to beef up the security, right?" I asked after a second of silence and deep thinking about his broken items.

He laughed at me, and I looked at him while frowning my brows. "I don't think so. I think we need to fix the things that were damaged. It wasn't expensive. Don't worry too much about it." He shrugged his shoulders, rubbed his smoke out on the ashtray, and stood up. He tilted his head towards the door outside. "Come. I want to show you something."

He didn't wait for my response and only walked away and back upstairs. I put my smoke in the ashtray and my mug down. I followed him behind, but my eyes were being pulled by the big cage. When I heard the metal stairs clinking, indicating that he climbed up. He shouted my name, so I glanced one more time at the cage before walking toward him.

He left the door open, so I entered immediately. I didn't notice the first time how much of a mess this was too. The stuff on his cabinet was on the ground and scattered. Some of them were broken, but most of them were safe.

"Was this all my doing too?" I asked while walking towards Cypher who clicked some keys on the computer table. I tried to be cautious with my steps as most of the things were all over the pathway.

"Yeah, sadly, it's already been added to the bill," he said without any hint of seriousness or joke. He got busy typing on his keyboard. When I stopped at his back, I tapped his shoulder to let him know that I was behind him now. He glanced at me and pointed to the monitors using his head.

"Check this out, dude," he said. I looked at the monitors like he said, and to my shock and amazement, I was stunned at my feet.

I watched in amazement as he fast-forwarded through the footage. The footage showed how I changed into something. It was very detailed about what I did to make my hair stand up all over my body.

Screens were showing all different angles, and Cypher played them all with a serious face. He pointed out something that he noticed in every video. I couldn't believe what I saw and couldn't imagine how Cypher felt, who witnessed it in person.

In the last minutes of the video, I saw that Cypher went downstairs to the cage. I saw how his body was moved by a couple of steps by my loud growl. How his shop had become a mess, and how the camera shuddered at the impact of my movements and growls.

My heart got heavy as I saw how the beast of me broke free from the shackles. How I saw the beast trying to rake my best friend through the bars that protected him.

I even wanted to shout at Cypher on the monitor to run away like I went to watch a movie in a cinema. But I knew how frightening it was.

We both experienced the same life-and-death situation a couple of months ago. We both knew how terrifying it was to face your death and fight for your life. To think that I let my best friend experience it once again, I couldn't help but bite my tongue and close my fists. I was so disappointed, mad, and upset at myself.

If . . . if I forced him to leave me alone, he wouldn't . . .

"Dude, I know what you're thinking, and you can fuck stop. I want to help you figure this out and I'm well aware of the dangers."

Cypher cut off the darkness welling up inside of me. I looked at him with sorrow in my eyes. I couldn't express myself enough. I knew I couldn't repay him for the help he had given me, and in all. But I was impressed when I saw him sitting down in front of the cage while smoking and laughing to himself.

"The fuck, dude? Why were you laughing in there? You could've died, you know?" I asked with irritancy in my voice.

Cypher laughed at me, and he became serious once again. He played the video where I changed into a beast. Now that my mind thought of nothing, I could see my bones expanding, breaking, and reforming into something bigger. It was painful to watch it as it brought the feeling of the pain back.

I breathed hard as Cypher played the part where I tried to break the cage to attack him. He grinned at me now while wiggling his eyebrows and trying to be funny like he always does. I shook my head at him and hit the back of his head. He said, "Ouch," in a funny way but still laughed at me.

I turned my view away from the screen and looked over at something. I noticed the wall had a couple of broken lines that I knew weren't there yesterday. I was thinking of how much damage I did when Cypher tapped my back. He handed me smoke and nodded at me to look back at the video.

I was hesitant to follow him, but he played the video again where I tried to attack him. He zoomed in and it went to his smiling face through the bars. I hit his head once again but stopped my mouth to utter a word as I saw how my eyes were wavering.

The eyes in my beast form were yellowish with a hint of brown. It was bright yellow that reminded me of the color of the sun I drew when I was a kid. But the brown I saw were my eyes, but they were flickering in and out like a battle went on between them. It made me curious when those unfocused scary eyes wavered after a few minutes.

Cypher talked to me while my body tried to break the cage. He didn't stop talking to me like he talked to the human version of me. I looked at my best friend who smiled a bit as he heard what he said. Miraculously, the beast inside me calmed down and turned its back on him. Instead of attacking the cage, I sniffed around the room.

"You see, man? Do you see that? You remembered me in that form and stopped attacking everything. You calmed down when I called you fat ass. Well, you growled but that's expected," he said full of pride with a playful smirk on his lips. I only nodded in amazement. And he laughed at me once again.

"Are you saying that I caused all that destruction in the first few minutes I turned?" I raised an eyebrow at him and turned back to look at the destruction in the room. Even though we both knew that I tried to change the topic to avoid praising his braveness and cleverness.

"Yeah, I watched you for a bit, but all in all you were pretty calm the whole time. Well with the random smash and howl away from my direction. Now, I'm not saying that you should be free. But what I'm saying is that I know that with time and training, you can control it little by little. You recognized me as not a threat, and with training, you can do better than this. This is the start, Angel!" He was obviously excited as he laid out his plan for my training, which he called Dog Training to avoid any slipping of the tongue in front of other people.

Great, right? I felt bad now that I noticed my guilt for trying to attack him. He didn't even ask me if I was okay with the name or my opinion about his plans. But again, he faced a scary situation yesterday, so I would let this go . . . for now. No, I hate the title of his plan.

"I'm not going to lie. That does sound very promising, except for what you call it. Can you call it something simple? Like 'training'?" I tried my luck to change his mind.

"Dude, that is boring. What if someone shows up? I will have to say Dog Training, so they wouldn't ask any more questions," he said, trying to explain everything with a serious face, only to keep his clever jab at me.

I shook my head, surrendering to his bickering. "Whatever you say, dickhead. But what's the catch?" I asked him as I lit the smoke, he gave it to me earlier.

"I don't see a catch?" he answered with uncertainty. He stood up and faced me while I puffed on my smoke. He looked me right in the eyes and said something that forced the smoke out of my lungs. "Unless you consider that I want you to change me," he said with a hint of seriousness in his voice.

I looked at his face. His eyebrows and lips were in a thin line. He didn't even blink nor did his blue eyes waver from the question he asked. After a second of not answering him and just minding my smoke, I noticed just how serious he was about this.

With that reaction, I started to laugh my ass off. I even coughed once from trying to smoke while laughing. Cypher just stood in front of me and watched me like I was some insane person.

"I wonder how long it would take until you asked me," I shook my head, leaned my back against the wall, and smoked. "Listen, man. I also thought of that idea, because I knew that having this kind of power is something that we have discussed for a very long time. I've already considered it. But we still don't know what is really going on and until then, I feel like we should have you monitoring my change like yesterday," I finished while glancing at my wolf form on the monitor.

The man was persistent, that's for sure. He kept on pushing and pestering me for days. He wouldn't shut his mouth for a whole minute without mentioning turning him into a wolf.

He followed me everywhere I went. He even sometimes spoke through the door of his bathroom just to pester me while cleaning up or bother me while taking care of my business.

"Okay! Okay! Seriously, dude? I told you my reasons, but are you sure you still want to do it? Because I'm telling you, it's not as easy as you thought," I said to warn him when after a week of getting annoyed at him, I finally caved in.

"Dude! I wanted to have powers more than anyone. I can handle it," he said, full of confidence in his voice.

I sighed heavily as he looked excitedly at me. "Okay. Okay, I will turn you." As I spoke, his eyes widened, and was about to celebrate when I cut him off. "I have one condition. We must figure out how to control it first before we both become one."

"What? How long will it take then? One week? One month? A year? Dude! I can't wait that long!"

I snorted at him and stood my ground about the condition. He tried to change it, but I firmly said no to him. The risk was just too high if we both changed during the full moon without even considering the worst scenarios.

When he tried to negotiate once again, I elongated my fangs—which I learned to control just yesterday—to scare him and shut his mouth. It was very effective though because he put his hands up to surrender and agreed on my condition.

I thought my mind would be at peace now but that only seemed to work for a few minutes before he started using that as a valid reason as to why he should have this curse. He even tried to cut himself on my teeth by convincing me to let him look at them to figure out how they work. But learned quickly that it wouldn't be enough for the change to happen.

"You are a crazy bastard. You know that?" I said to him as I recovered from the cattle prod to the back.

My teeth were out, and I wanted to get him, but I knew that's what he wanted. He irritated me on purpose so that I would attack him and infect him. I knew his plan like how I knew the lines on my own palm.

"Really? Nothing?" He squinted his eyes at me, hands up, holding the still-sparking tool.

"I told you; I would turn you when the time is right," I said as my teeth went back to normal. "Stop pissing me off before I break something, which might be useful to you." I narrowed my eyes on him.

"Well, you're no fun," he said as he stood up while glaring at me. "You're right. I will amplify the electricity to the full five hundred thousand volts next time, just to be sure." He turned back smiling wide, generously waving his finger in my direction.

"Dick," was all I said as I laughed at his reaction.

CHAPTER 9

VOICE

Cypher

Angel and I met at work one day and it didn't take us long to become friends. We had a lot of the same tastes, except when it came to women. But we will leave that alone for now. We would go shopping while working and would occasionally hang out after work or play a game online together.

Working on the truck for as long as we did lead to some pretty long days, some of those days would turn into giggle fests when we would get tired. Those were some good times. We would bicker back and forth so much that most of the customers would accuse us of being married which was pretty funny.

Our monthly camping trips started because we like a lot of those survival shows, the ones that pitted people against the harshest of elements. So naturally, we figured that we would have no trouble doing it ourselves. Which led us to where we are now. Funny old world, eh?

So, I thought that cattle prod would do it. I knew he would be pissed, and he would most likely try and kick my ass. He didn't.

Angel was adamant about making me wait for him to control his 'curse', as he calls it. Which I preferred calling it a gift. He was so firm on his condition that even though I bribed him with fresh meat, not to mention the lifetime supply of bouncy balls.

He got pissed at me as I was non-stop pestering him about the timeline of our agreement. So, when he went silent the whole day and didn't even look at me in the morning, I knew that he was really pissed at me. I didn't have a choice but to stop pestering him and let him at least deal with his work calls first.

I know I shouldn't complain about it. Considering, I did have all faith that Angel could learn to control it in time. He was one of the most persistent people I've ever met, well besides Ninja, but he was a different kind of persistent.

Anyway, I mean like in terms of learning new things and understanding them completely. I'd seen him focus his mind on every word and detail that could help him in any way. He never disregards small information, saying that it was all part of understanding it to its fullest.

Unlike Angel, I was super impatient. A man who would always try to find the quickest way to do something or cut corners where he could get it done. My mood would turn upside down while waiting.

Especially in anticipation of what I know I would have, like Angel's powers. And, man, would it ever piss him off if I learned how to control it before he does.

I bet it was his main reason for denying my idea. Though I understood why he wanted me to wait, I couldn't imagine two wolves locked away in the cage would go over very well. And what if one of us got out? That wouldn't end up good. But I still think he would be pissed if I did control it first though.

"What's so funny?" Angel asked as he caught me chuckling at my own thoughts.

"Oh, nothing. Nothing, dude," I said with a playful grin.

He snorted at me and got back on repairing the cage bars to get all the sharp pieces smoothed out again. We have been working on this one for more than a week now. We had been smoking, drinking coffee, grinding, and welding up a storm.

Though, I admitted that this cage was a good investment. It was sturdy, durable, and enough to keep a big monstrous animal like Angel in place.

We did, however, have to beef up the shackles a little bit since that clearly didn't work out for us last time. We can't always rely on the hopes Angel would calm down at the sight of me, more likely he will attack and eat me on the fact I won't stop bugging him so much. Maybe a scratch would do?

"I can't fucking believe you shocked me with that stick. Well, I can believe it but why? Did you have to go there? Dude, I can still sometimes feel my side twitch," Angel said to me as he lifted and placed the finished gate back into its original position.

I moved in to help him, but then, I saw him lifting the gate without any sweat or strain. I hated that he could do that.

"Because of that right, there," I said to him pointing at the gate in his hand. He looked at me with a curious look at first—but when he realized what I meant, he shrugged his shoulders.

"Fair enough," he said as he brushed his hands off after hanging the gate on the big hinges. I looked at him in amazement. He stood up away from the cage and stretched his body. He went for the pack of smokes in his back pocket, leaving me with a jealous look on my face.

"It is a blessing that we don't need anything to lift heavy things. If you and I became a werewolf, I'm sure we can both lift my house," I jokingly said, trying to insert my secret motive with a swift move.

He knew right away what I did. He crumpled and threw the empty pack of smokes at my head and frowned at me. I laughed at him and continued my work. He didn't help me with welding the bars together.

Which was unfair on my side, even though the heavy stuff was his work, it didn't seem heavy to him at all. Wasn't that unfair?

After what felt like an eternity, we finally finished fixing and setting everything back up in the shop that he broke that night. The place looked better than ever, even before all of this started. I thought Angel's destroying everything was a bad idea, but I guess I should've let him break more things so I would have an excuse to reorganize and purge stuff that I didn't need in there.

We reinforced everything we could. I was satisfied with the outcome but not Angel. He walked around the place looking like it wasn't enough, or something was missing.

Or maybe, he looked at the mistakes I made to make me redo it until he was satisfied. He looked at the part that I did with intensity which made me laugh and nervous at the same time. I'm not a professional welder by any means, but it wasn't noticeable, so I wasn't that scared.

I thought it was just the fact that we had been cooped up in this place for almost two months now. We only left this place when it was essential to restock food, some smoke, and beer. We tried to avoid those friends of his in the city so most of the time I went out to grab stuff.

When we did go out together because he would get stir-crazy, we were cautious. We didn't want to attract any undue attention to ourselves as long as we could, we never talked to anyone. We even sometimes wore hats to avoid people looking at us or recognizing us.

There have been quite a few times we would have had to play dumb or hurry away from ex-girlfriends or old acquaintances.

I couldn't believe how difficult it was to search and buy all the things required to build a giant cage. There was almost no one who would sell a cage with the specs that we wanted, we had to be pretty creative when asked why we would need something like that.

You wouldn't believe the amount of weird looks we got from some people when we mentioned what we wanted exactly, they probably thought that we were some kind of serial killers.

"The place will hold, man," I said as I tried shaking the bars. It produced a low creak sound, but the whole cage didn't look like it shook from my force.

I nodded my head as I tried shaking it again, and the cage was still intact and steady. I walked over to the table and poured coffee for the ninth time in the day.

"Oh, I know. I have a bad feeling though," he said, making me look at him with curiosity while drinking my coffee.

"Bad feeling? What do you mean?"

"I can't explain it, but I feel like something bad is going to happen tonight. I can't help but feel helpless at that thought. It was a new feeling, but it felt surreal," he said with a serious voice as he walked over to me and took a seat.

I grabbed a chair and sat down. I drank my coffee while looking at him. He stared empty like something was missing and he was lost in his thoughts trying to figure it out. I put my coffee down on the table and gave him my full attention.

"Do you think we should call for some help?" I asked with a serious look now too. I couldn't help but offer that as my guts were saying to believe what he said. I've learned very quickly over the years to trust his gut feelings.

"Who will we call?"

"Ninja? Chris? Maybe all the boys? Whoever is available," I replied. I pulled out a pack of smokes from my pocket and took one. I offered one to Angel which he accepted. We were both now thinking through a cloud of smoke.

"No, I don't want them involved unless we have no other choice. Plus, Ninja is skittish. I don't want to spook him," he shook his head and laughed as we both imagined how Ninja would react.

"Yeah, that's true. I wouldn't want the boys to shoot you when you turned and tried to attack them," I said as I laughed with him.

It felt good to laugh every now and then. We could forget that something wasn't right, and our situation wasn't normal at all. Everything has been so tense lately.

With all that had been going on, so much had changed in such a short time. Angel looked like a mature man now. He got quieter when he was alone and always frowned his forehead as if he thought so deeply. He felt like he had a different aura now, but whenever we were together, he still felt like Angel.

Since it's been a while since we had talked about other people, we got lost in conversation about Ninja, Chris, and the boys that we had known for years. We were laughing as we reminisced about the funny and unforgettable moments with them. It was a good way of resting and recharging the batteries from all these native happenings.

We ate lunch while still talking about the good old days. We also checked everything and tested the machines that we would be needing for tonight's full moon after what felt like a long week. We had been talking for hours while working and we didn't notice the sun was already out in the sky.

"We should get you ready. It's starting to get late," I said as I looked up at the clock. I noticed that it was an hour before the night started.

"Yeah, I thought the same thing. Listen, dude, be careful and leave if you must. I don't want to see that crazy shit you did last time, Mr. Smiles," he said seriously.

"Yes, Dad," I grinned at him and saluted like a soldier. I laughed while he looked at me. I could see the concern on his face while I placed the shackles on him.

"Don't worry, dude. I'll keep your squeaky ball safe." I pulled the ball out of my pocket to show him before it threw it on the ground, bouncing it a few times before putting it back into my pocket.

"You're not as funny as you think, you know," he said as his eyes tracked the movement of the ball.

"I'm fucking hilarious," I replied and laughed at him.

"But seriously, Cypher, something isn't right. I have been feeling this the whole day now. I have this weird smell I can't pinpoint but it's giving me some really bad vibes. Maybe you shouldn't stay and watch?" He looked around as he spoke.

"Sorry, fast-food gets me every time," I said with a hint of silliness while holding my stomach. I tried to make light of the subject. He overthought once again.

"Funny. Just be careful," he said as his skin started to go red. I looked out the window and saw the full moon waving at us now.

I muttered a curse as Angel started to groan in pain. The alarms of the thermometer, and other cameras were starting to make my heartbeat louder. I glanced once at Angel who drooled and bent his body. I ran out and made my way upstairs to monitor him.

When I saw that the monitor blinked, I muttered a curse once again. I ran back down and shut the gate. Then the lights started to flicker, then the emergency bulbs activated. More curses came forth as I went down to the cellar and primed the generator, firing it up. The light bulbs become normal again as always. It's good to have backups. I came back up and a chill ran down from the back of my neck. I looked over to the wide-open door.

"Cypher! Get out of here!" Angel yelled so loud, but it was too late.

"Well, this is an interesting turn of events." A low rough voice came from my back. I turned my body to search for the voice. I positioned myself in a defensive style while my eyes were roaming around.

"Here we are thinking, we were hunting a stray dog, and we had a bonus. We found dinner." The voice came from behind again. My heart started beating faster as I turned around once again to find nothing.

"Good. That's good, get that blood flowing. It will make it all that much easier to drain you." The voice started to laugh which echoed throughout the whole place. It had a resonating sinister voice.

I reached down slowly for my sidearm. I tried my best to move in a quiet manner, but my hand clasped air. I groaned as I tried to push down the curse words I wanted to say, but I didn't get the chance.

The voice laughed once again, and my eyes found the weapon. I looked up at my desk where it sat, it seemed so far.

"Please do. Food without a fight just seems so dull."

"Who are you?" I spoke.

I tried to make a plan to get my weapon. I looked over at Angel who helplessly watched. His chest heaved in his attempt to break free.

It stopped him from transforming. I couldn't help but smile at the thought of him controlling his power.

"If you touch him, I will kill you!" I heard Angel scream from his cage.

"I don't think you are in any position to make any demands. We will get to you soon," the voice said from my back once again. "And as for your question, well, it doesn't really matter who I am. You won't be around long enough to care about such things," he finished.

I thought for a second, turning towards the voice again. I knew that wouldn't work so instead, I faked a sharp turn and turned back to maybe see who talked. It didn't work, unfortunately. I leaped towards the table and the gun was gone. I rose to my feet in laughter.

"Good try, let me help you."

The voice sounded like it was everywhere at once. The gun was on the floor in front of me. I don't get scared easily, but whatever was in this room with me, all I could say was it terrified—and it knows it. Fuck it! I picked up the gun and shook the gross feeling of nerves off me.

"You know, I don't know who you are or what you are. But if you are going to dance around with me all night and be annoying, I might have to off myself," I said to no one as I stared down at my gun.

"Pretty brave for a breather. I applaud you for that one."

I spun quickly as the voice sounded like it was right in my ear. I started to get pissed off when I saw nothing once again.

"Cypher! Get me out of here!" Angel screamed. I thought about it for a second. I doubted I could make it to the release.

"Your friend must be very strong. How have you kept him hidden for so long?"

"Oh no, that's not how this works bud, if you aren't going to answer my questions . . ."

I stopped my sentence. I got pale when I noticed a passing shadow right in front of me. He had a mean gaze on his face like I talked badly about his mother.

He wasn't very big, but I'll admit he dressed well, very well. He wore a suit and his hair hung down. I looked him dead in the eyes and he smiled creepily. I saw his fangs, so I shot him, or at least at him.

You know how when you fire a gun, you can't help but blink as that small explosion of percussive sound emits from the weapon? Well, I never mastered the ability to stop that from happening, and right about now, I really wish that I had.

I shut my eyes for a split second as that bullet left my chamber and he now stood somewhere else. Even worse, there were two of them. I kept firing and they kept multiplying until I felt the warm sting on my neck.

"Cypher!" Angel screamed in a voice I'd never heard come from his mouth before.

I couldn't move. My body was fully paralyzed, but I could feel the burn of my blood leaving my body.

"I am impressed. I haven't been shot by a mortal in a very long time."

The words sounded prolonged and echoed in my ear. The world moved at the same speed but also slowed down. This must be what death feels like. I've always wondered, but I never thought it would happen like this.

A huge roar snapped me out of my final thoughts. I looked up and noticed people were all over me. In my state, I couldn't figure out why, until I looked at Angel.

His eyes burned with hatred as he howled and stood. In one swift action, all his chair restraints slid off as if they were wet toilet paper draping his body. Even with everything going on, I couldn't help but be amazed at how easy it was for him to get free.

Angel walked through the bars as if they didn't exist. Few of the people looked up at him. It looked like they were getting ready to engage and face him. He started a full sprint towards the last set of bars and swiped with his huge claws shredding the steel like a piece of paper.

"Get him," the voice said from behind me.

The two men lunged towards Angel within a blink and just as fast were completely ripped into pieces from Angel's pure ferocity. I felt myself start to fall and hit the ground losing sight of the battle. I was so weak and could barely concentrate but I willed myself to look over at the devastation Angel caused on the men.

Blood poured down all over me from pieces of flesh flying. It burnt all my open wounds. I stared at the ceiling as I felt my heart slow down.

I looked back over to the fight and saw less than five of them on Angel. One was on his shoulders, looked like he tried to rip his head right off while the others were holding his arms. Angel's jaws wrapped around one of them tight enough to touch teeth.

With one powerful head shake tore the man in two and the other exploded upon impact with the wall.

I noticed that one shackle was still on Angel's arm. It took every ounce of will I had to reach into my pocket and pull the switch out, and even more to push it. I watched in slow motion as five hundred thousand volts crept through the line and spread out between all of them.

Angel howled in pain and the others screamed. They fell on the ground giving Angel the chance he needed to gain the upper hand.

I smiled as I watched him step on two of their heads and they became crushed watermelons, my eyes grew heavy, and I strained to keep them open. The pale man stood and watched as his last man got serrated by Angel's claws before he blinked out, my eyes grew dark and black took over my vision. Angel howled and brought me back to the light, my vision cleared, and he was right over my prone form staring down at me.

A very concerned look flashed across his features and in his eyes before the rage took him over again. My eyes were getting heavy again as I watched Angel smash through the door and in the direction of the stranger, my eyes closed for one last time.

CHAPTER 10
UNINVITED

Angel

I woke up in a daze. I felt my back laid down on a rough, bumpy, and hard surface. I groaned when the back of my head rolled onto something spiky. My vision got blurred at first as if it told me to close my eyes for a second and remember what happened to me.

The bad news was—I sat upright, feeling lost and fuzzy in a foreign The bad news was—I sat upright, feeling lost and fuzzy in a foreign environment. Good news, I expected to shiver from the cold but curiously, my body was still in clothes, well parts of them that I wore from yesterday. I'm so glad we tried stretchy pants.

I placed my hands on my head to try and shake out the cobwebs. I stood up slowly while my mind still figured things out and made sense of everything going on. I sighed when I remembered fragments of faint voices in my ears. I took a big intake of air and let it out slowly, I let the refreshing air do its work.

"Where am I?" I said to myself. The air was strangely familiar. A fresh, earthy, and humid air that filled my body with calmness was something I always felt outside of Cypher's house. At that moment, I frowned when I tried to orient myself to the previous happenings.

I looked at my surroundings, trying to figure out where I was. Big trees surrounded me as I took in everything that was around me. The sounds of the animals and the trees dancing together in the whistle of the wind were all playing with my sensitive hearing.

I looked around the area and saw a tree wrecked by force. With all those clues, my mind was still lost to me at the moment.

It felt like I must remember something, but my mind wouldn't allow me. The last thing I remembered was Cypher locking the shackles and chains on my body. My hands went to my face to scratch my jaw, when I got a vague scent of familiar blood. I lifted my arm and noticed that I had a piece of fabric in my hand.

With much curiosity, I tried to sniff it to see if that was where that blood was coming from. Its scent was unknown to me but somehow familiar. I tried sniffing around the surroundings, I could see the sun taking over the horizon, and the power I have enhanced through multiple hours of practice finally paid off.

When I pinpointed the direction of where it came from, I sniffed at it for a second before it finally clicked in my mind, Cypher was in trouble. I looked down at my dirty blooded hands and the cloth I held tight. I remembered now. This cloth was from the guy I chased after. We had a fight, and the wrecked tree was my doing when I kicked him, and his back hit the tree.

I gritted my teeth in annoyance and felt my fangs manifest in my mouth. The guy I fought was nowhere to be found, only some torn clothes blowing around. I remembered Cypher going upstairs and out of my sight after he made sure that all the restraints were properly attached and locked.

That was the very moment when I heard several footsteps and whispers. After that, the rest got scattered in my mind. I shoved the cloth into my pocket and headed back towards his place.

Cracking my neck with motivation to get to Cypher's place while sniffing the blood I was sure was his, I started to sprint. My supernatural speed let me fly through the trees at an incredible rate. Everything seemed to be in slow motion, except for the big and small branches I found, trying to block my face before I could duck, those were faster.

Amazingly, my feet were moving faster than my brain. It avoided the big rocks and stuff blocking my way in an instant. My mind wasn't the one controlling my body, it was my high-level instinct pointing in the direction of the blood.

In what felt like less than half a minute, I was out of the forest. A green-matted vast acreage of Cypher greeted me, but that was least of my concern. I looked at the giant hole in the shop where the door used to be and saw the mess inside from where I stood. The smell of the blood got closer and closer to my nose.

I rushed towards the opening and stopped with my foot on the inside, careful that whatever was around could still be there. I jogged inside further to search for Cypher, thanks to my overly sensitive nose, I found him immediately. He laid on the ground surrounded by blood and what appeared to be white fine dust, but I had no time to look around at the carnage.

I picked up Cypher and rushed him to his house and laid him on the kitchen table. I looked over at him, checking his body for any possible open wounds. I searched with obvious franticness all over, panicking because of all the blood he laid in. I couldn't find any open wounds on his body, but I could have sworn that man bit his neck and many others joined in.

I looked at his neck, there was nothing but a scar, a very fresh-looking scar. All his wounds were scars. There must have been multiple puncture marks over his body with dried blood all over. I leaned my face near his nose to feel if there was any air coming, but to my dismay, I felt nothing.

My heart started to grow cold as I tried to give him CPR according to those videos that I'd watched thousands of times already. The moment my palm touched his chest, I sensed nothing but a cold body. I froze up and all I could do was stare down at my best friend's lifeless and pale body.

His expression was so peaceful as if he was . . .

A single tear drop fell from my eyes. Then I snapped out of my daze and started to get angry. My arms felt heavy, and my chest felt hollow as I sat there hoping for a reaction or any movement from Cypher. I miserably sit on the cold floor.

Just . . . what the hell am I doing? I have the power that normal people wish they had to save the important people in their life. And yet, here I was . . . letting one of my best friends die.

I blamed myself and beat the hell out of the floor with my fists before my anger set in for another reason. The images of the men who attacked us vividly came into my mind. The gunshots from Cypher and how he tried to fight for his life despite knowing that he was at a disadvantage was a real act of bravery.

But, now with only his cold body left, I didn't know what I was supposed to do.

"What am I going to do?" I thought to myself as I ran my palms over my face in frustration, guilt, regret, and sadness.

I didn't have the slightest idea of how Cypher had lost his life in a blink of an eye. I didn't know why I chose to chase the man before saving my best friend. I didn't know what to choose or whether I would bite the hell out of Cypher to turn him into a werewolf.

But then, would it still work if he's dead? What if I told someone? Would there be a person who would believe in every word I said?

Nobody would believe what happened, especially since all his wounds were closed, which by itself was very weird and questionable. I looked at Cypher's neck for a long time. I must have sat there pondering for hours before I decided to make a phone call.

I stared at my phone after I ended the call. Looking at Cypher's pale body made me scared to death. If I wouldn't tell anybody about this, my mind and heart wouldn't be at ease.

After debating for an hour on what I should or shouldn't tell, I decided to stand out on the front porch to smoke—I didn't know how many—cigarettes when I saw lights pulling up the driveway.

I killed the smoke on the ashtray beside the window as I saw the car parking in a slow manner a meter away from the house. I rubbed my hands in my back pocket while looking back in the house towards Cypher's body on the table, before deciding to stride and greet the man I called.

"Thanks for coming so fast, Chris. I know it's a bit of a rush, but—"

"Angel, what happened here?" He cut me off as he looked around at the destruction that had happened to Cypher's shop. "Are you going to tell me what's going on?" he asked as he walked up to meet me in the middle.

I looked at one of our friends, Chris. His hair was messy, and he left his house in a hurry, without changing into normal clothes. I looked back at the house and gathered my courage to talk.

"Come on in. I will tell you everything inside," I said as I lit another smoke and took a lead to get inside the house.

Chris was an old army medic and a good friend of mine and Cyphers. He was in special operations as well. The reason why I chose him among the boys, is I know that he could keep his mouth shut and maybe help with hiding the issue if it comes to that. I trust his army instinct in these matters. I only hope nothing bad will come from this.

"What the hell happened?!" he exclaimed to me as he looked over Cypher's lifeless body. He immediately went to the body and checked the pulse's points. He tried to open one of Cypher's eyelids before he muttered a curse and tried to give him CPR, as I did.

"It's no use . . . Chris is," I said with full emotion before shaking my head at him.

He looked at me, bewildered by what I said before he removed his hands from Cypher's chest; and, ran his palm on his face.

"It's a long story, man," I replied looking out the window as I caught a strange scent.

I looked around outside as I tried to move my nose to sniff into the air. When it was gone after only a second, it left me with a frown. I guess because of my confused mind right now, I must be paranoid or something.

"I need to know my options," I finished and looked at him with a serious face. He looked at me puzzled by my words.

"Angel, Cypher is dead. His body is as cold as winter. I couldn't even begin to tell you how that happened. By the looks of the stained blood on the floor, I could tell he lost a lot of blood. But I can't seem to find any open wounds on his body." He searched all over our friend's body as he spoke with a bewildered voice.

I fought within myself for a few moments about whether I should tell him the truth about what happened or make up an upfront lie about something that was obviously not true. I debated multiple times and decided to spill the beans.

Fuck it. He either accepted it or he didn't.

"Listen, Chris," I said in between puffing on my smoke. "See all those little scars on his arms and around his neck?" I pointed.

"Yeah, what about them?" he said as he lifted a stiff arm of Cypher.

"They were fresh wounds last night. I saw it with my own eyes, Chris. When I got back to him this morning, he was already dead, and his wounds were all closed," he snapped back at me quickly as I finished the words.

"That's not possible, man. How the hell will that be possible?" he asked.

"Listen, there are a lot of things you . . . don't know."

I turned and approached him slowly. I looked into his eyes and slowly showed him how my fangs extend. He stood up fast and backed up putting his hand down on his firearm. His eyes were frightened as he stood in a defensive way.

"Woah, woah!" I put my hands up and withdrew my fangs. I glanced down at his hand which was ready to pull out his gun and shoot me if I tried to move. "I'm not going to hurt you. We have been friends for a long time, and you're the only one I can trust. Please, Chris. Listen to what I need to say. You will understand everything. Please?"

He watched me with his sharp eyes. He weighed my voice and sincerity before he decided to move his hand a bit away from his gun. "This shit is crazy, man. What the fuck are you? The last time we met, you didn't have those . . . those fangs," he said to me and then looked back over to Cypher.

Chris's face showed all the emotions he had. His brows were furrowed, and his eyes were unfocused. He looked at me and went back to Cypher's body.

He opened and closed his mouth as if he wanted to say something but fought himself to say anything. After a minute of silence, he shook his head at me.

"You know what, never mind. The less I know, the better. In all honesty, I don't know what to tell you about Cypher. He's gone . . ." he trailed off with his statement and sighed the hell out of his emotions.

"You think I don't know that?!" I said with a bit more aggression than intended.

He looked at me with a bit of fear in his eyes at my sudden outburst. I took a breath, calming myself as I watched Chris take a step back.

"Listen, man. I'm sorry. I'm . . . just having a hard time with this—wait, hold up a second," I said as I caught the weird scent again and made my way back to the window. Chris followed me with his gaze puzzled even though he remained at a distance from my back.

"Something isn't right," I said to him as I turned from the window quickly and headed to the nook under the stairs. I pushed my foot into the trim releasing a small lock that opened the wall, revealing racks full of firearms and other lethal equipment.

"Holy shit," Chris said in surprise. He investigated the room before turning to me "Wait a minute. Why would we need these?" he said with a small nervous chuckle.

I pulled out two basic Armalite rifles and handed him one, with a vest and a bunch of preloaded magazines. Chris accepted all of them with a question mark all over his face. But, without any questions said, he started to put the gear on and ready his gun.

"Sorry for dragging you into this, but shit might get a bit hairy," I said to him as he finished putting on the gear.

"No sweat, dude. You know I got your back. You and Cypher are my brothers. I only need to know one thing," he stopped what he did and looked right at me. "Are these the motherfuckers that did this to Cypher?" His eyes were serious, and I could see the anger build in them as he waited for the answer.

"I'm honestly not sure, Chris. But either way, I have a bad feeling about it," I said solemnly, looking towards Cypher's prone form.

Chris put his hand on my shoulder, squeezing it a bit as if sending an assurance on my whole body. "It doesn't matter either way, Angel. I got your back," he finished by checking the sites and pulling the slide back.

"I knew I could count on you," I said with a smirk as I headed toward the back door.

Two trucks pulled up into the driveway and not more than ten men got out. They were all armed to the teeth but had a very casual look. I noticed they were the same men I had an issue with before and immediately turned my rifle's safety off.

Call me paranoid but I disliked getting shot at without shooting at them first. They all spread out surrounding my sight. The main guy I went to assume was their leader, made some hand signals to his men, and turned towards the house.

I looked at Chris who looked at me at the same time. Chris mouthed something I didn't understand. I was about to ask him what happened when we heard a loud voice coming from them. "We know you're in there. We don't want any problems. We only want to talk to you," the main guy said as his hands kept on giving signals to his men while his eyes were roaming around the house.

I glanced at Chris who pointed his rifle towards the men and looked down at the sights. He looked at me and nodded as if encouraging me to answer.

"Oh, yeah?" I replied. I copied Chris' position and got a clear view of their faces. Without a doubt, they were the guys who were following me and shot my truck. "Then, why did your men fire at me and try to take me off the road?"

The man combed his hand through his hair as he spoke. He moved his head toward another guy. I moved my weapon to the side he looked at—and I saw the guy who drove the truck.

"Yeah, I'm sorry about that. You see, Brog, over there is a little hot-tempered and he liked that truck you totaled." He chuckled as he pointed back at the other man with the mean scowl on his face. I remember that scowl.

"But in all seriousness, we only want to talk with you. I believe that we can answer some questions as to what has been going on with you lately. We know what you're experiencing right now, and I assure you that we can help," he said, explaining his side.

I put down my gun and looked at Chris who looked at me now. He had a curious stare which wanted to ask what happened to me. Fortunately, he didn't ask me anything.

"Okay then. Even though I wasn't convinced of your reasons," I said as I lowered my gun to my side to stand up straight, hiding behind the walls while peeking at them. "Who the hell are you, guys?"

"Well, to put it short, we are like you," he said with a cold voice.

Like me? Did he mean a werewolf or something else? He didn't sound like he bluffed me. With his bulky figure and confident stance, I had a feeling that he wasn't telling me any funny jokes.

"I see . . ." I was hesitant at first, but his last answer was a bit convincing. "Is that why I sensed you, guys, coming?" I asked.

The man nodded as he shifted to his feet. "We have come to offer our guidance and to help you adapt to your new life," he said as he started to walk closer.

I looked over at Chris one more time. I signaled him using my hand to make his way back to the window at the front of the house. He nodded and slowly headed in the direction I pointed.

"Well, if we are planning to get closer, why don't you tell me your name?"

"That shouldn't be a problem. I'm Kor. Now, will you come out and talk to us?"

I thought about it for a second. I looked over at Chris who shook his head in disapproval. I shrugged my shoulders at him and turned my back. I opened the back door heading out into the yard. I made sure that I had cover because I still didn't trust them.

"You know, we are going to have to trust each other. Nobody is going to harm you," the man said as he watched me make my approach. He waved at his men to lower their weapons as the sight of me all geared up must have spooked them.

"All the same to you, but you need to earn my trust and so far, the track record isn't looking too good," I replied as I planted myself behind my truck. I raised my rifle tight to my shoulder and chest and kept my eyes on the man who spoke to me.

"That's fair enough," Kor said. "I'm a lieutenant and these are my men. We are a group of species like you. Our job is to recruit any strays that get changed without consent I suppose. You can say I'm offering you a place amongst our ranks," he finished.

Lowering my weapon, I pulled a smoke out of my pocket and lit it.

"A stray, eh?" I said through a plume of smoke. "And why did it take you this long to come to talk to me civilly? You could have told me this when we first met."

"Well, we usually wait until after the first turn because there is only a minimal survival rate, but we caught wind of some shady characters that wanted to get to you first. That's why we trailed you and tried to get you to pull over. But once again, my men got a little heated," he said glaring back at Brog who only chuckled.

"Maybe, you should have better control over your dogs," I said flatly as I washed my cigarette in a mocking way in front of the men.

"Fuck you, you puny fuck!" Brog said as he tried to step forward, but Kor was fast to stop him.

I cocked my receiver back in a show of intimidation which worked beautifully as they all raised their weapons once again, it made me smile. "I got to say you're not doing too well in the convincing department with that barking dog behind you," I said with a smirk.

"I'll fucking break your ne—"

"That's enough!" Kor interrupted Brog with a commanding shout and stared hard at him.

"If you speak again, I will rip your throat out myself. Do you understand?" he warned as he grabbed Brog's neck. He lifted the oversized man up off the ground, his feet dangled there for a couple of seconds before putting him down, Brog stepped back in line.

"Listen, Angel. We prefer to be called soldiers, rather than . . . dogs."

I scoffed at him and puffed on my smoke. Kor found it offensive, but he didn't say any words. The other men fell in line beside him, gritting their teeth and looking as if they were ready to attack me with only a snap of a finger from Kor.

"Let me be honest, you obviously have some exceptional skills, Angel. We don't want to see them go to waste. I believe you'll be a very good addition to our army, and I implore you to take this opportunity," he narrowed his eyes in my direction.

"And if I refuse?" I asked.

"Well, we can't have strays roaming outside the pack that we cannot control. So, if you say no to my offer, you leave us no choice but to eliminate you," he said without batting an eye.

The afternoon air was cool. I could see my breath as I took a deep inhale and released it. I looked up at the house where my friend had lay dead and I saw Chris looking back at me. He knew exactly what I thought and nodded.

Chris had been in his fair share of fights overseas and knowing that he could read lips I mouthed the words, "The big guy is mine".

I focused my attention back on the men gathered a meter away from me. "Well, Kor, all I'm going to say is that if you wanted to recruit me you shouldn't have shown up last night and killed my best friend because that just made me despise you. And as much as I'd like to learn how you, guys, didn't change like I did last night, I would never join forces with you, even if you kill me." I stared right into Kor's eyes as I finished my words.

His features changed to confusion. He looked at his men beside him with a curious look. "Last night? What are you talking about? We weren't here last night?"

"I'm done with your lies and this fucking conversation," I snapped back at him.

I bit the pin off the round black cylinder and sent it flying. I crouched down and closed my eyes as a brilliant flash surrounded the entire yard. Not a second later, Chris started firing out from the window sending rounds into the first man beside Kor.

I stood up and followed suit by sending a triple round burst into the chest of the man rubbing his eyes frantically and attempting to aim his gun up at the window.

Six more to go as the other men fell to the ground. A stream of bullets started their course toward me and Chris. I picked up a piece of mirror from my truck that got shot up and looked through it.

I saw Kor and Brog make their way to cover each other. Kor made gestures to have the men flank me. Two men turned and headed to the other side of the garage, but Chris put a shot into the back of the head of one of them.

"I love that man," I murmured to myself as I stood and lit up two more guys that thought that taking a direct approach was a smart move, brave but dumb. I'd give them that. I sat back in cover and felt a pain coming from my arm. I looked down to see a fresh bullet wound steaming through the new hole in my shirt.

"It doesn't have to be this way!" Kor shouted from behind the cover.

I shot a burst in his direction. I was done listening to his shit and I let my bullets be my reply. I was caught in the moment as I realized how comfortable I was in this situation, I was mad.

I caught a glimpse of him raising his hand and waiving. I immediately turned and checked the back side of the shop where the last guy disappeared and as I thought, he came barreling out like a man on a mission. I fired my gun only to hear a click.

"Fuck!" I said as I dropped trying to make a smaller target for him to shoot.

I heard the gun go off and a thud. I looked up to see the man's head had a new hole. I turned and saw Chris smile from the window, my eyes went wide as I saw two guys enter the room behind him. I mouthed words to warn him as he stopped smiling.

Chris pulled his knife and disappeared from my view. I stood up quickly and headed for the house only to get stopped by another hail of bullets. Apparently, he had more men hiding, two more guys were walking up and shooting at me. I quickly reloaded my weapon and shot both their feet out from under the truck then took both their lives as they fell.

I stood and peeked out. Kor was still behind cover with Brog as four more soldiers came running up and got into cover. I checked my weapons and reloaded my gun when I heard a scream from upstairs.

I shifted my attention towards the window and watched my friend get ejected out and slam hard on the ground.

Two men exited the house and one of them had multiple wounds and a knife sticking out of his neck. The man with the knife in his neck pulled the blade out and went right for Chris but I put a round into his skull. All of them opened fire at me. I fell quickly trying to think of what I could do to save my friend. I didn't want to lose another one, the bullets stopped, and I heard Kor speak.

"Angel, this is as far as you go. I won't lie, I'm quite impressed at the display you put on and quite disappointed that such talent is wasted but there are always more men," he said as he walked toward Chris. "Come out and drop your guns or your friend is going to die."

I stood and glanced at Chris who looked up at me with a smile and winked playfully but with meaning.

"I'm dead anyway," he said as he drew his sidearm out and placed a shot into Kor's shoulder and another into the man's head who held him. Kor lashed out and struck Chris sending him flying and striking the truck hard and falling limp.

"You have made an enemy today that you'll regret, I will promise you that," I said through gritted teeth. I stared long at my friend lying there on the ground not moving at all.

They started to fire at me again. I sat back and lit another smoke as I thought back on the times we all had together. Thinking that this was as good of a day as any to die, I reloaded my gun and took a long hard pull from my smoke.

The sun was barely visible over the treetops and darkness gathered all around the woods, everything around me slowed to a crawl as I took in the scene in front of me. I pulled all my available strength together and stood proudly. I turned to start firing when the kitchen window just exploded out.

CHAPTER 11
BLOOD RAT

Cypher

When my eyes opened, I could actually see a cloud of dust falling in front of me. I tried to move my body to the side and heard a creak. It wasn't a normal creak I often heard—it was the kind of sound that was so vivid I could identify the differences.

I looked at my side as I couldn't move my whole body. My eyes felt like everything they saw zoomed in and out. I could literally see a leaf falling off a tree from meters away in extreme detail.

I looked around my house as I could see some scratches and voices near . . . or far? I couldn't identify if it was near as I couldn't see anyone talking near the front door. Though, the voices were all clear and loud in my head. What the fuck happened?

I literally felt like I just woke up from the worst nightmare ever, but then I got slapped with a strong fist of fucking reality. My body couldn't move, and I couldn't speak. My eyes were looking around and everything around me moved in slow motion—making everything clear as crystal.

I was in my house on the kitchen table, I think. I could feel each light from the sun's rays fall from the ceiling and penetrate my eyes. Then, time became normal as I watched Chris approach.

"What was Chris doing here?" I murmured to myself as I saw Angel staring out of the window now. "Holy shit, cold hands," I wanted to say but couldn't. Why the hell was Chris touching me?

I tried to tell him to stop, that I was fine and to take his fucking hands off me, but nothing came out. I didn't even think that they noticed my eyes were open. I wanted to at least make a sound, but all the nerves in my body were being restrained by something.

I felt like I got locked in my own body and I got frustrated as the seconds passed by. I concentrated on forcing myself to take back control and as I did, all of reality around me slowed right down again. It went back and forth like this for what felt like an eternity trying to gain control of my surroundings. I finally slowed myself down and managed to stand, but time was still.

I had been amazed by the scenes in movies I've seen that had this effect, but now that I experienced it firsthand, it was creepy as hell to be moving at full speed while everything around you crawled slowly. I looked down at Chris and my eyes grew wide as I saw myself still lying on the table.

"What the fuck? This is freaking me out," I said, and I heard a vague echo as the words left my lips.

I tried to get their attention, but they were moving at a super slow pace. Angel faced Chris now and had a very concerned look on his face as he tried to give me CPR. Was I dead? Should I be expecting some reaper to come to usher me forth to my final judgment?

Well, all I got to say was, I wouldn't be going down without a fight. I haven't quite lived my life by the expectation of 'going down quietly', and I'd be damned if I don't go down swinging.

After I realized that nothing came from me, I started to wander around getting a feel for my situation and trying to piece together my options. How would I get out of here? Why was I even here in the first place?

Questions could make a man go insane, but I had this itching feeling that I was no longer a man. What kind of normal man would experience this? I ended up boiling it down to get back into my body. I ran back into the kitchen and looked down at my unmoving pale body.

"How do I do this?" My mind raced through ideas on how I could get back. I closed my eyes and stopped myself from overthinking. "Fuck it. It's now or never."

I jumped on top of myself and immediately regretted my decision. The pain started flowing faster and faster through my whole body. It felt as if lava flowed through my veins.

As time caught up to me, the pain just kept on increasing. I wanted to scream out in agony, but nothing came out, everything around me was shrouded in darkness, but I could hear what's happening around me.

Angel talked about some uninvited visitors. Wait a second . . . did he show Chris my secret gun stash? Douche, but understandable, I suppose? Chris could be trusted, and he's one hell of a shot. But that wasn't making me feel any better at this present moment.

The pain turned into a dull ache. I could start hearing more clearly on a normal level. I tried to move, but not even my eyebrows moved.

Speaking wasn't working either so all I could do was listen and wait. I heard trucks pull up and I heard footsteps walking past me. I tried to reach out but still, no prevail.

A man started to talk as a new surge of pain started coursing through my body—tearing my concentration away from what was going on. This time all my muscles seized up. The only words I could use to describe the pain would be multiple stab wounds per every inch of my body, mixed with millions of creepy crawlies underneath my skin. This was fucking awful.

I got distracted for a moment as gunshots could be heard outside, but I had no time to think about that as my body reared up. My spine arced up on the table but came back down just as quickly in the blink of an eye and went back to zero movements but still in immense pain.

"Of course, just my fucking luck. I just want to scream and maybe, a fucking smoke too, but no. I can't even move my fucking finger." My mind screamed my thoughts while my mouth did nothing.

I started to get pissed and this started to get annoying. I laid on this table, looking fucking useless while my friends were having a grand old time outside with some new uninvited guests. I was already over whatever was going on with me, but what were my options really? Did I even have choices? I couldn't do anything about it.

My mind went deeper into my head to block out the pain and hopefully, overcome this nightmare; but the deeper I went, the less I could hear outside. I decided to take the pain to make sure my friends were still alive. The pain died down around the same time the bullets did.

I listened intently when a surge of light went through my eyes followed by more unbearable pain. My eyes ached with pain and they seemed to swell in and out of focus, but on the bright side (no pun intended), my eyes were starting to gain visuals. I still couldn't move my body but blinking was most definitely a good start.

When my eyes stopped pulsing and came into focus, all I could see was the ceiling. It was a glorious, beautiful vintage thing, even if it was a shitty old ceiling. I chuckled to myself.

Well, it's in my head so the choice was small for it being to myself. After a second, my head fell towards the front room as I saw the door open and two big men walk in. I saw Chris pull his knife out, sidestepping and dodging the first man's attempt to attack him. The scene sent him into a series of moves that gave a bunch of slices from the man's stomach to chest down to his arm.

"I love that man," I thought to myself.

Chris had some serious training, and he wasn't afraid to use it. He looked amazing with a blade. I used to have sparring matches with him, but of course, he had some proper training while I always relied on my muscles.

Watching him fight the first man-made me reminisce about all the times I got knocked down on my ass. The second man sent his foot into Chris' side, and he fell hard. As I watched him get on all fours, I noticed that he held his side with a frown on his face. His breathing looked like it was labored. Broken rib?

"Get up, dude." I cheered him on from my mind.

He lashed out putting his knife into the foot of the man that kicked him, sending him to the floor in pain as the first man snatched him up by the throat, and lifted him right off the ground. I stared in amazement at the feat since Chris weighed at least two hundred pounds and yet, this man held him up with one arm. Chris' eyes were getting heavy until he looked at me, we locked eyes for a moment, then he smiled.

He reached behind his back and pulled his spare blade out and sent it flying at much speed into the man's neck. He screamed in pain, and I caught the man yelling, "Stupid human!" as he threw my friend out of the window.

I got angry and my body started to vibrate, getting warmer and warmer. I could feel the sensation flowing down to my toes. I tried to wiggle them, and I felt a slight twitch.

I shot a glance back at the men. The one helped the other up and headed towards the door. I screamed and cursed at the top of my lungs, but no sound came out.

Then I stopped. I wasn't breathing or feeling the air entering my body. I quickly stored that concern for later.

I needed to get up and I needed to do it now. I shut my eyes and forced my mind to send out signals to all my body to get the gears rolling and for freaking fuck's sake, it started working.

I could feel the energy from outside. I could sense Chris and his weakened energy. I could also feel Angel and his increasing rage. I could discern the other men outside with energy that matches Angel's.

"Are they the same?" I thought as I sat up from the table. I didn't know but something from them made my senses tell me they're the same. Though, with different levels of energy, they had the same smell, temperature, and aura.

I looked around even though my body was sore. It felt like I haven't moved my limbs in ages. I stretched out my arms and legs feeling the tightness leave. I thought I'd give standing a try but no, I fell right down onto my ass after a millisecond.

I could hear vivid voices from the outside, but I tried to focus on getting back my mobility. I stood up again and used all my will to stretch my body out and circle my neck around. For all the aches my body had, I felt good and stronger than ever. I turned to look out the window as I heard the gunshots start again.

I watched as a man with a fresh bullet wound to his shoulder backhanded Chris hard and sent him flying into Angel's truck denting the side panel and falling limp. My rage came back in full force and my body stopped aching as my adrenaline kicked in. I turned and ran towards the guns.

The burst of speed I got sent me flying right into the shelving and almost through the wall, I didn't know how to explain the uncontrollable speed I just experienced.

"What the fuck?" I cursed to myself as I stood back up brushing the dust and debris off me. I looked around, no damage to myself but my fucking gun room was destroyed.

"Fuck," I cursed once again as I dusted off my rifle.

Sighing when I noticed that I broke the gun in half with my impact. I dropped it and when it hit the ground, the gunshots started back up. I looked down at my Berettas and picked them up immediately.

"This should work." I put some clips into my pockets and checked my guns.

I turned and walked towards the window. When I looked out, I could see men firing at Angel's truck while my friend sat behind it calmly smoking a fucking cigarette. I laughed a little at that until I started to crave one myself.

I looked at the men and closed my eyes, bringing my adrenaline flow up in my body. As I opened my eyes, everything slowed down and I swore to the heavens, I could see the bullets flying with ripples of energy as they impacted on the truck. I took a few steps back and unleashed my speed and went out the window.

I dove straight out concentrating on the light from the guns because it was the easiest to target, even though I could see the men as clear as day. My first two shots hit the closest man's chest sending him toward the ground. I kept firing as I flew tagging two more men with shoulder and arm shots.

I'm also certain I took off a few fingers from the last guy in the line before I hit the ground into an epic battle roll that got me to my feet quickly. All the men's attention was on me now. I started to make my way to cover.

The dive sent me all the way to the end of Angel's truck which was a pretty impressive distance. I rushed behind it and got into cover. I reloaded my clips quickly before I looked over to Angel who stared at me wide-eyed, smoke hanging out of his mouth pointing his gun at me.

"Hey," I said to him with a grin.

He shook his head. "Holy shit! Dude, you are alive!" he said to me with an exaggeration in his voice.

"Yeah, man. I saw you out having a smoke and figured I'd come to join you," I grinned playfully at him as I stretched out my arm. "Got an extra?" I held my open palm up as a gesture to toss me a smoke.

"Dude, what the fuck? What happened to you?" he said to me as he grabbed his pack and threw one in my direction.

"I don't know, man. It's a long story. Maybe deal with the fuck heads first, no wait, scratch that, send me a light first, and then we can deal with these fuck heads."

He nodded in agreement and threw a lighter. I sparked one up and took a long drag. Man, that felt good but weird considering I had to force myself to inhale. Angel poked his head out when he heard a voice and opened fire, but the man screamed a cease-fire.

"Friends of yours?" I tilted my head towards the men surrounding us.

"His name is Kor," Angel said to me as he reloaded his gun. "Shit. I have one clip left," he breathlessly said. I threw one of my pistols and a couple of clips out of my pocket.

"That's all I was able to grab," I said to him. I was about to say something when an unfamiliar voice interrupted me.

"Well, well, well, what do we have here?" I peeked out my head to look at the man who spoke. I looked back at Angel, and he nodded as if confirming that man was Kor. "Where are your friends, you little blood rat?"

I looked towards Angel and we both mouthed the words 'blood rat?' with a confused look.

"What does that even mean?" Angel said back as I chuckled.

"I'm not talking to you, soldier. I'm talking to that dead thing that's back there with you," Kor spat out with pure hatred dripping into his every word.

"I know you, guys, never really work alone, so where are they?" Angel looked at me and I just shrugged my shoulders and shook my head at him.

"Hey, man. I'm just the angry homeowner you woke up with all this racket you and your buds there have been causing," I said to him.

I heard a long gasp. "Heresy. Our kinds don't mix," he spat out again, clearly getting upset.

I looked over towards Angel who nodded towards the man that he shot. His legs were twitching. We started looking around at all the bodies as they were doing the same.

"It doesn't matter now. You have made your decision and after this new knowledge, well." Kor paused for a moment before finishing. "You, two, will both be dead soon enough."

I looked at Angel who smirked at the words of his buddy, Kor. "Hey, man. Throw me your knife." He looked at me with a raised eyebrow reaching down and unsheathing the blade and sending it my way.

"Don't worry, I'll give it back," I said as I caught it with my one arm. I grabbed the downed man's foot and pulled him towards me with surprising ease.

"Holy shit," Angel said as he noticed the ease at which I did that. I held the knife as I looked at the head wound on the fallen man whose twitches were starting to get more violent.

"They look like they are collecting their buddies," Angel said to me as he looked out past the truck.

"But why?" I said as I analyzed the man closer. I heard the wound bubbling then the bullet popped out as his eyes shot open and looked right at me. I got startled for a second. He grabbed my neck until a round entered his skull again putting him back down.

"Thanks, man," I said to Angel.

"Saving your ass is what I do apparently," he said back with a grin.

"We need to do something about this issue," I said as I flipped him the bird.

"I agree, what do you suggest?"

"We might have to do some hand-to-hand with these guys. I'm unsure how much ammo they have left but considering the number of rounds wasted on your truck I'm assuming much more than us," I said as more shots hit the truck while we talked.

Angel turned and planted some shots at them. I looked towards my garage and saw my old barbeque grill sitting up next to the wall.

"I'll be right back," I said to Angel.

I dove over towards the garage. I didn't even think the others noticed me. I hurried and unhooked the propane tank. It was hard to tell if it had any in it with the fact my strength has increased a bunch, so I assumed that it was full.

I looked back over at Angel and gestured that I went to head to the other side. He nodded as he put his last clip in. I looked down and saw an ak-47 on the ground.

Must be from the man with the head wound. I picked it up without any hesitation and threw it to Angel. He smiled and searched the body for clips as I headed the other way.

I heard the rapid fire of the gun start as I got to the corner. I peeked around to see two men slowly making their way toward me. I put the tank down and picked up a couple of short pieces of rebar I had laying in the pile of junk.

I twirled them a bit to get the feel of them quickly. I glanced out one more time before striking the first one across the face with a vicious blow, cracking his skull wide open. Before he even realized what happened, my other hand came up and drove the sharp end right through his temple dropping him like a sack of potatoes.

The other guy processed what happened, jumped back in shock pulling the trigger of his gun as he did, thinking nothing of it. I launched the last piece I had in my hand, sending it straight into his forehead. He kept squeezing the trigger as he fell sending an arc of bullets towards the sky.

When I brought my gaze back down to what had just happened, I noticed the bullet wound I had on my side. I didn't even feel it, maybe because of adrenaline. I hurried towards the ladder that went to the roof of my garage and headed up.

I slowly made my way towards the edge and looked down. Angel had been making some good work of the men down there, but they were slowly advancing toward him. I knew I was going to regret my decision of what I had planned.

My poor house . . . I fed my adrenaline as I launched the tank over the edge. I pulled out my gun and shot at it. Nothing, the fucking bullet just hit the tank and the tank hit the ground.

I looked in amazement at my utterly epic failure, not even thinking all the men stopped firing and were now looking up at me. Time was still as I watched all the guns aim up toward me.

It was then I caught a small little object rolling out from where Angel was. A grenade? My fucking grenade! I only had fucking one of those.

Not easy to acquire. In hindsight, I should have been preparing myself for the explosion, but I was pretty bent over my bad plan and my not using my own grenade.

I got ejected back and hit my roof hard, and I didn't stop there, no. I went all the way through to the concrete floor. It wasn't pleasant, but probably not as bad as what happened to the men outside. Angel came in through the new hole in my garage and over to me, I just laid on the ground staring up at the ceiling.

"Hey, man. Are you okay?"

"Is that my grenade?" I said calmly while still looking up.

"Really, why am I not surprised?" he replied while shaking his head.

"And, yes. I did use your grenade and your flashbang," he finished as my eyes shot towards him, shocked at the words he said even though I shouldn't have been surprised.

"You could have left that last part out," I said as I took his hand and got up. "You know how hard it is to obtain those," I said clearly irked.

"Yeah, yeah. I'll find you another one. I feel like we have bigger problems," he finished as he pointed out to the wreckage that was my yard.

My garage had some serious damage and my house was on fire. There were body parts everywhere. All the bodies of the dead men were gathered around the same spot the grenade just so happened to make it to. I looked over to Angel who looked at it as well.

"Blind luck," he said to me with a chuckle. I looked over to where Chris' body lay and dropped my head. Angel came over and looked.

"I'm going to miss that guy," I said with a sad and regretful tone.

He nodded in agreement as his fangs were now showing. "They will pay for this," he said to me with venom in his words.

"We're going to have to do something about this," I said to him pointing at the mess.

Luckily, I lived pretty off the grid, so I wasn't too concerned with anyone hearing the gunfire and the explosions. I knew we had time to go through some stuff after all of this. I paused for a second while I looked at all the carnage and blood everywhere.

I felt a tug towards the crimson liquid, and I leaned over and took a big whiff. My teeth shot out and my sight got super crazy. I got flashes of what looked like veins and then back to normal in an instant. Angel turned to me and looked shocked.

"Dude, what the fuck?" he said to me as I raised my hand and felt my teeth. They were long but not as long as Angel's got.

"Your eyes," he said quietly.

I looked at him puzzled, seeing flashes of his veins throughout his body but he had a pulse. He turned and grabbed a piece of broken mirror off the ground and my eyes widened when I saw my reflection. My eyes changed color as if it wasn't my eyes anymore. They were very pale blue with a thick red ring around them. I suddenly got a really sharp pain in my gut and fell to my knees.

"Woah, what's going on? Are you ok?" Angel said as he tried to help me stand up.

"I don't know," I said through gritted teeth as my back bent. "My stomach is hurting pretty bad."

I once again felt a tug in my mind that forced me to look at Angel's neck as he tried to help me. I could see the blood flowing through his veins, and it called to me. My mouth suddenly felt dry and thirsty.

I could clearly see and hear the transparent blood flowing in his vein. My lips opened as I was about to lean forward at him but pushed him away.

"Get away!" I shouted at him.

"I'm just trying to help, dick!" he said to me with irritation at my sudden reaction.

"I know! But I'm getting this urge to tear into your throat and, uh, drink?'" I said and held my throat that never stopped gulping.

He looked at me with a raised eyebrow. "Excuse me?" He chuckled.

"I think I need blood . . ." I said to him in a low voice as I was so unsure of myself. "And I don't think I'm being too picky on where it comes from at this moment," I finished as I looked at his neck plumped with healthy veins and flowing blood.

"Well, that's not fucking weird at all," he said to me as he looked around.

I caught some stirring going on in the back area and I nodded in the direction of Angel to look. He pulled out his weapon and headed over. He investigated a bit and came flying back at me.

I quickly rolled out of the way and Angel struck the ground hard where I was just a second before. He looked up at me in a bit of pain.

"I think one made it," he said as he tried to get back up to his feet.

I looked up as I was still on one knee. I saw the biggest man I've ever seen come out and it looked like half his body was fresh BBQ. I started getting flashes again as he approached, overwhelming my senses.

I couldn't react quickly enough as he grabbed me and lifted me straight up off the ground. I could see his blood flowing fast and saw his heart beating so fast. Because of our small distance, I could vividly hear the beats of his heart which made my thirst uncontrollable.

"You're going to pay for this," he said angrily to me, pointing a finger towards his face. "Burning fucking sucks," he finished as he slammed me against the side of my garage.

I saw Angel finally make it to his feet and aim his gun. The bullet went right through the big guy's arm, and it happened in very slow motion. The guy let me go and the blood started flowing out from his wound. I latched on to him with my teeth before I even hit the ground.

"What the fuck?!" the man shouted, trying to shake me off.

My teeth sunk deeper into his skin. I drank heavily even though it tasted a bit tangy, but it was still delicious. Until I thought to myself how gross this was but couldn't force myself to stop.

After a full second of losing myself, a giant charred fist went into my face and then tried to pry me off. Angel came up and hit the man over the head with his gun. I'd assume that he's out of bullets. He swung me like I weighed nothing right into Angel.

I was his weapon that was used against us. Before he even lifted me for the second time, I forced myself to let go and rolled to my feet.

I got a surge of energy, and I could feel the blood coursing through my body. It felt great. I got a warm, satisfied feeling as I smiled widely and ran at the man at full speed and watched as his hand shot out to strike me.

I moved to the side just enough for it to miss me. I came up with all my force and drove my fist straight up under his jaw. I heard and felt a shatter in his bones, and the sound amplified my smile more.

Right as my fist passed through his face, Angel's knife came down into the man's forehead. He stumbled back a few steps and fell. The knife lodged further into his head with the wet impact on the ground.

"Fucking gross," Angel murmured.

"Weird, it's actually not too bad. I'm quite surprised at how numb I am to this amount of carnage," I said as I looked around and then at the man we had put down.

"I'm talking about the blood-drinking, you fuckin' weirdo," he said to me with a laugh.

"Really? Out of everything that's happened lately, you think that's gross and weird?" I said to him with my own laugh. "Fuck it, let's clean this mess up before more people show up. We have much to go over and discuss."

"Still gross, dude. You can't change my mind on it," he finished as he turned to start towards Chris. I shot him in the finger.

We spent a decent amount of time gathering all the bodies. We decided that burning them all was the best solution, but kind of got spooked when we couldn't find Kor among the remains. We tried to search every nook of the place, but there were no signs of him anywhere.

We watched the blaze in silence as we wrapped our friend up, we walked him behind the shop where we placed a bed of wood down. Angel and I were tensed up in anger and sadness as we lit the funeral pyre for our fallen friend.

CHAPTER 12
FROM WOLVES TO BATS

Angel

It's been a long time since I put anything in this book.

Cypher kept telling me that it's important to write down anything that could be useful to us in the future, but in the past couple of months, the days have been blending together. Frankly, I wasn't the type of person to just forget the days and move on, but since it had been a while, I felt the urge to update what has been going on. Besides, it's probably a good idea, especially if it'd get Cypher off my ass.

"Dude, you better be writing something down and not just complaining and talking shit about me," Cypher said over my shoulder.

"I'm doing it now, you douchebag," I replied with my middle finger waving around towards him.

"Do you see what I'm doing?" Anyway, where was I? Oh yeah, the night that changed my life.

I remembered that night vividly playing before my eyes, and I doubted that I would ever forget it. I was sure that if someone have made it to this part, they would have read my accounts of the events so there's no need to get into all the details again, but I would say this, the number of bodies and destruction we dealt with in such a short amount of time was something that will stay with me for a long time.

Cypher seemed to be taking everything in stride and by that, I mean that it didn't seem to be bothering him at all . . . or was he just acting that everything was alright? Come to think of it though, we both have become quite numb and cold to whatever had been happening as of late.

I looked over at Cypher. He now filled his mug with a dark smoking liquid. The aroma of the newly made coffee fueled my senses with a reminder of how I'd missed my smell.

He lifted the mug right in front of his face and the faint smoke blurred my vision of his face. After a second of watching him sip his coffee, our eyes met.

"Does anything that happened in the past few months bother you? Like do you think about it at all?" I asked.

"No? I tried to think a bit about it, but really, I think that when I—well died, something felt off about me. The feelings that someone would normally have given at the events that have taken place aren't there for me if that makes sense? Since you know—I'm not quite a human being anymore." He leaned back on his chair, lit a cigarette and sipped his coffee.

"And the blood?" I lit my own smoke and asked.

"You know what? I probably would've thought it was something to be concerned with or would even cringe at but considering the circumstances that lead to my first feed." His lips formed a half smile, and his eyes went distant.

"The taste. The power it gave me made the thought of it pass right by and I've just tried to not dwell on it too much. We have been through too much shit, dude."

He said it as if he wasn't really thinking too much about it even though I found him sometimes looking at his teeth in the mirror, but since he said it with full confidence, so be it. But for me, I knew that my mind was busy thinking about it.

The scene flashed in my eyes of him drinking blood, and the truth that he needed to keep drinking blood made me feel a bit weirded out by it. I voiced it out to him last time. My concerns about the way he was supposed to live now.

We debated about it for hours because he couldn't give up drinking blood from the humans. It felt so weird saying that. The thought of stopping himself from drinking blood made him angry and his power would always surface.

We would have to take some time to ourselves for a bit because we would get into bad moods, but after realizing how difficult it would be to acquire human blood on the regular basis, he agreed to find an alternative to human blood. I doubted it would be that easy for him to go and milk innocent people of their crimson essence just because he gets thirsty, or would it?

We came up with a temporary solution, or rather, it was just the only alternative that applied to him. We have both been hunters for a long time, mostly deer, elk, and sometimes moose but now we are classified as super predators. Before I became a werewolf, I never thought of eating just any wild animals as a part of my meal.

But let me say that when I saw Cypher take down that bear with his bare hands, I was quite impressed and it really made our new way of life truly sink in. And don't even get me started on all the gloating I've had to endure after that happened.

I did have to snap him out of some pretty weird looks he had towards my neck every now and then. I guessed me being what I was didn't make a lick of difference to him, and since this was all rather new to us, we had no answer to his situation, just pure speculation and lore that we found online and in some ancient books we have.

With what happened that night, Cypher and I started to think that it would be in our best interest to go off-grid. We weren't sure if they would attack us again and we really didn't want to take that chance until we were ready. We both agreed to leave the area and city for a while as we try to figure things out.

A lot had already changed since the destruction of Cypher's house which we had to classify as a fire caused by a vehicle malfunction to the insurance company. Cypher got a nice chunk of change but refused to sell the land because of its history. I didn't think it would be an issue, and I totally understood why he wanted to keep it.

While dealing with that, I ended up selling my company for a pretty penny as well. I met with my workers and informed them of my plan. I gave them compensation and their benefits which were almost thrice my income for that month—but I didn't have any regrets at all.

They were such great workers that made my company successful for years. A simple bonus and some compensation wouldn't hurt me.

Once we danced around all the legalities and a close call with my monthly issue—which I didn't want to get into right now—we started to plan our escape from the town, and away from the people we know. We didn't want to repeat what happened to Chris. We argued about Chris a lot because I couldn't help but blame myself for his death and Cypher wasn't buying any of it. To avoid that, we needed to get out of here.

It would be tough for me to transform somewhere whenever there was a full moon since we lost the shop. But luckily, we brainstormed to figure things out before leaving. Upon searching estate offices around town, we had an idea that led us to find a little island while searching the areas from the online mapping system.

Its location was out in the mountains which was far enough away to not attract any attention and trapped me during the change. I did find that my energy got drained when I awoke and didn't kill anything during the full moon, not even any small game. Like humans, eating was a big factor in my survival as well.

My calorie intake was many times more than that of a normal human for my body to function properly, but it wasn't nearly as bad as Cypher's needs. It wasn't a pretty experiment on that little island. Cypher needed animal blood, and I needed meat.

We agreed to just share one animal as we would eat different parts of it. But we also started to realize that animals sense predators and the longer we stayed in the area, the fewer animals were around, so to balance it out, we resorted to buying from butcher stores, where some fresh pigs and cows were ready to be our food. A little bit expensive and lots of work, but it was still worth it.

It was quite nice camping out on the island for the time that we were there. It's very peaceful since no animals would get close to us. But finding a new place soon would be in our best interests since we weren't getting any closer to our end goals.

We ended up finding a nice property even further into the sticks under a couple of new names we obtained using some of our older contacts. I believed they were Auron Asteroth and Theo Raziel. I had no idea where Cypher came up with them, but it was only for the deed of the property we wanted to buy.

I already started to feel like I've been writing too much, and if it wasn't for Cypher's stinky eyes on me at this exact moment, I'd mostly call it quits on this whole thing, but I'll just keep writing in hopes that he'll ended up getting distracted by doing something else.

So, Cypher was much stronger now, not as strong as I was but not far behind. We pieced it together rather quickly that whatever had been happening to our overall biological issues had also been affecting our minds— which wasn't very appealing to think.

Cypher suffered from what we have been calling flashing. We came up with that term after experiencing and witnessing it happen. Now and then, flashing would stop him, and he would get a terrible hunger which was scary because he would always target my neck.

Even though we did go hunting very often, we had collected a great abundance of deer meat from the forest and more importantly blood, which seemed to be what he wanted the most. Like what we did to figure things out about my werewolf issue, we also experimented with different things about Cypher's vampire issue.

We knew that he was a vampire the moment he drank the blood of that man. We found out that he could eat normal food, but it didn't quite stop the hunger. It always left him feeling drained and weak. We had no choice but to stick to blood-drinking as his meal.

Cypher's healing ability was incredible in comparison to mine. The difference between my regeneration ability to Cypher's was the speed. My ability to heal wasn't dependent on anything. His ability always depended on his energy level.

I guess that was the reason for all his fat also melting off him within a week and his muscle grew new attachments, which made tearing impossible. We basically tested everything that we could think of to come to that conclusion except for the sunlight thing. We had read and found some lore books and stories on websites about the abilities of a vampire.

We pretty much tried it all and there were similar traits of the lore to

Cypher. The last thing on the list tried to go out where the sun waived in the sky. We really didn't want to risk anything, considering how volatile the movies and books make it.

The good thing was I could go into the daylight. He didn't need to risk it. We would go out at night quite often into the woods to do some training while hunting. I couldn't believe how fast he was.

I tried to keep up but in my human form, I wasn't quite as quick as he was. I also required fresh meat, apparently. Just because of my curiosity, I tried drinking blood the way Cypher did it. It worked quite amazingly for me too, but it's just gross to think of it. I think I'll just stick to eating raw meat.

His new abilities were starting to get better, but they still needed work. He had a very hard time at first keeping his speed to a perceivable level and controlling his hunger when there was another person we encountered at night. It was pretty cool, but the walls and broken tables and chairs would disagree.

Our new property was pretty amazing. A nice big house that we didn't ever use and came up with a shop near it. It was more like a showpiece for anyone if they ever did stumble across it.

I believed it was set up to be some author's house or something. I thought Cypher was saying something like that. The shop was massive and surrounded by trees—you could barely see it from the house.

We spent a great amount of time sitting out by the fire with smokes and coffee, just thinking to ourselves in silence and enjoying our new surroundings. Those moments made us feel normal again. Anyway, back to the point, the most interesting thing about this new place was the bunker it came with. Apparently, the previous owner was a bit paranoid.

He built an intricate tunnel system between the house and the shop. It also came with a secret escape tunnel that led out past the shop, which was impressive by itself. But the coolest thing was the bunker itself. It was massive and perfect for the doghouse—which was a jail to keep me by the way—as Cypher liked to call it.

Nothing better than a reinforced concrete room that had very few escape spots, to begin with, if something did go wrong. There were a few issues that we have been working on addressing, which was mainly the fact that Cypher's fluid intake has been increasing. He almost attacked a few hikers that camped out the last time that we hunted.

But the upside to it was his abilities getting more under control. He learned to control his abilities at that moment because I happened to punch him in the face. I thought he would get angry at me for that but instead, he muttered thanks for waking him up.

The other thing that concerned me was when I changed over, apparently, I acted crazier than normal when Cypher was around—which I assumed had to do with his new self. I noticed that ever since he became a vampire, I had a deep surge of the feeling of picking a fight with him all the time. I got the suspicion that he felt the same way toward me and it was harder to control the hungrier he was.

Come to think of it, does he really feel it? Like, does he want to bite my neck off my body and drink my blood? That was a scary thought but . . . I looked at Cypher's back as his shoulders moved as if he did something secretly.

"Hey, do you get the urge to kill me?" I boldly asked out of nowhere.

He stopped what he was doing and slowly looked over at me. "Uhm— what?" He raised his eyebrow and looked over at me.

"Well, I do notice the looks you give my neck sometimes. And I also have the weird feeling like we should be fighting each other. If that makes any sense at all." I chuckled a little bit to try and make light of what I had just said.

"I don't mean to stare at your neck, but I have tasted wolf blood. And man, it was really something. Besides, I can't really help it at times, but I am getting better."

He turned around fully to look right at me. "I do have the same feeling as you, but I'm just chalking it up to my whole hunger thing. I'm having a hard time controlling my urges and I feel like every time I drink blood, the time before I need more becomes less."

"Yeah, I've noticed that as well. I guess it must be difficult since it's only the two of us here." I nodded as my mind started realizing just how difficult it really is for him.

He nodded and turned back toward what he worked on. I stretched my neck to see what he did or made. It was a red smelly bloody water-infused creamer.

I smelled some aroma of coffee so I guessed it was for his coffee. Blood creamer for coffee? Weird but I could respect that. We spent a lot of time researching and training, trying to perfect our skills for any upcoming battles— and not just from unknown groups of people like the ones that killed Chris, but between the two of us.

Now with our new enhancements—I guess I'd call it that—which made for some interesting sparring between us, we also branched out to various alternative weapons to master that complimented our unique abilities as we felt that shooting guns off all the time wasn't the best way to avoid attention.

Cypher loved this idea because he loves his sharp toys. Now, obviously, running around the city with a sword on his back wasn't the greatest idea but knives worked just as well. Just not as cool in his opinion which I just shrugged it off.

As for me, I preferred to be more physical. I found myself interested in some knuckles but that's overkill considering my strength as it was. We didn't slack on our gun training at all. We had an awesome range set up in the bunker that we spent a lot of time putting together.

We spent sleepless nights, well I did, I don't think Cypher sleeps and a great amount of coffee to finish it as soon as we could. We use it a lot to keep our gun game sharp, or when we train with high and low-level noise to test our hearing ability. I can't express how much our enhanced hearing sucks in an enclosed area firing weapons.

Cypher dropped his rifle skills for pistols since it allowed him to be more agile. I went in the opposite direction. We got pretty good, and I think we're closer to being able to venture into the city without worrying about Cypher losing his control. We figured this out after our last pretty heated sparring session we had, which was pretty intense. The good part was Cypher finding his control and the bad was the constant repairs to our bunker.

"Are you ready to get stinky?" Cypher circled around me. His eyes watched my stance and tried to figure out my next move.

"Stinky?" I raised my arm to smell it. I didn't notice anything out of the ordinary. Yes, we were sparring so I was a bit sweaty—but as of late, I ran pretty hot.

He took this time to act, launching at me in a second. His fist moved at lightning speed, giving me a hard time tracking it. He almost got me too, but I moved to the side quickly enough to get my hand on his shirt. Without any second thought, I swung him back around and towards the wall.

I could swear he nullified gravity as he positioned his body to land on the wall as if he floated before shooting back out towards me, stopping out of arm's reach.

"Yeah, ever since I changed, all I can smell is a wet, stinky dog." He laughed as he fixed his shirt. And then blinked out of view.

I turned fast knowing he would come from that direction. I sent my fist towards where his stomach would end up, and it didn't fail my instinct. I hit him with enough force that he rose above the ground from the impact of my punch.

I felt like if he breathed, he would have the wind knocked out of him—but I was wrong. My eyes followed him as he started to lift my punch. His hands wrapped around my arm as he reached the apex of his rise. He pushed up, flipping his body around and over my head. I knew what was going to happen next was going to hurt. I braced myself for the pain.

"Oh hell," was all I could utter as he used the momentum of my hit to propel my weight over him and onto the ground.

"I think you broke a couple of my ribs." Cypher stood over me while I looked at the ceiling. He held his shirt up and all his bruised stomach returned to his pale and paperwhite tone. I could also hear the bones setting themselves back into place.

"The sun was in my eyes," was my reply as he reached his hand out to help me up.

"Sure, it was," he said, turning and starting to walk towards the door.

"And where are you going? We aren't done here." I hate that he always tried to end our training with him getting the last kick in.

"I'm hungry. All that ass whooping I've been doing has developed a hole in my stomach," he said, opening the door to walk through.

"No, actually that was my fist!" I yelled to his back, to which he responded with a good, cursed place finger aiming in my direction.

I looked down at my arm as the adrenaline slowed down. I noticed that Cypher's nails pierced them in his throw. They were already closed but blood continued to drip a bit. At that moment, I realized that Cypher wasn't drooling over it.

It was then that I thought we might be ready to head into town and test our abilities. We discussed a lot about what our plans would be when we both came to the realization that we could potentially use our abilities for the good.

Not that we care about that too much, but when I think about it logically, getting rid of the low-life criminals in the city would be the easiest way to keep our needs a secret.

Cypher did an admiral job of quenching his thirst, but I could tell that it was taking its toll. The last thing we wanted to do was to have him lose control and garnish us some unwanted attention. It was already known that we were being hunted.

So, the only thing left to do was to prepare for our first night.

CHAPTER 13
BLOOD

Cypher

I started to get a bit antsy on our way to the city in anticipation of doing some real hunting.

I pushed back my hunger by going into my head and looking back at the last few months and how much has actually changed in our lives. We often talked before all of this happened, about how we would be if we ever had the chance to fight crime like some of the heroes we've read about in comics and watched on the TV. Miraculously, it happened now.

Obviously, our situation was a bit different considering the circumstances around our individual "powers" or whatever you may call it. Angel and I were on two separate sides of the spectrum when it came to our abilities but at the same time, built completely in a way that complement each other.

The one thing that always came to me though was the fact that we have become pretty numb to the idea of normal people being food for us, well me mostly. We have talked over the weeks about between our training sessions that being vigilantes would be the best and easiest way to get two birds stoned at once.

"I think this spot is good enough." Angels' words snapped me out of my head and back to our task.

"I agree."

We parked our truck at the edge of town and headed in on foot. We figured there was no better way to test out our training than to stretch out the legs a bit in the outside world. We knew we could make it to the city core where all the action was without wasting too much time and effort.

Since I was faster than Angel, I naturally leaped away to the first building and then the next. I immediately noticed how our training had improved my mobility, I felt like a piece of paper flowing with the breeze.

I landed on a ledge and turned back expecting a finger pointed in my direction but instead, I was surprised to see Angel following. It took him a little longer since he had to get used to the landings because of how heavy he was. I was just glad that my weight didn't drastically change like his. I mean, I used to be bigger than him before, but technically I was still not fat, so I did drastically change, just not in a bad way.

I turned back to look towards our destination, I could see the city lights in the distance. We got wind of a local gang that liked to prey on helpless young women. This city was great for degenerates like that, kind of reminded me of Gotham City from the Batman comics because of how bad the crime was.

"You know, if this was Gotham, I don't think I would enjoy knowing that Batman isn't going to like what we were doing in his city." I laughed nervously at the thought.

"Agreed, fuck that," he said, stepping onto the ledge to look over and gauge the distance to the next building.

"It actually makes a lot of sense as to how our kind have been able to get away with this secret world of theirs with the amount of crime there is." I chuckled as I joined him and looked over the ledge. I stared down and watched all the people walking on the streets.

I had to close my eyes and relax my eyes from all the bright lights of the city landscape. The noise from the vehicles and people all around the city started to catch up to me. I tried to take a deep breath through my nose and immediately regretted the decision. Animal blood held no sway over the aroma entrenched me.

It was a bit overwhelming at first for me to push my urges down being around this much human blood. I opened my eyes and my vision started to auto-zoom on random people. I could see how their blood was different from each other, how darker or lighter the color was, and how fast It flowed in their nerves.

If I just stared for a second at someone's neck, I would eventually hear that person's heartbeat urging my thirst and making my throat get dry. Before this night was over, I would have my fill.

"Hey, man? You alright?" Angel looked over at me, clearly noticing that I was pretty much drooling over the edge.

I gritted my teeth and looked away from the people below us. I licked my lips while a grin formed. "Oh yes. I was just thinking about the light snack I plan on getting in a bit." I looked over at him with my grin getting wider.

I could see that Angel was hesitant about feeding on people, but I convinced him that he must try it just in case it had a positive effect on him. His feeding wasn't like mine. He didn't get the hunger I do but I knew that his abilities were directly related to his hunger in a similar fashion to mine, and when he didn't eat his other half got grumpy. I also think it was the fact that we were going after bad men that made him agree.

We got to the top of the roof and leaned over to watch and listen. I concentrated on sensing fresh blood in the area while Angel used his exceptional hearing. He had his sense of smell back in full force, but I had a much easier time with blood.

Our abilities were both matched in those departments, but he grew sharper the closer to the full moon we got while mine depended on hunger.

We both looked in the same direction at the same time, nodding to each other. We launched ourselves over the edge and onto the building below, surprised at how Angel had landed, not making any sound as if he was a feather. I glanced at him and gave him a thumbs up.

He just shook his head at me, making both of us grin at each other. We both jogged over to the edge and looked down. I immediately spotted two men trapping a woman against the wall.

They were all standing near a large trash bin. The city lights were reflecting at the end of the closed alleyway. One smacked the woman around while the other laughed and fumbled around with his pants. I tapped Angel's shoulder who looked so hard at the trio. He looked at me and I pointed to the men, smacking my lips together.

"I hate a lot of people in this world, but I have to say that rapists are on my top list of people I really wouldn't mind if something bad happened to them,"

I said with a sneer.

"Really, huh? And what number are they?"

"Number 3," I said with disgust on my face.

"Really? Number 3?" Angel looked at me for an explanation.

"Yeah, people who fuck around with children and hurt animals for no reason are way worse." I looked at him as if it was obvious. I shook my head and clenched my teeth as I imagined what I would do to people I caught doing that.

"Fair enough. You're not the only one, dude. They were like number 2 on my list to punish," he said as he turned toward me, nodding his head in approval and putting his fist out.

I just laughed and did the same. We proceeded to play rock, paper, and scissors to see who got down first. Angel won.

"Fucker," I said as Angel smiled at his victory. Angel waved to me as he stepped off the ledge.

"That's so bad for the knees," I whispered under my breath. While falling, I saw his finger come up. I forgot we had earpieces on to communicate from a distance.

Even though we both have hearing ability, we still thought that having an earpiece was better if we got separated for some reason, we could still communicate with each other. I shrugged and chuckled.

When Angel hit the ground, the attention of the men suddenly changed to look over at what that sound was. Angel walked towards them slowly and menacingly; he held a calm face with a slight furrow in his brow. Fortunately, my eyes were very clear when it was night. I could even see the pores on Angel's face.

"What the hell?" The guy who smacked the woman earlier looked at Angel. The guy looked up and our eyes met. Instead of hiding, I grinned and waved my hands at him.

The men looked at each other. The guy who looked up said something to the other guy. And now, they were both looking up at me. I couldn't help but wave my hand at them which made them take a few steps back.

"What—what the fuck do you want?" The first man stumbled out, turning his knife towards Angel.

"Yeah, mind your fucking business before you get hurt!" the second man added trying to do his pants up quickly.

Angel said nothing. He just kept walking calmly towards them. Only tilting his head. I heard his lips forming a smile at the man pointing the knife at him, paying no attention to the one fumbling to tighten his belt.

"Fine then. Do you want some fucking trouble? I'll fucking give it to you," the man with the knife spoke as he headed toward Angel.

"Bad move," I said to myself as I saw the man get closer to my friend.

I saw the second man finally fix his pants. He bent over and picked up a knife he either dropped or placed down to undo on his belt before we even saw them. The second man didn't seem to be in as much of a rush as the first. You could always count on these guys to be cowards often.

Angel stopped his walk as the first man started to run towards him. For some strange reason, the guy didn't attempt to stab Angel when he reached him. Instead, the guy threw a haymaker to the side of Angel's head.

Now, I suppose a regular person would be affected by such a hit, but we both knew that Angel isn't a regular person anymore. His head didn't move an inch, and even worse was the guy's hands that literally shattered upon the impact forcing him to drop his knife and grab his bad hand.

"Fuck!" the guy screamed while holding his busted hand in the air. He looked up at Angel, clearly in a tremendous amount of pain.

"Fuck you—" he shouted but got cut off.

Angel's fist hit him so fast and hard that I could see his knuckles enter the man's skull. It didn't take a genius to know that it was a killing blow. But to my surprise, the man fell instantly and started to scream even louder while rolling around violently.

"Fucking show off," I said into the earpiece. I caught a slight smile from Angel as he turned his attention to the other man.

The second guy stared, open-mouthed at his buddy that just got dummied. His eyes looked up and met Angel's gaze. My friend's eyes were glowing bright yellow.

His intense and fierce look made the second guy pee; the fucking guy actually pissed his pants! Angel took one step towards the man, which snapped the guy out of his frozen fear. He dropped his knife and ran while screaming like a kid.

"That one is mine, dude," I said to Angel, who stopped his walk and just nodded slightly before turning back towards the woman who crouched in the fetal position.

I stood from the ledge and began my run; I watched as the man tried to disappear into the shadows. It didn't work as well as he thought. I smirked and launched myself off the ledge. My feet landed right in front of him, making him scream in terror and fall backward onto his ass.

I smiled widely with my fangs extended as I approached. I opened my mouth as I stared at his neck. I could see the dark color of his blood, as I could also hear it flowing like water inside his body, his heartbeat was undeniably music to my ears. I took a step, but the man just fainted.

"Are you fucking kidding me?!" I cursed to myself as I looked down at the pissed-covered man.

I leaned over and grabbed the man's arm. I turned away and started walking back toward Angel. He stood by the woman. I walked up and released the almost lifeless man. The woman stared at me confused as I pulled out some zip ties and placed them on the unconscious man.

"Dinner," I said with a fanged smile. The woman's eyes widened at my words.

"He's just joking. We're tying them up for the police to come get them," he snorted while giving me a stern glare.

"It's safe now. You should hurry and go home," he finished as she took his advice and left as quickly as she could.

"What?" I said to Angel as he stared at me while I made my way over to the other man who was clearly dead now from the blood loss.

I tried my best not to get distracted by all the blood splattered on the ground. It wasn't worth it to lick it off the ground, but I knew I wanted to. I practiced my restraint since I knew we had a live one.

"You know damn well what!" he barked back at me. Barked, man I am funny.

"C'mon, that was funny. And you know it." I looked at him innocently. "You should go get the truck so we can get these guys back." I finished as I leaned over and lifted the dead man.

He just stared at me. I was sure he contemplated hitting me or not. I smirked at him as I squatted in front of the dead man. I lifted his cold and lifeless body. Angel's eyes grew wide as I sunk my teeth into the dead man's neck and took a swig.

"What are you doing!" He looked at me with surprise.

"Uh—I'm eating? Duh," I said as I pulled away with blood running down at the corners of my lips.

He once again began to stare at me. Without a word, he turned and left to grab the truck. I continued to feed myself.

The blood flowed down my dry throat. I could feel my fangs getting deeper and deeper on the skin of this man. I enjoyed the blood when suddenly my stomach started to twist and turn.

I could feel a thousand lightning bolts, shooting and twisting through my nerves, and my head started throbbing so much that my clear vision now got blurred. I dropped the man and bent over in pain.

I fell to my knees and started to vomit up all the blood I had just drunk. I lay there for what felt like an eternity waiting for Angel. When he pulled up, he immediately got out and ran over to me.

"Are you alright?" he said, looking down at me.

"I don't know. As soon as you left, I started to drink again, then my stomach twisted, and it all came back up," I said while clenching my stomach.

Angel helped me get into the truck. He ran back and loaded the men up, while I sat there in pain wondering what the fuck just happened. I got a clue from something I read from our research. Vampires don't drink dead man's blood.

The rest of the ride was quiet. I forced my body to expel the rest of the blood out of my system. On the bright side, I felt immediately better once it was all out. We pulled into our bunker. We each took a body from the truck.

"I'm going to put this one in the incinerator. Take that one to your pen," I said as I lifted the dead man onto my shoulder.

"Copy that," was all he said as he did the same and headed in the other direction.

We had decided a long time ago that installing this incinerator was the best way to get rid of any evidence we might have. Sure, it was a risk traveling with the bodies, or not working if we ended up in a bloodbath—but for the most part, it was a solid idea. Nothing like flash-frying a corpse.

I laughed to myself as I pushed the button and headed back toward the kennels. Angel already had the man propped up in a chair and restraints put on.

"Should we blindfold him?" he asked as I walked into the cage.

"I don't know. Do we plan on letting him go?" I chuckled as my rhetorical question left my mouth.

Once again, he just stared at me. This time, he clearly fought the urge not to hit me. I walked over to the man and pulled out one of my knives.

I dragged the sharp blade across the man's exposed cheek, watching the blood immediately start leaking as the skin started to split. Before I finished the cut, the man woke up and started to scream, making my cut all wonky. I immediately placed my hand over his mouth and leaned in with my grin, teeth, and all.

"Hush now. You don't want to wake up the neighbors, do you?

The man stared at me wide-eyed and passed out again. I couldn't help myself and just burst out laughing. I could see Angel from the corner of my eye, trying not to laugh at himself. When I looked his way, he went serious.

"Should I be concerned that you are enjoying yourself this much?" He looked at me then the man.

"Maybe I should be concerned that I'm okay with this and might possibly be enjoying myself as well." I laughed at him. I turned back towards the man releasing my hand from his mouth.

I looked down at the blood that covered my palm, hesitant to try it after the last time. My urges got the better of me and I started to lick the blood off. It was amazing.

Words cannot begin to describe the taste as my taste buds ignited off every single drop. I thought when I drank during our fight at my old place was good, but this was something totally different. I could feel my body accepting the blood, and I couldn't help myself. I started wiping more off his face and into my mouth.

"Really, dude?" Angel walked up and pushed me away from the man. "Let's try and act a little civilized. Okay?" he finished as he pushed a needle into the man's arm.

I shook myself out of the daze and started to help him. I grabbed the hose and strung it neatly along the chair. Setting up some coffee mugs underneath before opening the valve.

I watched as the blood slowly made its way through the tubes and started to drip into the cup. My mouth watered in anticipation as the blood worked its way to the rim. I leaned over to grab the cup and replaced it, fighting all urges to chug it down as fast as I could.

"Here, I want you to try," I said as I lifted the cup in Angel's direction.

Angel was hesitant to grab the cup. After a second of looking at it, he reached out and took it, staring down at it again. The other cup filled up and I slid another larger container to catch the blood.

I lifted mine and fought myself to start sipping it slowly. The liquid coated my stomach with pure ecstasy. I felt my body and nerves getting energized in an instant. I looked up to see Angel still staring down at his cup as if it was poison.

"Don't be a bitch, man, just drink it. You won't know unless you try. Plus, you've done worse for less." I looked at him with a raised eyebrow knowing full well that my words were intended to goad him into it.

He looked up at me and scowled. "Fuck it." He pressed the mug to his lips and slammed back its contents.

He emptied the cup and rested it back down to his side, waiting to see what happened. I quickly finished mine off as well and watched as he started to smile.

"I feel pretty good, I'm not going to lie," he said with blood-stained teeth. "Still fucking gross though." He threw in quickly before reaching for a top-up.

We both laughed and filled our cups back up, enjoying our victory over the night. It was hard waiting for the blood to fill and not just tear into the man. He started to stir a little bit and we both took a step back, cups in hand, trying not to make him faint again. We had some questions that needed to be answered.

"What—what's going on?" the man softly said, weakened from the lack of blood.

I looked over at Angel and tilted my head. Basically, I told him that he should be the one to talk to the man since I've made him faint twice now. Angel nodded and took a couple of steps toward the chair.

"You should tell us where your main hideout is," Angel said bluntly.

The man squinted at Angel and started to look around the room frantically 'till he locked eyes with me, and he immediately looked away. Doing that made him notice the tube sticking in his arm and the blood running out into the container.

"What the fuck are you, guys, doing to me?" His eyes grew wide as he started to shake his arms, attempting to break free.

"You should just answer the question." I walked up and rested my hand on his shoulder as I spoke.

I lifted the cup of blood to my lips making sure he saw the contents while my eyes looked right into his. His eyes grew extra wide as he let forth all the information that he had. We found eight different locations for his group of assholes; we would be going to be busy for a while.

Then the incinerator burned for the second time that night.

CHAPTER 14

BLIND LUCK

Angel

You know when all of this started happening, I always kept thinking to myself, that it was just my luck, that being locked up once a month to stop me from causing havoc and mayhem wasn't exactly how I saw or wanted my life to go, but then something changed. I didn't know if it was when Cypher changed or not, but now spending one night a month in a cage is a fair exchange for everything that we have now.

I mean, who would ever imagine themselves inside of a cage? I spent the whole night while the full moon was up in the sky, not that I could really remember those nights anyway. Like, don't get me wrong, one night is nothing in the grand scheme of things, I just didn't quite think it would turn out this way.

For years, both Cypher and I would always bring up the topic of what superheroes would really be like, apart from the obvious fact that it was comics and not real life. I doubt Clark Kent would get away with hiding just by wearing glasses, but then again people are dumb. We could both go on for hours back and forth about the whole thing, and it seemed like so long ago now.

I suppose we were technically superheroes. Well, there was that grey area where we ate our victims, but that's just a little minor blip. I kept telling myself that anyway since I still hadn't gotten used to the whole feeding aspect. I coped just fine living off the land. We had a great abundance of wildlife around and I found it fun to hunt like a predator.

Cypher, though had a different perspective on the matter, I think it had to do with the difference in each of our biology which I wouldn't even know where to begin or attempt to blabber on about the scientific things I didn't even really understand yet. All I knew for sure was that he needed a great amount of blood, and human blood was his priority and most of the time to the last drop.

At first, the animal blood seemed to do the trick, but it died out fast, human blood seemed to be the ticket. He wasn't wrong though, in the sense that when we ingested human blood, it sent our bodies into an overdrive of sorts, him especially.

He went nuts when he was around blood. It took a long while for him to build up the strength to not tear into any person he saw, but a lot of patience and more than one close call seemed to work out for the best, well besides the fact that he apparently gets thirsty quite often.

"Are you going out again?" I looked over to Cypher as he zipped up his jacket.

These past few nights, I often noticed that Cypher was always going outside at the same time of the night. Though I knew that he just checked things out near the area, I couldn't help but still ask the question.

"Yeah. I need to get out of this bunker for a while. My body got a chill and as you know shouldn't be possible so I'm assuming it's a gut instinct of sorts." He loaded his pistols as he spoke.

"Do you want me to come?" I started to stand as I waited for his reply.

"No, it's alright. I think I want to do a little recon and see if I can smell some dogs." He looked over at me with a grin.

"When your stinky ass is around me, I have a hard time pinpointing anything." He shook his head and scrunched his nose as if he smelled spoiled food.

"Copy that. Just be careful and call if you have any issues." I sat back down, leaning over my coffee.

"Yes, Dad. Do you want me to be back when the streetlights go out? You know, streets are very dangerous for a handsome man like me," he said in a placating manner.

I replied with my finger, which he answered back by shadowing over and snapping my finger to the side. Shadowing was what we call his ability to move so fast he was essentially a blur, which he likes to use frequently. The break was like lightning passing through me.

The impact on the air as he cut through the wind left me dumbfounded as dust got into my eyes. I rubbed my eyes and frowned in front of me as if he was still standing there. And he wondered why he was so hungry.

"Ouch! What the fuck!" I said as I stared down at my finger sitting at a perfect 90-degree angle.

I groaned and cursed under my breath. I glared at the opened door where Cypher went out. I shook my head and took three long breaths in preparation to straighten my finger.

"1 . . . 2 . . . fuck, that hurts." The audible pop my finger made going back into place resonated through my arm. I stood up quickly to shake out the pain and walked towards the door to close it.

I could hear a faint maniacal laugh echoing down the concrete walls and out the opening. I went to get him back. I raised my hands and rubbed them together trying to numb the little bit of pain left on my once-curved finger. I healed fast but fuck that was annoying.

I stood in the doorway staring out into the wood, I could hear all the water rushing down into our collectors. I looked at the dark sky and twinkling stars. The night wind blew past me. The sound of the crickets, dancing leaves, and animals echoed through my heightened senses. It really was a nice night.

"Next time close the door, you animal!" I yelled into the forest before turning and shutting the door.

Hours seemed to go by as I kept an eye out on the local news channels that were flashing on the small TV next to the radios and local law scanners to see if we could find any weird animal attacks or sightings. But these guys were good, and it proved to be very difficult to locate them or even get a hint as to what they were up to in our city.

"Nothing but the usual crazy person and drunk drivers. Humans were nuts," I said to myself chuckling because I finally got the chance to admit that now since I wasn't one of them.

I stopped suddenly and perked up a bit, I could smell something, like the fresh rain as if the door opened for a split second. I tried not to move and smirked a little. Cypher thought he was slick and went to try and sneak up on me.

This should be fun. Just a little closer . . . I shot my hand back and latched on to a finger that was an inch from my head and as I spun around my momentum forced the finger to point back at Cypher, my smile grew from side to side as his eyes grew wider. I stood and planted my foot into his chest sending him soaring back into the wall.

"Ouch! Fuck that hurts." Cypher stepped out of his hole in the wall holding his sideways finger. He shook it out, and the bone popped back into place.

"It's all fun and games until karma bites you in the ass." I laughed at him.

"More like a rabid dog," he replied as he took a seat while massaging his finger.

I went to the sink and poured him a coffee as I laughed and topped up my own. I heard him mutter some expletives under his breath, to me that look on his face will keep me entertained for the next little while and it'll be even more entertaining to keep reminding him of this moment.

"So, did you see anything while you were out and about?" I slid him over the mug and took a seat.

He grabbed the mug while placing a smoke in his mouth. He took out a small flask and undid the lid placing it onto the table and reached for the lighter on the table, his smoke lit up while he added his special red creamer. He looked over and pointed to the flask.

I just stared at it for a few seconds, I could smell the aroma coming out of it and it called to me, but I shook my head instead in the negative and he shrugged, putting it back into his pocket.

"Not a damn thing, but what I've learned is that it is incredibly hard to smoke in this weather." He sat back and took a big inhale of his cigarette.

I looked at him with a confused look. When a second passed, my look turned into frowning at him. He laughed at me and shrugged his shoulders as if he was proud of what he accomplished on his trip.

"Productive," I said with a small chuckle.

"While I'm outside, I'm thinking though," he started to say while stirring his coffee.

"Uh-oh," I quickly cut in. I shook my head and lifted my hands as if trying to stop him.

"Oh, shut the fuck up!" he snapped through a cloud of smoke. "What if we created something to lure them in?" He raised both his eyebrows while looking at me.

"Hmm, I'm not saying it's a bad idea, but I'm listening." I crossed my arms and gave him my full attention.

"Very funny, dude. What I'm trying to say is what if we tried to do the opposite of what we're doing right now?"

I looked at Cypher who looked at me with a serious face but with a proud grin. I nodded at him as if encouraging him to continue his words.

"For example, we're doing things very cleanly. We leave no traces of our existence every time we go out. What if . . . we tried the opposite of it? What if we left our smell, and let them trace us?"

He went on to explain how he figured that they would have caught wind of our extracurricular activities by now but hadn't because we were just really good at what we do. We've been hiding here for a couple of weeks now. We've been monitoring our surroundings with caution. Fortunately, we didn't encounter anything at all.

When we were going out, we made sure that our faces weren't seen as we always walked on the dark side of the road and corners. For all the days we spent here, there were no weird or unusual smells. If someone from Kor's group would try to visit us secretly, I would still have the instinct to sense them like before. Or at least, they would have left a trace of smell somewhere.

Cypher suggested that maybe we should deliberately be messy. Trying not to be too careful and sensitive to everything. He did drag out the conversation a lot more but that really was the gist of it. He really did have a point.

"That actually might work, and it would be nice to hit them on our terms," I said as I scratched my chin in thought. I nodded as I processed the words he blurted out.

"Awesome, let's go!" Cypher jumped up excitedly.

"Woah, woah, woah, calm down. We should probably plan this out a bit better. Like step by step? Back it up with plan B maybe C?" I put my hands up as I spoke.

Cypher was known for being a repulsive person . . . or a vampire now? Either way, he still hasn't changed the way he acted as if he was still the same as before. Maybe that was the reason why I was still hesitant about his plan.

But it was actually a really good plan. It might work and we might find something by doing that.

"What's there to plan? When we plan, we get away with it. I thought we were going to make a mess?" I couldn't argue with the point he had just made.

"Besides, we'd been listing things about them. We tried multiple things on you that might work for them too. How will we get a chance to try it out if we're not having time with them?"

"Okay, you got a point at that. Well, it's almost dawn and I need to run into town to grab a few things and fill up the slip tank. So, how about we do it later tonight?" I said, hoping to calm him down a bit.

I sipped on my mug as I watched Cypher. He frowned his brows as he leaned back on his chair and glared at me. I shook my head at his reaction.

"Fine, but I'm coming with you to get some shit too." I watched his shoulders sag in disappointment.

"Do you think that's a good idea? The sun is coming up soon." I looked at him confused.

Now, we haven't really tested what sunlight does to him, but we did find out that if it's cloudy out like it is right now, he is unaffected. I was just worried that the weather might change, and the sun would suddenly invade the whole area with its blazing and hot rays of light. With the descriptions in the books of vampires, sunlight was their greatest enemy. Enemies that they couldn't fight or even had a chance of winning.

"You know I'll be fine in this weather. Come on, you always get to go get stuff. I'm bored when you're not around here. Instead of talking to the TV, why not take me? I'll be good. I swear with my pinky."

He looked at me all innocent. He blinked his eyes as if he acted cute, which in truth, sent shivers down my whole body. He acted like a child.

As if his parents would say yes to his face when he acted like a child. A very dangerous child that could rip a man's throat out before he could scream.

"Please, stop making that face. It wasn't worth seeing, dude."

I finished up a few things. I worked on some stuff while Cypher did some light training. He constantly taunted me to come spar with him.

He called me pussies names as he jumped lightly and flexed his boxing style by punching the air. I would just shake my head at him and laugh. After a couple of invitations to spar with him and a few times declining and ignoring him, he finally focused on shadow training.

We started our way up to the main house. When I entered, I was amazed at how little it had been used since we moved in. Everything was still in place from when we had it furnished.

The smell of dust and untidy houses welcomed us. Though we cleaned this upper part of the house occasionally, it was still left unattended for weeks. We headed out to the truck and got in.

Usually, I was the one to go and get supplies at the little town not too far off. But, since Cypher insisted, we took a trip to the city instead, since he hadn't gone out there in the daytime since he had changed. I didn't think it would be a bad idea since there was a nasty thunderstorm out, so I doubted many people would be out and notice us.

What worried me the most was the sun, but now that I couldn't even see any stars in the sky, that worry slowly died down.

"I wonder what those other guys do during their transformations. Like, do they have a big facility with a ton of cages and stuff?" Cypher was lunging back in the seat, throwing a ball he found somewhere in the air and catching it. He was playing while I was driving in the middle of this dark road.

I glanced at him, deciding to just let him be, but when I saw the ball was familiar, I immediately tried to snatch it from him.

"Will you stop doing that? It's distracting and mine!" I snatched the ball out of the air after trying for the third time and returned it to my pocket. I glared at him as he was just shrugging his shoulders. He looked like a bored child.

"And I'm not too sure, but I would like to find out. They could have some useful information." Cypher nodded his head in agreement.

"I'm surprised we haven't run into any others like me again." I nodded my head in agreement this time.

The truth was we were waiting for them to attack us. We're not letting them find us for weeks because we still haven't found a way to completely kill or win over them, at least. But after weeks of being caged and experimenting with a bunch of weird crap, we came up with a list of things that could work on them.

The rest of the ride was quiet as we were both thinking about how we would lure the wolves out. I was considering staging an animal attack and seeing who would come to investigate. When I voiced it out to him, Cypher didn't like the idea.

He said that he couldn't wait until my next cycle to do it properly. He was insisting on doing it as soon as possible, as the next full moon would be in two weeks. But for me, I was firm on my suggestion.

It would be better to attack them when we're both in top condition and not just him who would have the chance to fight them head-on. What was the purpose of having power if you'd just sit in the corner during the battle?

Cypher basically wanted to shoot off a roof and hope someone heard and came charging. Sure, on paper, it sounded alright but there was always the chance that they would just watch and follow us. He also said they were just trying to get the upper hand again by attacking us at an unexpected moment. We ended the topic when we entered the gas station's parking lot.

"You want to pump the gas and I'll go in and grab the supplies?" I asked Cypher as I got out of the truck.

"Yeah, I can do that. But you gotta get me some jerky and, uhm, maybe, you know what, forget it. Just the jerky." He got out and walked towards the back to get the slip tank ready.

"You don't even eat the stuff." I looked at him as I walked past the back of the truck.

"So? You're the one always telling me that I must try and blend in better, dick." He gave a serious look as he spoke. "Plus, I like to chew on it, don't ask me why."

"Yeah alright, doesn't sound like a bad idea. I might give it a try now too," I said as I made my way through the door.

I walked and grabbed all the stuff we needed. He didn't really give me the kind of jerky he wanted so I got a bit of everything. I watched him finish filling the slip tank and then start to top up the truck. We paid for everything in cash because we didn't want to leave a trail.

I paid for everything and made my way out of the store. I walked by the truck and noticed that Cypher left the cap off the tank. I placed all the bags into the back and walked over.

As I was screwing it on, I heard a group of loud men coming from behind me. I turned and saw a group coming out of the diner across the road. Now, when I said I had blind luck, I meant that it could go both ways, but today was apparently a good one.

The last man walking out of the diner was fucking Kor. That's the asshole who shot up Cypher's house and the reason why Chris was gone. I was watching them walk to their vehicle and get in. When I heard a door start to open.

I quickly looked over to Cypher who was looking at the same thing as me, but he had pure hatred in his eyes. I quickly made my way to the door and closed it, looking at his confused expression through the glass and pointing towards my nose. He reluctantly sat back and nodded.

We got in and started to follow damn blind luck.

CHAPTER 15

RAKAI

Cypher

I gritted my teeth as I was stopping myself from acting and moving my way past Angel. I found it very hard not to push and got out of the truck. knew attacking the fucking asshole would ruin everything we had been trying to accomplish. I reluctantly sat back in the passenger's seat. I glared freaking laser beams into the thing on the man's head.

Angel didn't want to tempt fate or even challenge it. He was overthinking things. He said that it would be better to watch them close and wait for the right time. Like, come on, dud?

Have you seen a hero in a movie who messed up the whole thing because they were waiting for that so-called right time? Wasn't waiting a waste of time? But then, Angel was good at explaining things that made sense.

We didn't follow -too closely behind them. Angel drove the truck slower than a turtle. My feet were restless. I played with my lips with my tongue repeatedly. I glanced at Angel who was looking straight intensely at the truck in front of us.

"Can you go a little faster? That old car just passed our truck," I jokingly said as I saw a car from behind us overtaking.

The car got in between our truck and the truck of our sworn enemies for this year. Though the car's color faded and had holes indicating it is overused, it was definitely not old. Angel looked at me with his widening eyes. He shook his head at my joke and focused once again on driving slowly.

I laughed at his reaction. If we ran after them, we could even hide our bodies in the streets than this big truck of his. I joked once again about running, but Angel's serious face made me feel the need to get serious too.

I looked straight into the street and carefully watched the truck. Luckily, the car was still in between us, we had a shield if they would get suspicious. Their truck seemed to be driving around to a lot of local spots. They were going in to look inside, then left after a couple of minutes.

In some stores where the windows were transparent, we saw what they were doing inside. I would bet there were five of them inside the truck. They were entering shops by two's while the other person was filling up their gas tank.

We tried to park near their truck, but that would be very obvious. I told Angel to park near that exit to the road; we would get on our foot to observe them while they were inside the shop. We hid in a bush across the street from a shop.

With our ability to see things clearly from far away, it helped us to be unnoticeable while watching. They were picking something up on the food racks and would line up to the cashier. Once they got near the person at the cashier, they would start talking.

It was also like this when they went to other shops. And before this shop, we got a chance to go nearby. We heard what the first two men of Kor asked. They were looking for someone.

They were giving some descriptions of two men, but not a specific name. When we saw them moving towards the door, we ran as fast as we could to get inside our truck. We didn't make a sweat out of it even though we ran faster than the wind. Not being an asshole to humanity but being something different felt good.

"What do you think they are doing?" Angel asked behind a lit cigarette.

"I'm not sure. I wouldn't doubt it if they had some racket going on to make money. Come on, they were leaving," I said and tapped his shoulder as I saw their truck leaving.

Angel moved fast. He turned on the engine and drove a couple of meters away from Kor's truck. We did the same thing as earlier. We hid, not too far away, but also not too close.

They entered several diners in just an hour. They ordered, and ate—but in a quick movement. They were split into two teams when entering the shops.

The first team was Kor and a man I didn't know. The other team was composed of three men including the driver. They were seated far from each other, and each of them was near a huge group of people dining inside the resto.

By observing them, they were really good at blending in with the crowd. One moment, they were ordering, and talking to the waiters who were just shaking their heads at them. Then, the next moment, while waiting for their food to arrive, they would start leaning their heads on the next table beside or behind them.

The other people would shake their heads or shrug their shoulders. Sometimes, they would look behind them and talk to the people, which I was betting they know, before seated back properly. They would talk for a minute, pointing at the person they've asked, and shake their heads.

I knew Kor, but the rest of his crew was unfamiliar to me. I asked Angel about them earlier, but he also knew about Kor and no one else. They were all new to us, but the feelings of the men who attacked my house have the same feeling as them. Ominous, and uncomfortable.

At first, it was hard to watch after them when they weren't together like this. The other men blended well in the crowd. They wore normal, casual clothes like a normal person. Some of them had hats on their heads and were hard to identify when they were in a crowd.

"Aren't they moving strangely?" Angel asked as we watched their food being served.

I glanced at him for a second but didn't answer him.

"What if they're looking for us?" He looked at me for my opinion.

This time, I looked at him. He gave me a look of worry. His brows furrowed together as his face was serious.

His eyes were getting deeper as I looked at it for more than a second. This jerk was overthinking things again.

"What do you mean? Why would they be looking for us at diners?" I tried to laugh at him, tried to shake off the worries etched on his face.

Angel said nothing and stared at me. He waited for me to understand a clue about something that he already gave to me. I stared back at him, confused by his intense eyes.

From worrying a couple of seconds ago, he looked at me with his glowing yellowish eyes. He gave me this kind of eye when he wasn't taking any jokes from me. I shook my head and faced the diner.

Kor's group was now eating peacefully with their triple-pound layer burger. I gulped the drool that formed in my throat as I watched them bite into their food. Just what the hell, right?

That's the third time they were eating burgers in a row, and every time I watched them like this, I couldn't help but to think of the whole night we were following them. The only thing I ate that night was a pack of jerky and candies. How could a vampire live properly with just that?!

I shook my head, as I was trying to calm myself down. Especially now where I started to hear the flow of the blood on the people passing by. I tapped Angel's shoulders to get his attention and said what was on my mind now.

My eyes were still inside the diner, but my vision started to give me a signal to drink my vitamins of the day to ease my thirst. Angel didn't bother asking. He pulled his hand away from me which made me turn my head to him.

"Dude? Seriously?" I asked him, my eyes widened in disbelief at what he did.

"You get serious, Cypher. This is a life-or-death situation. Can't you take this a little seriously?"

I laughed at his reactions which gained me a finger in the air. I shook my head and tried to remember what we were talking about earlier. He was saying something about the strangeness of eating at a diner.

What's wrong with eating? Angel sure overthinks most of the time. I opened my mouth to tease him about it, but a series of events flashed through my head. Then it hit me, Angel said they were watching him at the diner the first time they attacked him.

But, how did they know that Angel was in a diner? Were they watching him for a long time now? I mean, he does look like a person who frequents diners.

Angel saw the dawning of recognition on my face and nodded his head.

"Plus, there's no telling how many guys they have actually out looking in other places. What if there were two or more other groups than this one?" he said as if it was a matter of fact.

I nodded in agreement. I turned my head and eyes back to the diner. They were eating silently with eyes roaming around with caution.

This went on for hours. They went to different shops, and diners doing the same thing all over again. It was actually good for me, if I was just not hungry, and bored.

It was starting to get late and there had to be thousands of diners in this city. Might be a small city compared to the place we grew up, but this city had a quite number of places to go. They couldn't check them all, could they?

Not with any hope that they would find anything anyway. I mean, Angel and I were tailing them and just decided to show up now. Though people who passed in front of us didn't even care to glance a second time, we still wore hats and hoodies.

I was starting to get antsy; Angel had always been the more patient one out of the two of us and today was a testament to that.

"I'm telling you man if they go to another fucking diner, I'm going to lose it." I was almost pushing the dash in with my hands as I spoke.

"Patient, man. We will get them in no time. I want to kill them after what happened to Chris and your place. I was as antsy as you but try to keep it low." He looked over at me as he spoke firmly.

"I want to kill them all, not just Kor. That's why I'm saving all my patients for them." His eyes had a steely glaze on them.

His angry but contained words relaxed me, but not fully. I, as well, shared the same feeling as him. I wanted to kill them all and not leave anyone alive.

I have been pushing back a lot of aggression I had over what had happened at my place that night—which reminded me of my grenade. I turned and gave Angel a dirty look. I raised a brow at him and punched his shoulder once.

He cursed at me and shot a glare. "The fuck, dude?"

"You still owe a fucking grenade!" I shouted at him.

I was trying to keep my mind from all this waiting, and I couldn't find it more interesting than to annoy Angel. Besides, we're inside our truck, while looking for the Kor's team to fill their tank with gas.

Angel slowly turned towards me with a raised eyebrow. "Do you think this is the time for this?"

I shrugged my shoulders and smiled. I figured if I was stuck in the vehicle playing stakeout, I might as well make the best of it. I turned on some music and started playing air guitar.

My head was banging into the air as Angel looked at me. He shook his head as if didn't want to be part of my small gig. But instead of letting him go, I started to shake his shoulders.

He laughed as I lip-synced the music in front of his face. He was trying hard to maintain a serious face, but I didn't let him. I continued my crazy escapades when he pushed me hard enough to make me sit back.

"They are on the move again." He turned back to see the vehicle we had been following pull out of the driveway.

This drive was a bit longer than the rest as we passed similar places. We figured they would stop somewhere after a couple of minutes, but they didn't. We followed the river towards the docks and kept driving as the vehicle turned into a warehouse.

We kept driving a little bit and pulled into an old shipping yard before exiting our way up to a better vantage point.

"What do you think they are doing here?" I asked while lying prone on the container. Angel is at my side looking through some binoculars.

"Um, I feel like that's what we are here to find out," he said sarcastically while not taking his sight away.

"Well, you're right." My reply was all I could muster as I asked the retarded question.

I remained quiet as we both watched the warehouse for some movements. I did notice that some of the men walking around were human, which I assumed had to do with the fact they needed some security when the full moon was overhead.

The facility was massive. It looked like it could house a lot of holding areas for the wolves and at night in this part of town, it wouldn't be hard to mask any noises. But it made me wonder if they would even use a place like this for that kind of stuff anyway.

They might not even have a holding area because Angel has been learning to control his abilities. They might be able to as well, or they had a better area outside of town where they wouldn't have to worry so much about prying eyes.

"I think I should come back here while the moon is running so I could get a better look while the others are preoccupied," I finally said after my eyes and brain finished thinking.

"I don't think that is a very good idea, but I don't see the value in that plan," Angel said reluctantly on what I suggested.

"Good, it's settled then, we will leave, and I will come back in a couple of nights to have a look around."

Angel rolled his eyes at me knowing that he couldn't stop me anyway. He was getting much better at control during his cycles, but it wasn't to the point where he could be free from his cage yet. The next few days consisted of a lot of driving and sitting. Angel insisted that we watch the place a few times.

I agreed that it's a good idea, but man, was it boring? The storm broke free so I was back to only night visits, which was better anyway because I liked the night more. What we learned was that there were anywhere between fifty to one hundred men in that facility at any given time.

It seemed to be where they would go to rearm and resupply themselves. Lots of military-style trucks went in and out loading and dropping off supplies. It was amazing to see this group of men be organized very similar to the military.

We discussed a few options and ways to get into the building, but I was still thinking that going back there during the moon would be our best bet to get a clear image. We wanted to take this place out since it seemed important to them, but Kor was still the prize. The night came and after making sure everything was set for Angel, I decided not to waste any time and left.

It took about an hour to reach the warehouse. I headed up to my perch to watch what they were doing for some time. The place seemed to operate as usual with less than about half the manpower we saw from previous observations—which confirmed my early suspicion.

Seeing a lot of the men going didn't give me much hope that Angel would be able to fully control his abilities any time soon, considering these guys look like they have been doing this for a very long time with the setup they have. I was thinking hard about what to do next, and trying to figure out what they were doing as they gathered like usual.

Kor walked out of the building. My heart flickered for a short second at the sight of him. Surprising the hell out of me. I didn't know it could do that.

I knew Kor was a wolf without a doubt, but the rage I felt put a pause on my logical thinking. I had to stop and forced my lungs to breathe in oxygen I didn't require. Kor was down there barking orders, no pun intended, and the men were rushing to get into line.

They started to all get into vehicles and make their way to the exit. I decided to follow. Amazing . . . that's the word I would use to describe the feeling of flying, or at least close to it. Leaping from building to building and keeping up to moving cars wasn't something I thought I was ever going to be able to do.

Regardless of the dreams I've had about such things, here I was, fucking yes. I saw the trucks stop. I landed on the ledge peering down the street at them.

I didn't want to get too close as I've learned these dogs have a really good sense of smell. I suddenly got this chill down my spine which was extremely unsettling considering I haven't felt the cold for a long time. I looked around and opened my senses before losing my concentration as bullets started erupting down in the street.

I immediately looked down to see Kor's men firing. Glass shattered all around them. I looked down at the street and couldn't see who they were fighting.

I did notice the location was one of the old run-down areas of the city, with a lot of homeless people and rarely any cops in sight. It's one of the spots me and Angel haven't made it to, yet. It was on the list though.

I looked down as the fighting grew more intense. When I finally caught a glimpse of who they were fighting, my eyes grew intensely. They were fast. Very fast that chill went down my spine again before I heard a voice from behind me.

"It's the smell that gets me," a woman spoke as I spun around bringing my gun up fast to face the man, but I wasn't fast enough. I turned to see no one in sight. I hated this game.

"Please, you don't need that here," she said as I just stood there taking in my surroundings.

My eyes scanned the area and my ears picked out the sounds, which is difficult to do as the hellfire from down below wasn't slowing down.

"Very perceptive," the woman said with a chuckle. "I am like you." She finished her sentence only when the words came from a different direction than the first.

I decided to put my gun down and as I did, I closed my eyes and slowed everything down around me, a trick I was starting to get very good at. I put my hand on my knife and waited. I heard the quick swoosh coming around me and I acted immediately.

I moved with my own supernatural speed and this time thought that I had him by surprise—I didn't. She spun back around and smiled at me. She was a petite woman with a southern drawl, blonde hair that passed her shoulder, and piercing blue eyes.

Her fangs were etched with weird symbols that I couldn't read out. The blade of my knife hit the ground as the hilt was still in my hands and at the guy's throat.

"I'm very impressed, you are very good for someone your age," she spoke as she took a step back, so we weren't face to face.

Her hands were still clasped behind her back as she moved away. I didn't see her move them at all, so how the hell did my blade break? I couldn't imagine the speed she must have to pull something like that off.

"What do you want?" I said with a scowl.

"Oh, no. I was just curious as to who you were. Considering you are just standing up here watching the battle below like you're waiting for an opportunity," she said plainly. She walked towards the edge and looked down.

"I really don't think that is any of your fucking business," I said keeping my eyes locked on her.

"Perhaps not, but you are a vampire and by the looks of it, you're alone. I find that very interesting. What Order are you from?"

I raised my eyebrow at the question. Although I didn't understand any of his questions, I still gave him a firm answer.

"Also, not your business." The woman smiled and nodded at my reply.

"There is so much to learn young blood, and manners can help you age better."

I laughed at her remarks, but my guard was still up. "Is that a threat?" I asked, tensing my body in anticipation of a fight.

"Oh no, not at all."

She walked back over to the edge. "I'm, unlike the others of my kind, I don't get mixed up in these squabbles they have with the wolves or each other. I'm a Mind not a Soldier," she finished as she stepped up onto the ledge and turned away from me.

"And who exactly are you?" I thought if I should take the chance to attack while she was looking away.

"You can call me Rakai." She turned to say with a smile as she stepped off the ledge.

I ran over and looked down, of course, she was gone, typical movie bullshit. I went back over to the over ledge to continue watching the fighting below which had seemed to have died down quite a bit. From the looks of things, the wolves weren't doing very well.

The gunfire stopped, and everything went quiet. I started seeing the remaining wolves all change into what looked like some beast form but not quite full werewolves. Some of their body parts turned into wolves, but their whole body remained a human form on it.

My eyes grew wide as I spotted Kor walking up as the rest of his team blew past him at an alarming rate, smashing through the glass and into battle. Kor looked up and locked eyes with me. I was unsure if he could see me or not, but he smiled as he slowly turned into the beast and headed into the building.

CHAPTER 16
PLACE

Angel

It never gets any easier when walking up from the uncontrollable rage nightmare I must deal with. It's getting easier though. The pain got less intense every cycle that passed. The throbbing headaches and body soreness were giving me less sense of pain when I was conscious.

The feeling of being lost and the scared feeling that I might have escaped and brought catastrophe to the city brings uncomfortable beats in my heart. Just by thinking of the probability that I can kill someone in an instant and what's the worst, I will never remember doing that. Thanks to my friend, and this sturdy cage that I have been using for months now, my sanity and humanity are still intact together.

I'm also starting to get the hang of this writing stuff. I think sometime soon, I will have to go back and start from the beginning. Thanks to Cypher who always shouted at me for not writing in a day, I have my own records to review in the future.

I inhaled some smoke from the cigar I was puffing at from earlier. I tapped the ashes down to the tray and continued to write in the notebook. I described what I felt different from the last change to now.

I stated what I vaguely remembered when I was in the wolf form. With all Cypher's instructions on what to write, I just write whatever I thought of. I finished before the mother's hand of my clock hit a number completely.

I stretched my arms in the air and took a last puff from my smoke. When I smelled something awful, I doubted myself at first—but when the wind blew, my nose smelled my opened armpit, and my heart sank. I smelled like Cypher now.

A sad reality I didn't want to. Shaking my head, I stood up. I looked around and noticed Cypher wasn't around. So that's why I finished peacefully, huh?

Walking past the training room, I heard some noises. I peeked my eyes at the slightly opened door and saw Cypher's intense shadowing. He was in pure sweat and his eyes were blank as his body moved.

He showed off his skills. He failed a couple of times and tried to figure out how to perfect his newly discovered move. When he tried it one more time, he laughed at his victory.

Because of that, he didn't stop doing the same move all over again. I shook my head and just turned my body away from the room and headed towards the shower. The water felt amazing against my heavily heated skin.

I lifted my head up, and let the water fall from my face down to my entire body, leaving no space to feel the runny water. Satisfied with it, I still turned the water to the coldest level. When I was a pure human before, I liked showering at a balanced temperature.

I like it warm but at the same time, I like it cold. I always loved to take a shower and smell like soap. I loved the sound of water dripping down to the tiled floor.

I loved the secluded room with very minimal sound coming from the outside. It was a good place to calm your nerves and be cleaned at the same time. But as things changed for me, I started to dislike the warm temperature.

I mostly took cold showers after a change because my body burned like hell whenever I transformed. The cold shower helped a lot to make me feel comfortable and normal. While humming a song in my head, I got out of the shower room.

As soon as I opened the door, Cypher's distorted face greeted me. He was breathing heavily. I saw a drop of sweat slowly travel from his forehead down to his neck.

His shirt was soaking wet as if he was taking a bath with a shirt on. I frowned at him and planned to walk past him, but he immediately slid his feet and blocked my way. I glared at him. I took a step backward when he shook his head and his sweat splashed all over me!

"Dude! I just took a shower!" I shouted at him as I wiped my arms where I saw his sweat drop.

He grinned at me, and instead of stopping what he did, he shook his head one more time. I cursed him and tried to push him away, but his feet just moved half an inch away from me.

"You're just a killjoy, my man," he teased as he stood straight and draped his shoulder on me. "Let's spar! I discovered a new technique that will kill you in an instant."

"No, thanks," I said with a full, uninterested voice. I tried to take off his hand on my shoulder, but he made it heavier.

I turned my eyes to him and glared at him. "I just got out of my shower, Cypher. I don't want to sweat again."

"What the fuck, dude? Are you becoming a pussy now? A shower is only for the weak!"

"Yeah, yeah. Whatever you say, dude. Just don't bother me."

I used a small force to take his hand off, and I succeeded. I immediately started walking away from him, but he caught me. He laughed so loud that it echoed in the small hallway.

He uses half of his strength to bring me into the training room. I walked into the training room and realized that Cypher did some sword dance thing. This wasn't what I expected.

Earlier, he didn't have this. Was he practicing this when I took a shower? How many hours did I stay inside the shower?

I didn't know what it was, but it reminded me of the Sith light saber flurries from an old game I've played. I continued to watch him as I walked in. I looked around the training room.

It was a spacious studio type of room. Perfect for a training slash practice room. We used this room most of the time. The floor was scratched, damaged, dusty, and completely worn out.

With our multiple pieces of training that required a hard and intense fight, the floor would be like this. I walked towards the weapon rack in the far corner of the room, where I grabbed my hatchets and spun them in my hands a bit. I watched him jumping and jogging slowly as he was encouraging me to walk in front of him.

"You're making me regret my decision to take a peaceful shower. If I had known that you'd be like this, I should have kicked your ass earlier." I shook my head and started to walk closer to him.

The thought of sweating all over again, and feeling hotter than normal, made me doubt if I could give him good training. But his face was excited to show me something. Sometimes, I got envious of his ability to remain at a constant temperature regardless of activity, but I would keep that to myself.

"No words. Just fighting." He grinned at me and started to attack in the blink of an eye.

The training was a common occurrence here, just because we had supernatural abilities and used firearms didn't mean we shouldn't perfect all abilities, bullets ran out. We both agreed to not rely on the guns especially when facing enemies like Kor. We did our very best to surpass our limits and discovered things we didn't know we possessed.

Cypher smiled wide when he saw me walking towards him. He crouched down into his stance as if he knew what I would do next. We both locked eyes and felt excited about what was about to happen next.

I thought I'd regret training with him and got annoyed as sweat would bathe my body once again. However, I felt the opposite of it. My heart beat so loud and crazy in my chest. My body anticipated moving and starting the fight.

My mind heightened as I watched and observed the little details of Cypher's moves. Cypher blinked out, which I prepared for since this is something we have been training for. He came out right above me slashing down hard. I quickly sidestepped and dragged my blades across his sword which resulted in a shower of sparks.

"So, I found out some really interesting things while I was out last night," he said, standing back up, wrenching his sword from the ground.

"Oh? What happened to your 'no words, just fighting' motto?" I smirked at him.

He rolled his eyes at me which made me laugh at his reaction. "Is this a social call?" I said as I raised my eyebrow and weapons towards him.

"Depends . . ." he replied as he also went back into his stance.

"Okay, I'll bite. What does it depend on? Depends on who wins?" I decided to indulge his answer instead of attacking.

"Depends on how hard you hit me, obviously," he said with a wide grin.

"And yes, I know you bite, you're a dog. I expected that from you, doggy." He quickly threw in for a good measure.

I didn't reply, I just attacked him. I threw one of my hatchets at him, which started its flight toward his head. Everything was in slow motion, even the surprised look he got while deflecting the projectile.

I moved fast as lightning, but he was still able to stop my fist half away from breaking his ribs. He flew back, dropping his sword but not before sending a stray boot to the side of my face. We both stood to recover from the attacks.

Laughing like lunatics over the outcome of what just happened. I wiped the sweat dripping from my chin using the back of my palm while watching Cypher who was trying to catch his breath. His pale body looked paler as sweats form all over his body.

He didn't mind his shirt dripping wet from his sweat and proceeded to wipe his face with it. I shook my head at him and grabbed a water bottle near the racks. I was heavily breathing as I emptied the bottle in just a second.

My body temperature leveled up. I could feel myself burning like I was near a fire. I grabbed another bottle and poured the water from my head. I felt refreshed after doing that a couple of times.

"Fuck you, dude! Can't you take a shower there? This is a training room, not a room to pour water on." He frowned at me as I threw the fourth empty bottle on the floor.

"This is the consequence of forcing me to spar with you." I shook my head and took off my clothes. I squeezed the water out and smirked at Cypher's reaction.

"Seriously?"

I laughed at him and continued my cold shower in the right place. Cypher followed me, and we both took a shower together. We reminisced about some scenes from our old city and from our old friends we left behind.

We also talked about Chris and shared some unforgettable experiences we had with him. We stopped for a smoke after taking a shower. He went on to tell me everything that happened yesterday.

He told me how he followed the wolves to some massive shoot-out they got into with the vamps. He also told me about the other vampire that he ran into named Rakai, who was much stronger and quicker than Cypher, who looked pained at admitting that.

He told me that he spent the rest of the night watching and listening to the news on TV to see if the shootout he witnessed made its way there, but nothing showed up, not even on our old police scanners. I found that to be very strange but at the same time not that surprising.

What really caught my attention was the fact that he saw the wolves changing at will. I was curious if that was something I could learn to do. Was it only during the full moon?

I started to feel silly that until now, I just accepted the fact that I would only change once a month and possibly would learn to control it. It had become such a routine that I'd mindlessly go into that cage and shut down my mind to the torture I went through every time my skin stretched.

If they could change whenever they want, then I could do it too, right? I should learn how, but when I remembered trying that before, I ended up losing hope. But then, they could. All I had to do was to find out how they could do that.

Another question that formed in my mind was, why didn't they change during our battle at the acreage? They could have defeated us more easily if they did that. They wanted me, right?

Then, instead of transforming into wolves, why did they let us escape and win the fight? These were all questions that I needed to answer immediately. I see the bright light on the horizon now.

I'd be more adamant about channeling my strength into control for this cursing gift I have. Cypher was talking about potentially infiltrating the building. He laid out to me his plans and strategies he thought of trying. I tried to listen, but my mind couldn't stop thinking about my abilities and control.

"Hey? Earth to Angel!" He waved his hand in my face as he spoke.

"Ah . . . yeah . . .? Sorry, man. I'm here just thinking about what you were telling me," I replied while still staring at nothing.

"Well, what do you think then?" He sat and waited for my reply.

"I like the idea of breaking in, but I feel like our problem is with Kor for now." I finally turned to him while I spoke.

"Agreed on that. I would like to get him here alone if we could and have a nice little chat with him." He had a big smile on his face as he was clearly getting excited.

We talked more about the subject and concluded that Kor being a lieutenant means that it would most likely be difficult to get him to talk. It would be nice to pry information out of him, especially with respect to our abilities but I didn't have my hopes up on getting it.

Instead, we thought that taking some of the lesser soldiers might be a good plan, we knew that we would have to make it worth it because they would eventually catch on to what we were doing. It basically came down to more watching and waiting to choose the best person and the right time.

I really didn't like that Cypher said Kor might have looked up to him and smiled. Maybe he knew we had been watching them? It was very suspicious, so we decided to look for a different vantage point. Luckily for us, there were countless places to watch from that had easy escape routes.

We got up to one of the many roofs in the area to begin our surveillance for that night. There wasn't much activity going on. At first, it looked like they had vacated the place and abandoned the space.

The idea of that gave me a quick heart ache thinking they might know we were watching or worse, we would have to start our search all over again. The movement started as trucks showed up. It did appear they were trying to be more cautious and kept a lot more happening inside than in the actual warehouse.

On the bright side though, there seemed to be quite a few men to choose from, but I had my eye on someone, specifically from Kor's unit.

We sat there waiting for Kor to show up. It was only a matter of time or so for him to come up and order his soldiers. I kept telling myself that anyway.

It grew deeper into the night as we sat there quietly waiting and searching. I was impressed that Cypher could keep his mouth closed for this length of time.

"No heartbeat," Cypher said out of nowhere, standing and turning fast.

I quickly followed suit. I turned and saw three people standing right behind us, two men and a woman. Where did they come from?

They suddenly showed up behind us and gave us an intimidating look. I wanted to smack myself in the forehead for not keeping my senses open to this kind of threat. I glanced over at Cypher and his face told me we were feeling the same thing.

Oh well, we're still learning, I guess? It couldn't help if they were ahead of us in terms of honed skills, and experiences.

"Well, this is strange," the woman said as the men behind her just stared daggers at me.

Cypher and I didn't reply. We remained standing on our ground. I could see out of the corner of my eye that Cypher was tensing up for battle and I did the same.

Instead of thinking that they were stronger and better than us, I started to think of our intense training. The woman looked at Cypher, then at me, and sniffed which put a scowl on her face as her eyes narrowed in my direction.

"What are you doing here with this dog?" She looked back at Cypher as she spoke.

"Excuse the fuck outta you?" I don't usually take insults personally because I hang out with Cypher but something about this woman bugged me to the core.

The way she said the 'dog' word was insulting and offending the hell out of me. Now, I understand why Kor's soldiers hated being called a dog.

"I wasn't speaking to you, vermin. You're lucky enough to even be breathing after laying your eyes on me!" She spat the words towards me with pure hatred in her eyes.

I'd admit that I got pretty mad at that statement. My hand went right for my gun so I could place a bullet into her fucking head. Maybe even her mouth first just for speaking to me like that.

Cypher stepped up first and put his hand up towards me to let me know to stand down for now. I glared at him as the feeling of shutting her mouth flowed on my nerves fast as my heartbeats. Cypher shook his head at me with a calm face which wasn't like him at all. I sighed and I reluctantly did so.

"First of all, you should watch your fucking mouth when you speak to my friend like that. He might be calm most of the time, but he tends to be a bit sensitive about his smell and gets enough comments from me. Second, who the fuck are you and what the fuck do you want?" he said to the woman, such an asshole. I thought as I just shook my head at his comment.

"Friend!" she exaggeratedly said with venom in her tone. "This goes against all that is sacred in our syndicate!"

Cypher turned and looked at me confused. All I could do was to shrug before he turned back toward the woman. The men in the back began to tense up as her words started to get more heated. I had a feeling that Cypher was about to start some shit anytime.

"Listen, lady. I frankly don't know what the fuck you're talking, and I really don't give a shit either. I don't have time to answer your questions or any of the other bullshit you have the need to send my way. How about you fuck off and book an appointment later when I'll be more than glad to show my foot up that nice-looking ass of yours."

I visibly cringed at Cypher's words. He sounded like a crazy psychotic pervert. The woman's face tensed up as she heard Cypher's words.

It was after that last sentence I knew shit was about to go down. He has always had a way with words and wasn't known to shy back when dealing with the opposite sex either. I chuckled to myself as the woman scowled hard at him.

Apparently, one of her men didn't quite like the tone Cypher was having with his mistress and tried to approach. When he got close, I punched him right in the face sending him back where he started only on his ass this time. I shit you not, the woman hissed at me. Fucking hissed at me.

I looked over to Cypher who looked back to me. We couldn't help ourselves; we busted out laughing like lunatics. I couldn't make this up if I tried.

"Your insolence is unacceptable, what order are you from?" the woman said to Cypher.

Cypher sat there for a minute thinking and was about to speak when a voice came from behind the woman.

"My order."

A woman with a Southern accent said as she sent her foot right into the other woman who went flying to the side. My eyes followed the woman to her landing spot and when I turned back towards this new threat, my eyes widened. She stood behind the two men with a dagger in each hand sticking into the men's necks.

Her clear blue eyes were glowing at the dark side. It was dripping with an intense and serious gaze. Her blonde hair follows her every move without any flaws. It even shone when the lights from the moon landed on her hair.

My eyes blinked in amazement as both men started to decay at a very fast rate. I looked toward the woman in the middle and noticed her hands glowed red slightly. Both men fell to the ground and the impact turned them to dust which the wind promptly began to take away.

I instinctively put my hand on my gun and looked over to Cypher in hopes that he was doing the same. Instead, his head was tilted towards the woman as if he was confused about what he had just seen, which I couldn't blame him because I was shocked as well about what I had witnessed but I didn't think this was the best time to be amazed.

"You!" the woman shouted from behind.

We turned to see her standing there with a stare I couldn't believe could get any meaner toward our new guest. No replies happened as the woman turned and jumped off the ledge and disappeared into the night.

We both turned back towards the newcomer as I waited to see her next move. She shook her hands in the air as if she touched something dirty. Her face was blank as she started to walk toward us.

"This is Rakai," Cypher said to me as he saw me tense up from the woman approaching us. His words didn't do much to quell my thoughts after what he just did.

We exchanged greetings. I introduced myself and offered a shake hand, but she just nodded her head at me. She looked at me and I saw her lips shadowing a smirk which gave me a thought that something wasn't sitting right with me about this Rakai. I was starting to wonder if I have some inherited hatred for vampires. I pushed it aside for the most part.

"We need to talk and we shouldn't do it here," Rakai said with zero emotion on her face.

I looked over at Cypher who just nodded towards me. I thought for a minute about taking her back to our bunker and decided against it, but figured that if she wanted to kill us, she'd have done it already there really wasn't anything at the bunker for her to want. I decided to avoid it anyway.

"We've got just the right place then."

I smiled at Rakai and stretched out my hand again. She looked at it first. She glanced at Cypher and accepted my hand after a second.

CHAPTER 17
TRAIN

Cypher

I used to think that I've seen a lot in my time on this planet. At my age, experiences of the harshness of this world bring me to a mature level, or so I thought. As days passed by, I realized, boy I was completely wrong.

I always had this feeling that there was more going on than what everyone sees with their bare eyes. So, when Angel ended up being a werewolf, it didn't surprise me as much as it probably should have. Naturally, when the vampires turned up and attacked, people would be shocked and wouldn't believe what was happening and question its existence.

But for my side, I didn't get surprised and just accepted the fact that he became something. When more than one thing happened in a day, it didn't give any sort of surprised feelings within me. Well, I was at the moment because I thought I was gonna die. Then again, I did die.

All those things that happened to us lately made us numb to everything or any shocking things. We had a full-on firefight with wolves like we just did on the weekends for fun. We practiced and trained our skills like it was just jogging in a park.

We ate blood and raw meat like it was the best meal in the whole world. Everything was fucked, but what happened tonight took the cake. I wasn't going to go into specifics leading up to it but all I could say was, what the fuck did I just see?

Rakai, the vampire that I met recently, pulled some supper vamp shit with Hoover vacuum daggers. Those blades literally pulled the blood from men on the roof, and the glow that came from Rakai's hands was awesome. In my years of living at the top of this earth, I finally saw the coolest girl.

Though she cheated because she was a vampire and more powerful than any girl, she was still totally cool. She would be likely to be my friend. If we got closer, she could teach me some tricks to be a true vampire like her.

We headed to a location out of town in the woods so we could hear her out. Angel and I struggled to run fast as there were more woods and huge branches blocking the way. Plus, it was night.

Angel might have the ability to see things clearly as crystal, but I didn't have that kind of ability. I could see through the dark, but it was mostly because of my senses. The sense of smell, hearing, and instinct gave me the power to move like Angel in the night.

As I was admiring the moves and abilities of my friend, Rakai zoomed out at my side. She was fast, faster than anyone I could think of. Her movements were fluid and she stuck to the shadows like she was born in them.

Her feet, although breaking the branches into pieces, were silent. Her steps and landings on the ground don't have any single note coming from them. She moved as if she was one with the wind.

I tried to outrun her, but she just glanced at me as if saying. 'Try it if you can'. Though, I knew she didn't mean that and gave me a blank glance.

My mind processed her glowing blue eyes into something bad. I tried and tried, but whenever I ran faster than I could, she would just slow down her pace, as if letting me win! In my irritation, I gave up on trying, and just focused on figuring out how she could do it.

I was impressed, maybe a bit jealous as well, but she had clearly been doing this dead thing a lot longer than me, that's for sure. I mean, how could you know that someone was this skilled? Of course, for her performance.

She proved to us that she could kill us whenever she wanted to, but just prolonging our death day for something more important. As we moved through the bright city, I watched her. Her moves, the ways her feet pressed on the ground, her breathing, her hands, and her face.

I watched all of them and observed how she was moving them so smoothly. I found myself wanting to learn more about her. I was also getting this feeling like we could actually trust her and a lot of it had to do with the fact that she was the first vampire that didn't give any grief about Angel's condition, not that we have met many vamps, but speaks volumes.

She never said anything about my friend, though her gaze at him was something. But I guessed, she was staring at us with the same look on her face. Blank, mysterious, and uninterested.

I looked back at Angel who was keeping up really well with her. He seemed to be having trouble keeping pace with Rakai. But there were moments where Angel almost outran the woman.

For some unknown reason, Rakai didn't let him win or gave any openings for my friend. I found it very interesting as Angel struggled. He hit the ground a lot harder than us, so he definitely wasn't graceful at all.

I laughed at him, but I could see him staring at Rakai. I offered him a hand and asked him what was wrong while whispering. He shook his head and stared at the woman vampire.

For years of being with him, his expression gave me his thoughts. He wondered if she could be trusted or not. I could understand the hesitancy since every unnatural being we have met so far has tried to kill us.

Rakai looked at us. She didn't say anything or even blink. She just turned her body around and started to move fast again.

I tapped Angel's back and we started to move together. Instead of trying to compete with Rakai, I slowed my pace to speak with my friend.

"How are you doing back there, big guy?"

"She's pretty fast, but I'll keep up in no time," he said to me without taking his eyes off the woman.

"You don't trust her, do you?"

I made my way to his side as we let Rakai get some distance. She didn't move her head to look or even glance at us. Though I knew there was a probability that she could hear us at this distance, I still asked my friend.

"Not at all. Not like that, instead, she gives me the creeps. What she did on that roof has concerned me about why she really wants to get us somewhere secluded. I mean, dude, how come we're following her willingly? What if she lead us to their headquarters? Or her leader? We're gonna be doomed, dude. I'm telling you."

He snapped his gaze towards me to answer my question with his questions.

"I doubt that she's going to kill us. She could have easily done that on the roof with the other men," I answered plainly, shrugging my shoulders.

"Yeah, we shall see." He picked up his pace to keep Rakai in his sights.

The truth was, I felt comfortable with her. She didn't seem interested in my friend, but she didn't also have any malicious intent for Angel. I watched her face for a long time now, and she never once glanced at my friend, unless Angel tried his best to outrun the woman.

Besides that, there was nothing weird or suspicious about Rakai. Or was it just me because we're in the same species? We leaped down into an old rail yard. The path led the walkers out of town.

The trees on both sides of the rail yard were unusually quiet. The shadows made from the light of the smiling moon gave out a design in a dark way. As usual, the animals, from insects down to the kings of the animals, gave out background music to the three of us.

The wind eerily blew at us, but we didn't give any concerns about that. This path was the first to go for my friend and me. We liked to use this way because there was always a chance to run into some dinner—meaning it's a good place for criminals to do their business.

I turned back and saw Angel jump down a second after me. He extended his claws out to catch the side of a concrete pillar, clearly for dramatic effect to pay for his awkward and funny fall scene earlier. He hit the ground and smiled at me, proud that this time, he didn't flatter or stagger.

I shook my head before shadowing back towards the woman who kept on striding. I loved running through the woods. The trees shrouded in darkness were always beautiful to me.

I had to force myself to breathe in the air before getting the feeling of the forest. Now, with my heightened sense of things, the emotions were unexplainable. I could sense all the wildlife in the area, and if I concentrated, I could hear their heartbeats, their small movements, their sounds, and even the animals who were under my feet.

All of these gave me a comfortable and warm fondness for my surroundings. I found myself more and more enjoying being dead. I got lost in my moment when I suddenly blew past Rakai who had stopped.

I looked back at her and saw her facing Angel. I quickly changed direction and headed back to her. When I got there, I noticed Angel was already there standing about a couple of feet away from the woman, who looked like he was preparing himself for a fight.

"This will do," Rakai said, her hands behind her back.

I could see Angel was starting to get really uneasy. His hands itched toward his weapon. I looked at them with a confused face.

Just a moment ago, I was enjoying the peaceful gift of Mother Earth. I was having fun running through the wind, while these two were irritating and annoying each other. What the hell just happened in a few seconds?

"Don't worry, young wolf. I have no ill intentions toward you or your friend. I actually find you, two, very interesting."

"Why do you find us interesting? I'm sure you have a reason behind that." Angel was so firm with his stance. His face was serious and with just a small move from Rakai, he wouldn't hesitate to bring out his gun and shoot her head.

"Who wouldn't be interested? In the history of the vampires and wolves, there are no stories or lore that the two species can befriend and get along together."

She smirked as she looked at Angel and at me. I confusedly nodded my head at her words and looked at Angel to convince him with my eyes. Her hands were up in a surrender position to try and quell Angel's nerves.

I looked between the two of them as we stood there in silence for a moment waiting for Angel to decide on his next move. I wanted to hear the woman out but if Angel felt the need to attack then I had no choice but to be with him on his decision. Even if I didn't doubt Rakai or have any sort of feelings for her, I would trust the instinct of my friend. I've learned over the years to trust his gut on such matters.

"Trust is earned," Angel said as I just nodded my head like an idiot back and forth between them.

"That's fair, so let me earn it more, then. Please let's find somewhere to sit. This is going to be quite the tale." Rakai gestured to some fallen trees to sit by.

I made my way over to one and sat down. Angel, on the other hand, snorted and jumped into a tree to take a seat. We both lit up cigarettes and waited for Rakai to start her tale.

The big amount of clouds in the sky was slowly getting near to the smiling moon, making the bright light to dim and shadow the shape of the cloud. It was quiet, but at the same time, I could hear everything around us.

"Sanguinem Magum which translates to Blood Mage, that was what I was training for when I was in the Order. I was born in Louisiana in 1857 and died in 1894. The vampires that took my life specialized in blood magic. At that time, I was a master in my field of voodoo dolls or a witch doctor, I guess you can call me that."

She smiled a bit as if she remembered something. I glanced at Angel who was busy with his smoke and listening seriously to the woman she just doubted earlier.

"My life was normal, not until they came to me. They turned me and added me to their ranks. It took fifty years for them to initiate me from a little worker bee to anything of actual use." Rakai looked distant as if looking at her life from beneath her eyes.

"So, you played with dolls?" Angel asked from his tree.

"Fifty fucking years!" I jumped in to say. I counted the years she said and the year she died. It was amazing that she worked for that long, but my capability to compute it using my mind only was more amazing than it.

"Voodoo is a lot more than just dolls, and yes, the initiation process is very long since time isn't as relevant to us as when we're mortals. You would be surprised how fast time flies when it isn't a concern anymore." She shrugged her shoulders.

"If you're saying that, then how old are you this year?" I asked after I puffed a smoke from my mouth.

Rakai violently looked at me. Her eyes were glaring at me as if I said the wrong thing. Her fangs showed up and acted like she was ready to bite someone.

I looked at my friend to ask for help or any reaction, but he just shook his head at me, telling me that he was disappointed.

"Okay. Okay. Next question. Did you say Order? And we heard the woman from earlier asked us what Order we are. What's that mean?" Rakain looked at me before answering.

"There are about 16 orders that I know about, and they are run by 4 pillars. I don't know the exact whereabouts of the Orders, but what I do know is that one of them is here and another is located in England." Rakai paused for a minute.

"I suppose knowing something is better than nothing at all," Angel said with sarcasm.

"Sshh—It's getting good." I looked over at Angel. He frowned at me and cursed, but he still got quiet.

"Yeah, well to some of us living folks time is relevant, so maybe let's get to some good stuff." Angel looked impatient.

"What makes you think time is relevant to you?" Rakai asked Angel.

"I'm not a vampire. I still have a heartbeat. I will age and die. I don't have fifty years to do anything and look just as young as a teenager," Angel said bluntly.

"Yes, I do heal wounds fast and can take damage that would kill most men, but I don't have the time you, guys, do. Every second is important," he finished through a cloud of smoke he exhaled.

"Then, allow me to give you some knowledge you might find useful. It's definitely no secret that vampires are immortal. It has been a tale as old as time, but something that isn't known by many is that werewolves are immortal as well," Rakai said with a smirk on her face.

The shocking part was Rakai smirked and had an emotion etched on her face, but of course, the most shocking part was what she said last. I looked up at Angel with a big grin getting excited for him. I watched his eyes go wide as the information processed through his mind.

"Are you saying I can't die?" Angel sat up clearly starting to get interested in what Rakai was saying.

"We can all die, young wolf. But time won't be the cause of it for any of us."

"Fuck! You mean, I have to deal with him forever?" I asked and pointed at him with a small smirk on my face.

"Oh, fuck you, man! I'm not that bad, I happen to think this is great news. You don't hear me complaining about your smell!" He shot back at me.

Angel jumped out of the tree laughing, headed over to a stomp, and sat down closer. He was starting to be less tense around our new ally.

"Please, continue." Angel gestured to Arlo to keep going.

"The information they gave me have been very basic like I said about the orders and the pillars. There will be a lot of time to go through the little knowledge I have but I want to get to the real point." Rakai looked at us seriously.

"There is a war going on that has been waging for as long as time itself. Do you notice that you, guys, have a primal urge to fight against each other?" she asked.

"I can feel something of the sort but not so much towards Angel. But I felt that urge on my nerves when I met the other wolves. I felt a pull of force to attack them. It was strong compared to when I met you and the other vampires," I said as I thought about it for a moment.

"I also agree with Cypher about that only for me, it's the exact opposite. I was close to being overtaken with a rage to attack you and it is still tugging at me. Cypher though, I haven't felt much about it besides the occasional time I want to slap him upside his head." He looked at me and laughed. I raised a finger to him and cursed him under my smoke.

"That's actually very interesting that the effect isn't very strong between the two of you, but that's my point is that this war has shadowed this world for a very long time, and it is absolutely forbidden on both fronts to be anything less than deadly with each race." Rakai paused for a moment and took in a big breath of air while thinking, it wasn't necessary, but I understood the reasoning.

"I'm going to tell you my reason for wanting your trust and I hope I will gain it from my story." Rakai stood and walked in front of us and began his story.

"About five years ago, I was getting prepared for my trials. They take place after learning all the requirements of being a blood mage. The last task I had before I could do anything was to hunt down a clan of wolves and bring back their heads. This wasn't as simple as that as you had to do this alone. I traveled and found a clan. There, I met the owner of my heart." Rakai held her chest before continuing.

"Her name was Arlo. He was absolutely the most beautiful man I ever saw. His sun-soaked skin and dark eyes sparked something in my chest that I had thought had long been dead. We fought and we fell in love, that merging between our species was beyond forbidden and was an absolute death sentence. So, we hid, and we made plans to run away together once I was done with my trials. We should have left sooner. They found out that we had been seeing each other and my trials were forfeited. I had barely escaped with my life. I ran as fast as I could to my love to find her mutilated by four other wolves. I drained all their blood as slowly as I could after ripping all their limbs off. I found an envelope with pictures of us in the pocket of one of them. I was days away from learning all the vampires' secrets before this happened, but I can assure you that I will do everything in my power to bring both parties to their knees," Rakai finished her story and looked at us for our response.

I looked over at Angel who was looking skeptical but also less tense. He was starting to believe, just like me, that Rakai might actually be able to help. It was a long shot, and it wasn't very easy to bring people into our group, but at this time, we could use all the help we could get. We couldn't take an army on alone even though I like to act like I could.

"So, what exactly do you want from us?" I spoke as I gestured to Angel and myself.

"Oh, that's simple," Rakai said quickly. "I want to train you both. I would like to teach you what I know about blood craft and improve your skills. I would like to share the knowledge I have with Angel about wolves."

Angel immediately perked up to that reply clearly interested in that knowledge. I couldn't lie if learning blood craft meant I could do what he did on the roof to those men, I was so fucking down. I looked towards Angel who smiled and nodded to me. I looked back over toward Rakai with a big grin as well.

"When do we begin?" I asked, not containing my excitement.

"Right now," was all she said behind a smile of her own as she shot forward and attacked.

CHAPTER 18

ANGEL

Angel

I wasn't quite sure I trusted this Rakai girl very much. She had pummeled those guys on the roof all by herself, and she could undoubtedly do the same to us. I'm sure her being a blood-sucking creature had to do with it.

Her abilities were heightened because of that, however, it all still felt surreal. And it was exactly why I couldn't seem to trust her. When I heard her story though, my mind kind of started to lean towards it maybe.

I kind of felt her. If some bastard had done that to the woman I loved, I would most likely do the same. Or something even more severe than just dismembering their limbs.

Cypher and I wanted to do that when our friend was murdered. How much more to a loved one bound by soul? Her story was very convincing.

If any of what she knew about werewolves held their weight, then it would be worth getting to know the chick. But everything vanished the moment her fist met my face. She pissed me off big time, yet I couldn't deny the fact that she was immensely powerful. I coughed as I cowered on the ground.

"What the fuck!" I roared as I stood and looked up to where Cypher was. She had just done the same to him in a nonchalant manner.

Lame—I couldn't think of any other word that I could use to describe myself taking that hit from a girl. I could only sneer in both amusement and displeasure. It wasn't that easy to knock me over, but with just one blow from Rakai, I found myself picking myself up from the ground. She's definitely strong.

"Holy shit!" Cypher exclaimed, massaging his bruised face. His expression though showed that he was having a fun time.

I was well aware that it was all for us to accept her training proposal, but boy, she's getting under my skin for some reason. Her doing this was probably to show us that she's capable of whipping us to shape. But then, did she really need to go all out?

We might be dead before we could even touch a strand of her hair! It might even take me ages before I could compete with her at speed alone. All I seriously hoped was that she wasn't really intending to kill us like everyone else we had met.

As my friend recovered from his knockdown, he opened his mouth yet another time. "Damn, dude! Are you sure you're a girl? You're more like a thug beating the hell outta people."

Rakai glared at him. Cypher quickly shut his mouth and hopped on his feet. He assumed his fighting stance, too. We both turned to face Rakai who was standing in her original position like she never even moved at all. A big smile was etched across her face.

"Seriously, you, guys, need to train hard if you intend to take down both parties," she said.

I could feel my forehead crease the moment her eyes landed on me before their blueness sort of absorbed my very existence. Shivers ran down my spine that instant. Her eyes . . . though they were the color of the sea, I could sense darkness creeping from deep within them.

Was it because she was a vampire? Nonetheless, I didn't think that I and Cypher could actually take her on even if we tried. And the fact that she was gorgeous didn't help.

Her look shifted to Cypher again before it darted back to me. "I am not even yet close to the strongest they possess in their ranks. If you can't take me on, then I fear all your efforts will be for nothing."

"There's someone stronger than you? You're kidding me! What would that make us look like then? Twerps?" Cypher butted in.

"Do not lump me in with you, dude. I'm way stronger than you are," I hissed sarcastically. "And I'll bring this vamp down, too," I added, pointing at Rakai.

Cypher just raised a finger at me, and said with a teasing look, "Oh, really, young wolf? I can sense you shivering."

"Shut it, sucker. I'll pound you harder than this girl who had whooped your ass."

The banters between us continued, not minding about our surroundings. However, not long after that, I felt a chill run down my body again as the female vampire's voice rang in my ears.

"What a rambunctious lot. Will you, two, quit it and just focus? Or do I need to knock some senses out of you both?" It's as if the coldest air just blew when she said that.

Hairs on my arms and back even stood up like porcupine spikes. I sensed the same effect of her words on Cypher. Not that I was surrendering to her, but right now, I knew she was stronger than Cypher and my strength combined. Rakai's grin was wiped off her face when our look darted to her.

She sighed before speaking calmly, "What I'm saying is that you must put your all into getting stronger. You're lucky that I found you 'cause Kasha back there is a very formidable warrior. He would have most likely killed the both of you if I happened to be late."

I heard Cypher muttering some words of profanity under his breath before he shadowed and attacked. Rakai, however, wasn't easing up on us and sent him flying to where I was. Should I catch him or just let him fall?

I was debating with myself whether I should try catching my friend or not. In the end, I did. He's quite the ass, but I couldn't leave him. Also, I couldn't stand the fact that a lone girl was thrashing us.

He repositioned himself back towards me very quickly as I sidestepped. I instantly asked him, "Sucker, you good?"

"Don't call me that, dickhead! I'm fine." Cypher's brows furrowed as he tried regaining balance. He still figured I was jokingly calling him names despite us being in such a situation.

It worked out well at first until I turned my head the other way only to find Rakai standing right in front of me, grinning.

"How the f—" Her action surprised the hell out of me, but she cut me off before I could even finish a sentence.

"I told you to focus," Rakai said before she sent her palm slapping onto my forehead. Her quick reflexes pushed me back, my feet almost burning as I tried to stop the force from sending me even further.

"Damn it!" Besides the pain in my forehead, I could also feel the friction between my feet and the stony ground. I was sure my soul would have been severely scraped off if I was still a normal being.

Fortunately, I wasn't. And thanks to that, I only felt a stingy sensation coming from there. This whole fist-fighting with this vamp is starting to make me mad.

I was about to counterattack when Cypher's voice reverberated through the woods, making us turn to him. "The hell's wrong with you, dude?"

He had mopped the ground with his body when I looked at him. It was probably the force from when the girl attacked me that caused him to kiss the ground. I forgot that he was leaning on me.

"Who told you to dust the soil, man?" I chuckled at him while still on guard. Cypher clicked his tongue before he stood back up to face the girl.

"You're so sloppy that she had almost whooped you again," he said. He then faced Rakai with his fists positioned in front.

"I bet we had a chance if we both went for her together." Rakai just smirked and gestured for us to come to get her. Damn confident, woman!

She had my blood boiling when she did that, so Cypher and I quickly jumped to punch her. I even think I threw trees at her at some point, and I could swear they were going right through her as she never moved. We fought like that for what seemed like an eternity, but we failed to land her a blow even with our combined attacks.

I admit, I'm stunned by this woman's abilities. She suddenly stopped attacking and just stared long and hard at us. Our cuts were healing fast; we were both breathing heavily.

Beads of sweat trickled down my forehead. My friend, on the other hand, looked cool as a cucumber. My eyes then drifted to the girl's sneering visage. Stupid vampires!

"As I have said, I'd like to help train you, guys, and join your cause. You do not have to answer me now, though," Rakai finally spoke to us. "I believe we can all help each other."

I looked over at Cypher, and he just nodded to me. I was still hesitant, but I can't deny that we could use her help in what was to come. The best course of action was to sit down and talk it over for a little bit, but I was almost certain that we had nothing to worry about Rakai's intention.

"Could you give us some time to think about it? If it's alright with you, meet us back here tomorrow night," I spoke first.

Though her proposal's great, it would still be best for me to discuss it with my friend over yonder. After all, our kinds had been at war with each other as she had mentioned a while back.

"Yeah, that would be best," Cypher said after he finished nodding toward me.

"Very well. At this time tomorrow, I will be here awaiting your answer. Take care." Rakai sped off as soon as the last word left her lips.

When she was finally out of sight, I looked over towards Cypher only to find a giant shit-eating grin plastered on his face. His eyebrows were curling up and down at me, teasing. I should not have asked because I know deep down what the expression on his face implied, but I've got no choice.

"What are you smiling about?" I asked him with a sneer, knowing I wouldn't like his answer.

"I saw you staring at her ass, dude. Like your eyes were glued to her butt. She's cute, isn't she?" His smile never faltered. This guy's definitely teasing.

"Well, she definitely hits hard. But it feels like we have more pressing matters to deal with." I tried to say it with a serious tone, but his grin was becoming infectious.

I was relieved though that he didn't press the matter any further. I was assuming it was because he realized we did have something more important to discuss than that woman's ass. We immediately made our way back to the bunker to do some serious thinking.

After a series of discussions and fighting in the pit, we decided to make use of Cyphers' idea. Ultimately, we have opted to trust the woman. When the next night came, we headed to the meeting spot a little before the set time.

She was already sitting with her legs crossed when we arrived. It looked like she was doing yoga of sorts with her meditation pose. Red energy was leaking around her floating body. Could I also do that kind of thing if I concentrate enough?

I was in awe and Cypher couldn't keep his mouth closed. I could even see the drool coming out of his mouth, but I cannot blame him. It was utterly cool!

"That's freaking awesome!" he blurted out. I could only chuckle at his amazement.

"And that's enough to have you drooling over her? You're crazy."

"Shut up, I know you're as astonished as I am," he said, eyes still fixated on the girl.

We quietly walked up towards Rakai with the man beside me still flabbergasted at that sight. I even heard him swallow his dried saliva a couple of times as we shortened the distance between her and us.

"There's no doubt about it, man! She is a fucking super Saiyan!" he exclaimed.

"A what? Stop fanboying over her and let's get serious," was all I could reply even though I had to admit it was really a cool one.

Rakai stretched her legs, and let her feet slowly reach the ground as the aura of energy began to dissipate. Her eyes opened, and a smile was plastered on her face. I could feel knots growing in my stomach for some reason when our eyes met, and it sent shivers down my spine.

It seemed like it would take me a while before I could completely trust her—at least I hope that's what that feeling was.

"Hey, there. Did you come here to kill me or talk?" Rakai asked after a short greeting as she placed her hands on her back.

"First of all, how the fuck did you do that? Second, teach me!" Cypher blurted out before I had the chance to speak. His eyes were blazing with amusement, and his weird hand gestures made Rakai chuckle.

"Snap out of it, Cypher. Your way bewitched by her that it might cause you to be a pushover," I said.

"I'm sure you also wanted to be taught that, Angel. You don't have to deny it, man, because I know. I know, boy," he replied teasingly. I didn't respond to him anymore and just turned to the girl.

"We have determined that it would be great if we work together as it would positively benefit us since both party's interests align. However, we're still unsure if we can trust you enough to bring you to our hideout," I said plainly. Cypher nodded in agreement to my words.

"You mean that old bunker you, guys, have in the mountain valley out west?" She looked right at me with a huge grin on her face.

I was startled at her words; Cypher let his mouth hang open again. My mind started to race about how she knew that, and if she did, others may as well. Her statement didn't help motivate me to trust this woman any more than I already did.

"How do you know that?" That question was all I could get asked with a whispering voice.

"I just discovered it last night after our discussion. By the looks on your faces, I can see that my knowledge of your hideout has brought up many questions and hesitation to trust me, but don't worry. I can assure you that its location won't slip from my lips."

"You fucking followed us?" Cypher asked. Anger was evident in his tone. Between the two of us, it was Cypher who kind of trusted the woman more. It's not a surprise if Rakai's action angered him.

I also tensed up a bit. I didn't know what to feel about that. What if we did come here to kill her? Or at least tried to? We could have been killed instead.

"Listen, you, two, aren't the only ones taking a risk here. I also needed to know who I was offering to work with," she said flatly.

Her words made sense. If I was alone dealing with the enemy and even offered to join hands, I would be very hesitant as well. It was all to make sure she wasn't jumping into a snare trap. I could see Cypher was thinking the same thing as his body gradually calmed down.

"That is understandable. I would have done the same thing too. By the way, we have decided that we will work together on this matter because we have similar goals. But then . . ." Cypher's words hung as he stared straight at her.

"But then, you must teach me how to do whatever it is that you just did when we showed up. Oh, and that shit you did on the roof too," he added before his lips curved into a smile.

She nodded and agreed to his condition. She then looked at me next, waiting to see if I had one of my own. All that stuff that she could do was pretty cool, but it was never really my thing.

I don't think I need it to fight, and I wasn't even really sure if I could actually do it. What really interested me was the information she held and the kinds of stuff she could show me about my own condition.

"I have no conditions. Just know that I'll be watching you," I warned her.

"I've noticed, and I'm fine with that." She winked at me with a grin as she said those words.

I didn't quite know how to take that, so I just turned about and headed back towards the bunker. Did she do that to annoy me? Or was that outright flirting? Well, I didn't care.

I could sense Cypher's smile at me growing wider as I took off. We all ran back. It didn't take us very long to sprint to where our hideout was, but I know for the most part that I enjoyed the trip.

It's a lot more enjoyable to take the woods than to take the highway route. When we got back, Cypher took Rakai to where she could set up a place to live.

"You can decide where to settle. It's spacious here, and there's no way that that ball of fire above us will be able to burn you while you're inside," he said as he took her on a tour around the bunker.

The girl chortled at Cypher's words. She seemed to understand that my friend wouldn't let her turn to ash or disappear without her teaching him those 'cool' things. Right now, he's kind of in a frenzy.

I couldn't quite ascertain if he was just doing this for her to trust us while we were in this unusual cooperation or if he was just really engulfed with the awesomeness of the girl's abilities. I snickered at his childishness.

"You sure are making sure you learn those, eh? Nevertheless, I'm honestly afraid that their coolness might diminish if you started trying 'em out."

It's true though that we have many rooms and plenty of space for her, so she may rest easy about the thing her kin's afraid of sunlight.

"Oh, shut up, you jealous, young wolf," he said without batting me an eye. Rakai chortled at our exchange. She seemed to be having fun watching us.

"You, guys, are close, aren't you?" she commented as she walked behind Cypher who was already in the last room.

The next few weeks consisted of a lot of bumps and bruises. Rakai was very adamant about not doing anything further until we were properly trained. Cypher was all for it.

He would do better than he had been doing for the training to move faster. His body was black and blue all over, yet it didn't diminish his will one bit.

"For the cool stuff, Cypher," he chanted for the twentieth time. That phrase had been his motivation for the past week. I cannot even count how often I heard him say those to continue with the hell training.

Conversely, I dislike having my body shredded and worn out with scars and wounds everywhere. No matter how badass he said they were, the fact that the fatigue they had caused my system contributed to how effective I could do tasks the next day.

"Can't we do this without me getting bruised?" I asked. They both chuckled at my question before Rakai charged at me to continue with our sparring session.

With all the training and stuff, an interesting development that I learned was those werewolves couldn't use blood magic as Cypher and Rakai could. I could instead learn how to harness my will to control my transformation as well as how to nullify blood magic. I wasn't sure I understood what she meant, but I was certain of my idea: I think the only downside was that I couldn't do anything unless I learned how to control my change.

"You haven't tried that out, boy, have you?" she asked as she looked at me dead in the eye when we took a break from training. Rakai already warned us not to lie to her as we're in cooperation. Even until now, she was somewhat scrutinizing my every little move.

I leaned my back on the tree trunk behind me, while she stayed standing and looking down at my battered body. I let out a sigh due to tiredness before I responded.

"Of course not. Complications may arise if I suddenly do that without proper training. I don't want to risk doing things that might kill me. Also," I paused and pointed at Cypher who still trained.

"I'm not a fool as that bloodsucker over there."

"That's good to hear." She nodded and reminded me again that I should not attempt it until I had my shapeshifting under control which could probably take a while.

Rakai then turned her attention to Cypher and called him from afar. She told her to rest for a bit as she settled herself on a fallen trunk near me. The latter quickly looked at her and gestured 'OK'. He dragged his feet to where we were and sat in front of me.

"Why are you overdoing everything, dude? Excessive training won't always be considered effective. You might strain yourself," I asked him, still catching my breath.

"For the cool stuff, men! Cool stuff!" he exclaimed with bated breath.

"And why are you thinking like a human being? I'm basically dead, you know. I don't care one bit about overworking myself," Cypher added, pumping his arms as if he had just achieved something.

"And why were you doing what a human does—pumping your arms like you had won a contest of some sort?"

"Because I have arms, man. There's not an issue if I do that, right?" Cypher sarcastically said before he jumped back to his feet.

"Alright, back to work!" We talked about how we changed, and the experiences we have gained along the road. She was taken aback by how strong we were already despite us being young.

"Just a little more push and you two could surpass me in no time," she said, smiling. I had seen her curve those lips of her various times, but it was only now that I found her face more radiant doing that. Not literally glowing, though. She seemed a little different from the first time we met.

One night after training, we decided to exchange tales from our past. I told them everything I could recall the night we were attacked by the vampires that turned Cypher into one. She told me that I should channel that feeling and utilize it to help control my shifting when I finish the story.

A strange thing I started to notice after weeks of being together was how she was always watching me. Her stares made me nervous. Her words fluttered something within me especially when she asked if she could watch me change.

"Can I? It's kinda fun seeing you get stronger. And Cypher's energy as he trained is strangely contagious," she asked through the rustling of the trees. A light wind blew past us, sending some strands of her hair flowing freely behind her.

She smiled at me as she tucked the ones dangling in front of her face behind her ear. To be honest, I was starting to enjoy her presence, and I could see that Cypher was as well. But I think that my feelings on the matter were a bit different.

He wanted her knowledge while I, besides her vast information about my kind, was starting to think that I wanted something else. I don't know. Everything still seemed vague.

I did as she asked and let her watch me as I changed. I don't really remember much from that encounter, but she praised me when she saw my color as a wolf. She also pointed out that I was a lot larger than she thought I would be at my age.

I told her that I don't know what that meant and that I would try harder to control my shifting. After all, I'm stubborn enough to persevere, so she can rest easy. Rakai's lips are quivering, and I cannot deny the fact that I like it when she smiles.

CHAPTER 19
CYPHER

Cypher

You would think ninety days would go by fast when you're an immortal stuck in an underground bunker. Most stories I've read have vampires coasting through the centuries living in very similar conditions. I was losing my fucking mind with all these walls enclosing me.

Besides the fact that it was boring when we weren't training, everything in here just seemed to make me go crazy. I didn't like being cooped up in a cement shell of torture. Rakai was persistent about us training and becoming more powerful to take on our mutual enemies. She would constantly remind us about things we often forgot. Honestly, she's been a great help.

"Make it snappy over there!" She side-glanced at Angel who was currently doing push-ups. The latter's shoulders dropped the moment she heard the female vampire's words.

He still continued working out despite his silent scream of complaint. Adding to the fact that she wasn't easing up on us, Angel cursed under his breath. He was doing his best though to get rid of his concern about his body getting worn out.

The woman was working her way into the group very well, and I think she and Angel have a thing for each other. It was quite obvious from how close they had become. Didn't surprise me though since we all know she was into dogs. My life, on the other hand, had become blood, and learning to become more violent than I already was quite peculiar.

Funny world, right? But her training was proven to be very useful. She's very powerful, and it has helped us immensely being able to learn and adapt from her beatings.

I still, however, couldn't get the fact out of my mind that she wasn't even close to the most powerful. If I wasn't already so numb to most things, I would have considered it to be nerve-racking.

Angels' abilities had grown significantly over these last couple of months.

I wasn't sure if it was the practice or the fact that he wanted to impress our guest, but either way, it was working and that's pretty fucking sweet. He had started utilizing his senses a lot more in anticipation of attacks which makes a lot of sense, no pun intended. He was a wolf, and his senses were one of his greatest strengths. Honing them would be the best course of action.

"Dude, what the hell!" I screamed when Angel threw me onto a wall. He was laughing sheepishly when he did that. A thunderous bang sounded the moment my body hit the solid barrier.

It kind of hurt, but the time of healing of the wounds we sustained was getting shorter. And it's not that I have to worry about dying. I honestly didn't know how I felt about how he would always grab me out of thin air when I think I'd got him, or the fact that he had grown comfortable with throwing me into the wall at Mach fucking four. He seemed to be enjoying himself though.

"That was sorta fun, to be honest," I added. Rakai just shook her head in disbelief at the way Angel and I played.

As for me, well, I've been getting much faster. Rakai showed me how to end my vampiric puberty a lot sooner which was awesome since those flashes were making me insane, to say the least. I have also learned how to adapt better to my vision so that I can now cycle my eyes to different views of my surroundings. The term was always at the tip of my tongue, but I forget about it every time.

I see no better way to describe it, but to compare its similarities to how one of those alien predators could change their vision from that movie I saw when I was still human. That ability was pretty amazing. I could now see thermal energy as well as the vein system in a person, but Angel would sometimes flinch as he thought It was creepy.

All my progress was only the tip of the iceberg as Rakai liked to keep reminding me. But what I really wanted was to learn the magic. I had been drawn to that super-Saiyan-like thing we saw her do, and I can't wait for her to teach me that technique. Rakai has shown me a few things that she could do but hasn't taught me how to do them yet.

It was a bit frustrating at some point, and my itch to want to do it just kept getting bigger. Because of that, I tried to do it alone in secret, but it doesn't usually end so well. Let's just say I'm glad that I could regenerate fast.

"You've been sneaking to do it, right? Boy, how many times do I have to tell you not to be stubborn?" Rakai roared when she saw me come out of my room.

"It's not some piece of cake that every vampire could easily do when they want. It takes patience and persistence." She has cautioned me a great many times, telling me that I have a lot of power that she can sense and that I shouldn't be taking it lightly. I just listened to her litany while occasionally shrugging. She sometimes looked like a nagging mother.

But her warnings—I have come to consider them bullshit as they sounded like some movie mumbo jumbo. Training and reading were all we did, and it seemed to be all we were allowed to do, and I'm starting to get bored. I'm going mad with all the restrictions.

However, I think it was better than burning under that blazing shit. Rakai had been going and getting food for us and wouldn't let us out to do any hunting. She said that we may be caught again in despair if we happen to run into those who were after us.

It was seriously cramping my style, and the fact that Angel had been defending her reasoning was equally annoying. She would always bring us back human blood and animal meat. We have also told her that we prefer criminals over innocents, but I guess whatever would be just fine.

And it's not that I would investigate its origin first before I take it in 'because that would be a hassle. I didn't really care where the blood came from. I find myself pretty numb to it either way. All I actually cared about was how satisfying they were every time.

Also, I was starting to think that Angel felt the same—the more we removed ourselves from our old mortality, the less human we became. I was surprised though that with all the time I've had lately, I chose to slack so hard on my journals. I think that was why I was playing catch-up right now.

Hopefully, this terrible writing of mine will someday prove to be helpful to somebody. I decided to take a break from my books and walk down to the training room. There was some sort of commotion going on as I heard tripping noises over my companion's voices.

I walked through the door and saw Angel and Rakai sparring. I leaned up against the door frame and couldn't help but be impressed with how fluid Angel's movements had been getting. Rakai saw me watching and decided to turn the table on him fast, which made me wince as he hit the ground hard.

"Are you just going to just stand there or get in on this action?" Rakai turned her eyes to me and nodded her head up without paying any attention to Angel who had sprawled out on the floor. She looked like some badass thug with that gesture.

I laughed at Angel as I walked by. He, on the other hand, shot me the finger while picking himself up off the ground. I made my way towards the weapons rack where I looked upon a plethora of various weaponry: swords, staffs, knives, you name it.

I do love my swords, but I have been trying to hone my Bo staff abilities, so that's where my hand fell. I caught Angel out of the corner of my eye picking up the previous weapons he had from the ground. I assumed that Rakai had disarmed him and kept the weapons from within his reach.

"Fighting sticks, eh?" I asked him as I walked to the center of the ring.

"Well, it was a staff before she broke it," he looked at it sheepishly, somewhat remembering what had transpired to the broken staff. I could see Rakai smirking over at the wall where she was leaning.

"Over his thick skull." Rakai threw in for good measure.

"Just a lucky hit!" He turned sharply towards her. Rakai chortled. They seem to have a lot of chaff exchanges lately.

All I could do was fight my inner demons about not bursting out laughing. However, I was utterly defeated in an instant since I let loose a torrent of laughter, which didn't help Angel's mood on the subject. He turned his gaze back at me.

I could sense him planning on getting some revenge on me in some way for his defeat against Rakai. He would always turn to me when he lost. Well, it doesn't look like he would magically win against her if he suddenly decided to retaliate.

We both looked at the woman, and she nodded at us. Before I could turn back towards Angel, I caught the edge of a stick on the side of my staff, barely managing to defend myself from the attack. I quickly recovered and let the momentum of the blow drive the back end of my weapon around and up toward his face. Luckily for him, the other stick had made it in time for a good block.

"I presume you are a little upset about losing to a girl," I said as I stepped back a bit to reset my position.

Angels' eyes narrowed to a slit right before he sent a well-executed spartan kick toward my mid-section which I easily sidestepped.

"Just a girl, huh? Why don't you fight her then?" Both sticks came towards me as he spoke: one aimed at my head the other towards the stomach. I brought up the staff and blocked them both while sweeping up toward his inner thigh.

It was at this moment that I realized just how much better we had gotten as Angel quickly removed his leg and sent the other toward my head. That move was quite amazing considering his weight. The kick forced me to turn on a higher gear and grab his foot which made me slide back with the momentum.

"We have both been getting our asses kicked by her." I smiled as I let go of his leg.

We went on like this for the better part of an hour, trash-talking to each other because that's what we do. It was only when Angel broke my staff that Rakai stepped into the ring.

"I am very impressed with your progress, and I think it's due time to see what you've really learned." She walked up towards us and threw some metal weapons on the ground at our feet. A steel Bo staff landed in front of me, and a pair of steel kendo sticks to Angel.

We picked up the weapons and inspected them by feeling their weight. Rakai, on the other hand, pulled out her special little daggers—the scary ones, the type that could drain you of all your vital juices. I was about to protest when she suddenly attacked us.

"That was dangerous, woman!" I complained though I was able to get a hair's breadth away from her.

"You were able to dodge that! Quit complaining, and double the attack, man," Angel howled as he warded off the woman's knife with his kendo stick. I sometimes think I'm here just to get yelled at.

Rakai really didn't ease up despite everything being a practice. I sometimes thought that she had some pent-up hatred against us, but she asserted that it was for us to know what to expect in an actual war. She would always say that no one will go easy on us on the battlefield.

"Be vigilant! Attacks come from every which direction. You'll be slashed in no time if you slack off for even a second," she reminded, still parrying our weapons with her mere arms. I heard Angel click his tongue before swinging his stick to counter her. But Rakai didn't let up.

"Damn, dude! Your stick won't even reach her!" I teased Angel.

He just smirked and said, "And, dude, your staff?" We both chortled as we admired the woman's strength and pro moves that she even dared to take on two guys together all on her own. It was she who charged first, to boot.

I was quite amazed at both of our abilities to keep her at a safe distance, but the battle is a lot more different when you know you can be seriously injured. We fought for a good long time before I caught a chance for an opening. Angel had the same thought as our sticks sparked off of each other while Rakai's head moved back with unnatural quickness.

"Not bad," she commented as she resumed showering us with counterattacks. She smirked and added, "But you need more than that to bring me down, though," before she started showing signs of retaliation.

Rakai tried to make us fall on our knees as she swept his right leg onto ours to make us tumble. Fortunately, Angel and I were both able to dodge it by jumping up while we still went on with the attack.

"Damn, dude we're sorta cool when we do that!" I exclaimed in amazement. Both Angel and the vampire woman chuckled.

Despite that, we didn't let up for even a split second and just kept pressing the attack. Sparks came flying when our weapons collided as we searched for the opponent's opening, fighting for momentum. Chance seemed to favor us for a bit when we caught her falter for a split second which was all that we needed.

She came charging at me with her daggers while I jumped and spun, swinging my staff around for momentum while dodging her strike. I watched her eyes jump towards Angel who had dropped his sticks down into the back of her knees giving me the chance to send my staff straight, spearing her in the chest. A thud resounded through the forest as the force from our combined attacks sent her flying onto the back wall.

My jaw fell as I dropped my staff. I was rather surprised by that back wall hit she had received. It was actually half-luck, but that was rather proof that our training wasn't just for nothing. That little achievement made me happy at some point.

My attention then shifted to where Angel was; a shit-eating grin was plastered on my face. He was pulling a dagger out of his side, panting heavily. It looked like Rakai still managed to send one of her daggers to him. With all her talent and experience, it wasn't any surprise that she still managed to land him a hit despite the situation she had been in.

"She got you again fucker!" I couldn't help but laugh at his agony. It seemed like the woman was targeting Angel more than me, and I, for some point thought they were sort of flirting with that. But then, my laughing at what had occurred to him came to an end when he pointed his finger at me and smirked.

I looked down only to see Rakai's other dagger sticking out of my side. Strangely, I didn't really feel it piercing me. And I think I wouldn't have noticed it either if my friend over yonder didn't tell me.

It's really odd and I considered it dangerous to not feel anything despite being stabbed. I think I could consider myself numb, but the fact that I'm a vampire may actually have something to do with it. Moreover, I had this conversation with Rakai from back then, and she assured me that I would learn to adapt to it. It's still very strange nonetheless.

"It's bullshit that you didn't feel that," Angel said walking up to me with the dagger in his hand. He was still limping a bit, and his breathing had not yet slowed down.

"Oh, I agree. A hundred percent," was all I could say while still looking down at the blade. I didn't even try pulling it out despite the odd feeling I have until now.

Rakai stood up and opened her palms, and both daggers flew over to her as if they had strings connected to her palms. I sensed another peculiar feeling as it ripped out of my side.

I could feel it starting to stitch up the moment the blade landed back on Rakai's hands. When I looked over at Angel's wound, it was also slowly closing.

"That was very well done," Rakai praised our performance as she walked up to us with a big grin etched on her face. She turned to face me and said, "I am thinking that me and you, Cypher, should spend a bit of time on some craft."

Her words were music to my ears. It had been since the beginning that I earnestly wished for her to say that, and now, she did. I couldn't help myself. I launched my hand toward the sky and brought it back in for an epic fist pump.

This was it! Physical training and sparring were fun and all, but I really wanted to learn this blood craft.

"At last, the cool staff!" I cried in elation. I felt the side of my lips curve upward.

My teeth were showing too, I guess. But I could only care less about those trivial things. Angel took his time before he made his way out towards the kitchen. I assumed he would be making some coffee.

He's kind of loving them lately. Rakai didn't mind him and just ushered me toward the center of the ring where we sat down cross-legged. I felt like I was ready to try it, so I sat there in silence and started to meditate.

"I want you to hold out your hands in front of your chest as if you are holding an imaginary ball," Rakai suddenly uttered which prompted me to open my eyes again. She gestured to me about what to do while explaining it. I proceeded as she said and stuck my hand out. It was pretty simple.

"Good, now you need to open your mind and feel the precious liquid that's flowing through you. Focus on your blood circulation, and feel it streaming through your every vein," she said another time.

Rakai's eyes fixated on what she was doing, but she spoke yet again, "We aren't like any other beings. Our body's normal uses have been altered to suit our needs—blood. Our old organs have been converted to work as storage so that we could store in more blood, and we have the ability to harness and control them to work for us."

As she spoke, I could see blood seeping through her hands and coalescing together before floating in between. I tried to fight the urge to stare in amazement at how cool that looked since I knew I should be concentrating, but fuck! That was sweet!

I couldn't quite understand it at first, but I tried doing it anyway. It seemed pretty simple, but I wonder if my organs will come to obey me. I closed my eyes and took a deep breath, which was unnecessary of course, and started to feel the blood coursing through me.

Once I became in tune with it, I started to direct it toward the center between my hands. I could feel it obeying my will and traveling through my fingertips. When I opened them, there was a pool of blood floating in between my palms.

"Interesting. I've never witnessed anyone who could do it on their first try. That's very impressive." Rakai looked at me in awe, and at the fact that I actually managed to draw the blood out.

"Very gross," Angel said, walking back into the room towards us. A cup of freshly brewed coffee was in his hand. He was staring in disgust at the pools of blood we had floating in place. Mine faltered a little bit as I chuckled.

"Concentrate," Rakai said to me calmly as she shot a death stare at Angel. I wanted to throw a banter at him, but I must not for I might receive a death sentence instead of just a dagger look. Angel just shrugged and blew over the steam in his cup.

I relaxed a bit and started to think of different shapes and forms for the blood to take. It might be an exaggeration, but I noticed Rakai's eyes go wide as she watched my pool take different forms and even dance around my hands.

"Very good," she said as she rose and stepped towards me. She leaned over and sliced my arm open without warning. I was about to say something at her nonchalant action but was rendered speechless as I watched all the blood race towards the wound and sealed it almost instantly.

"Okay, that's cool, but still gross," Angel said while sipping his coffee from behind us. The disgust on his face had somewhat dissipated already as he stared at us with a blank face.

I turned to shoot him the finger when Rakai suddenly rose and started to frantically look around. She closed her eyes and took a deep breath through her nose.

"They found us." Her eyes flew open, clear concern on her features.

"Who did?" I stood, asking. Meanwhile, I noticed Angel turn around and head toward the gun lockers. Everything was getting me confused, but the two seemed to know what was going on.

"There is no time to explain. You, two, must get out of here now. I will draw them away," she said. Desperation was evident in her tone and was even showing on her face.

"Not a fucking chance in hell. We are all in this together," I stated flatly, firming my resolve. We have been together for the past few months, and I've also come to consider her as a friend. If living meant them sacrificing themselves for a twerp like me, I'd rather not.

It's not that I'm considering myself as some hero nor am I just being childish. What I mean is that this is exactly what we have trained hard for. And it would be a waste to not take the chances we have.

"Cypher, you do not understand. Both of you have excelled well beyond my expectations, but you are not yet ready," Rakai spoke in haste as she kept urging me toward the escape tunnel.

I stopped in my tracks and looked her directly in the eyes. "I will take my chances." She looked defeated and her eyes went to the floor.

"Very well, just remember what I told you—our blood is bonded to us, and we can make it do amazing things; even over great distances," she finished while looking back up at me.

I nodded and turned back towards the gun room where Angel was gathering equipment. The place shook and rumbled as soon as I took another step. I also heard a blast from not so far away.

"Damn it!" I braced my hand on the wall while everything jolted around. Ten to twenty seconds, or even more. Everything shook. And it was then that my surroundings suddenly blurred—my sight funneled before darkness completely enveloped me.

CHAPTER 20

DECEPTION

Angel

Trust. One word with a deeper meaning. Easy to utter but hard to earn. As a man who lived in this cruel world with nothing but predators, I always believed that someone could gain trust through the days and moments they have shared, through tears of joy and pain, through doubts and fakes—and not just merely days of meeting without any special moment to give and receive trust.

So, the reason I trusted Rakai was a puzzle in my mind. If the people around me didn't know the answer, how the hell would I get the answer?

"Load it up!"

When I recalled that I hadn't even questioned Rakai's words and actions when she told me to load up, I sprinted towards the weapons locker to compensate for the lost time. Was it her commanding tone that admonished me? Or was it the panicked expression on her face as she yelled at me?

Regardless of the cause, my physical self began to move before my mind could come up with anything to do or say. I came to a halt when I reached the stockpile, closed my eyes, and took a deep breath in, even though the short distance I had traveled had not caused any tiredness in my body. Rather, I did so because I could feel something in this location.

The feeling that transported me from sweating summer to chilling winter, the goosebumps on the back of my neck, and the heightened awareness that I always exhibit when engaging in a battle with a friend all reminded me of Cypher and his reticent presence. Should I have put that much faith in Rakai? Was I right in believing so much in her?

At this moment, I completely comprehend what she meant by always being geared up; however, I will need to return to this topic later because it will require extensive and in-depth consideration. I realized that your readiness level and the extent to which you intend to be very well equipped are the two most important factors in any situation.

"What's the situation on your side, Angel?" Cypher shouted from the other side. I didn't know if he shouted, but his voice was loud and echoing in this deafening silent place.

I found a set of bags that had already been loaded and were prepared to be used. These bags were scorn bags, and they had built-in gun holders. They were a thing of beauty.

I checked the supplementary weapons that Cypher and I had and the ones we shared and filled an extra duffle bag with preloaded magazines for the rifles and handguns.

"Damn." When I discovered that we didn't have one clue about Rakai, I wanted to punch myself in the face. I only glanced in her direction and observed that she was occupied with a shadow moving through the darkness.

Despite this, I had a suspicion that she didn't require one, especially after I heard a loud yelp from wherever she punched.

"Fuck it, woman!" Cypher let out a scream of agony. He got back up, as if he didn't already have enough pain in his body, and tried to attack Rakai again, ending in his nth embarrassing defeat. I felt myself grinning at his stupidity.

As if the suffering in his body wasn't enough, he kept attacking her. Why did I ever believe she was just like us normal people? I was amused by the idea and stood there for a few seconds, chuckling to myself.

When I saw the long rapier, I immediately turned to our rack and grabbed some melee weapons to use. The musty scent of age lingered in the air, adding to the atmosphere of mystery and anticipation. The rapier's grip was a work of art adorned with intricate antique engravings that told a tale of forgotten battles and heroic feats.

As I reached out to touch it, the cold metal sent a shiver down my spine, and I could feel the weight of history in my hands. Its grip was decorated with antique engravings, and its long blade glowed brilliantly whenever a moonlight ray struck it. I gave myself a sardonic grin before draping the sword's scabbard over my upper body.

The rapier's blade was extraordinary, catching the moonlight streaming through a narrow window. The steel seemed alive, sparkling and glowing brilliantly whenever a moonlight ray struck it. It was as if the blade held a life of its own, waiting to be unleashed in combat.

Feeling a surge of confidence, I couldn't resist a sardonic grin as I draped the sword's scabbard over my upper body. The leather felt rough against my skin, and metal meeting leather sounded oddly satisfying. I knew that this weapon would serve me well in the coming battle.

I was well aware that if I didn't bring Cypher's sword with me, I would never escape the consequences of my decision. My imagination caused me to shudder with horror as I tried to picture his never-ending complaints and drawn-out temper outbursts. Even after ensuring I had everything, I still thought something was missing.

Therefore, rather than going, I bought some brass knucks for myself because why not? After loading everything and being content with how it looked, I turned around to go back. It was a good thing that I had enhanced strength because I had the impression that all of this luggage and weaponry would be quite hefty for a person who wasn't boosted in this way.

I was forced to take a few steps back since I could hear Cypher and Rakai bickering about something rather than attacking each other. Should they have chosen to debate with words or seen a funny reprise of Cypher's defeat?

I shook my head with a grin as I went to the doorway, intending to tease my dear friend, when an explosion rocked me a bit, causing me to lose my balance and drop a couple of bags. I grabbed onto the doorway for support as I dropped the bags and continued to shake my head.

"What the hell . . ." I became alert due to the powerful vibration beneath my feet. My eyes witnessed Rakai deliver a full-power blow to Cypher's neck, knocking him out and making him unconscious.

My friend's body dropped in a drawn-out move right before me. However, just as he began losing consciousness, our eyes met. He gave me a look that conveyed something I couldn't quite put my finger on other than the fact that this was a negative situation.

"What the fuck . . . are you doing, Rakai?" I was conflicted as I threw the remaining bags to the ground, extracted my weapon, and pointed it toward Rakai, doing it more out of reflex than out of a genuine desire to do so.

She gave me a sly grin and raised an eyebrow in response. She dropped her sight and moved toward Cypher's legs, who's lying still on the ground.

"You need to get him out of here." Zhe gestured down towards Cypher's unconscious form after she went near the doorway and looked for something. I tilted my head more, and with just one micrometre away, my finger would trigger the gun on her head.

"I tried telling him that you, guys, need to get out of here, but this fool is stubborn and wouldn't listen to me."

". . . why?" I couldn't help but inquire further about her because I was perplexed by her unexpected command to leave this place. I wasn't looking for a definitive explanation; I was curious about why Cypher was knocked out after taking just one hit. I'm sorry, Cy, but that must sting.

"They're coming. And I bet you two wouldn't stand a chance on their troupe. Well, maybe, one or three of them. After all, you both improved a lot . . . not just to the point of killing every single one of them," she said without sugarcoating her words. She grabbed a small knife and brought it under the moonlight before glancing at me with bright red eyes. "You should go if you still want to live."

". . . yeah." I couldn't immediately find my voice to answer her for some reason. My eyes remained on her as the breeze blew her tied-up hair. I feigned a cough before continuing my sentence.

"That sounds about right." I lowered my weapon, looked down at Cypher, and looked back at Rakai.

"What should we do?" She rummaged around in her pocket before producing a filthy object. I shuddered when I saw what was within the small vial when the light from above cast a clear image of what was inside the vial. It was filled with a dark, familiar liquid.

It was completely covered with blood. She flung it at me, and I caught it with my other hand. "I want you to give that to Cypher when he wakes up, and he will know what to do. I'm sure he would understand if he listened to what I've explained earlier."

"Blood? Why blood? Is he going to drink this and get powered up?"

"Ha, funny, Angel. Didn't know you got that humour in you."

I grinned at her and looked back at the vile on my palms.

"I told him you aren't ready yet, but that was a lie. You are ready but not fully ready to fight head-on with a troupe. I can't afford to let this chance slip away. This is the opportunity we need. The moment we've been waiting for. I can't let this go."

As I stood there, my eyes fixated on hers, the surroundings seemed to blur into a haze, and the world took on a dreamlike quality. Everything began to move at a glacial pace the moment she walked in my direction and started walking. The wind blew as I watched Rakai walk, but all I could feel was the numbness that slowly crept up from my toes to the top of my head.

Despite the wind that swept through the area, I felt oddly insulated from the external world. My focus remained solely on her, oblivious to the sounds of birds chirping or the distant heavy breathing of Cypher. It was as though time itself had slowed down, stretching each second to an eternity.

Her appearance remained as ferocious as if everyone were her foes, but despite her fuming with rage, I could still see how her face shone in the spotlight cast by the disco ball. It resulted in an instant enhancement of her beauty, which rendered me mute and speechless. Rakai came up to me and gently stroked my face.

As I gazed into her eyes, I was struck by a sensation I hadn't had in a very long time. My voice went hoarse, and just as I worked up the nerve to speak, another explosion spoiled the moment for us both. Instantaneously, she broke eye contact and looked away.

"Quickly get him to the tunnel and get out of here. I will distract them to buy you enough time to run."

Regretful at our truncated moment, I turned and grabbed Cypher's unmoving body, threw him over my shoulder, and turned back to see nothing but a space of darkness and fainted dust devil.

"Good luck, and be careful," I said softly under my breath. I reached down and grabbed our gear. We started to head towards the bookcase that hid our escape.

As I turned around, I heard grunts and hurls in the distance, both of which appeared to be coming from Rakai. My legs were itching to turn around and offer her some assistance, but I was certain that this wasn't what she desired. She had been preparing us to arrive at this point.

Even though my mind, body, and spirit started to become anxious, the very least I could do was keep to the plan and get away. A few days ago, Rakai explained how we would hide our hideout a secret.

"A secret tunnel would be a great hideout. The two of you will stay in there as much as you can," Rakai said, using a small, thin wood stick encircling a place inside the house on the drawings she did on the ground.

"Oh! A secret tunnel behind a bookcase door! That's a cool one, dude," Cypher let out an exclamation.

When I stared at him, I wanted to almost groan at his face when he didn't even realize something Rakai had spoken. After seeing the emotion on my face, he wrinkled his brows. "What?"

I almost rolled my eyes at him when I turned my gaze at Rakai. "What about you? Do the two of us need to hide? We've been training for a while, and I know I can help you fight them—"

"Totally agreed! What's the use of training so hard to the point of almost dying if we'll hide? Right, Angel?"

Ignoring what Cypher said, I continued, "I'm sure we can help you."

Rakai shook her head. Her eyes looked at Cypher before they settled on mine. "You will hide. You two, should be safe before we go to the main thing."

Cypher glanced at me while we were both befuddled. On the other hand, rather than continuing to push the same issue, he was more thrilled about the hidden hideout.

"So, how will we do this secret hideout?"

Rakai broke the ease of operation details for us. It's a straightforward one, much like the movies I've seen several times over and over again. We would establish a secret route behind the modest three-tiered library, and all we would need to do to access the hidden entrance behind the shelf would be to take one book out from under it.

It proceeded smoothly. Rakai took the time to explain the process to Cypher and me, and we were quite curious to see how it turned out. On the other hand, we needed more time to try and practice opening the passage, which was why I couldn't recall the name of the book that allowed us entry.

As I looked through all the books, I became annoyed at myself and threw our belongings and Cypher onto the ground. The sole light source was a little window in the ceiling, but due to my heightened scotopic vision, I didn't require any light. I was able to make out all of the letters and images.

Cypher groaned when he hit the ground, which I didn't mind because he needed to get up and help me!

"Wake up, you fool! I don't know the book's title," I said, whispering to myself, and kicked Cypher's arm. To no avail, he didn't even react, so I didn't have a choice but to continue this by myself.

I reached for the first book called Torn by Auron Astaroth, and nothing happened. I kept reaching for the book and kept falling. Irritated and getting impatient, I started to move faster. Book after book fell to the ground. The sound of the books hitting the floor mixed with the continuous vague sounds of guns.

"The art of deception," I turned around and heard it behind me. Cypher was sitting up and stroking his head when I turned around to look at him.

After locating the book and pulling on it, I heard the clicking sound made by the locking mechanism, and the bookshelf came loose. I then swung the door open and stared down the long tunnel.

"What happened?" Cypher stood up and looked around before turning his attention swiftly back to the outside when he heard what sounded like additional gunshots coming from within.

"No time, man. I'll explain along the way. Grab your shit, and let's get out of here." I got my backpack off the floor and put it on while I saw Cypher do the same thing. He swiftly looked over his weapons before finishing putting on his buckles.

"And Rakai?" he said as he sheathed his sword into the backpack slot.

"She is giving us time to get out of here." While going into the tunnel, I could hear Cypher muttering obscenities to himself under his breath. However, I didn't turn around to address him. After making it approximately ten steps, I turned around and saw Cypher still standing at the entryway with his gaze turned toward the direction of the shooting.

"Don't even think about it, man; we must go." I continued to make my way through the tunnel despite hearing him saying something under his breath and footsteps approaching me from the opposite direction.

"I just don't understand why we flee from our home, Angel. This is fucking retarded; we can take them." Cypher's voice rang down the tunnel towards me.

"Maybe we can, but maybe we can't. Rakai has a plan, I guess, and I would prefer to fight them on our terms and not theirs." I turned slightly to make sure he was still heading towards the exit with me.

"I suppose you're right, but I don't have to like it; I like this place, dude, and I don't want to lose it," I could hear the anger in his tone, and I could understand it. All I could do was nod at his statement as we pushed on.

We spent considerable time looking for the ideal location, and I was equally interested in learning how they discovered it. However, we couldn't think about these things right now since we didn't have the time. As we advanced toward the surface exit, I could hear an increase in the frequency of the gunfire that was occurring nearby.

That our tunnel only brought us around 200 feet away from the house was something I considered more than acceptable. As we got closer to the latch, I turned around to look at Cypher and signaled with my hands that I was ready.

Out of the corner of my eye, I saw him bring his gun to his shoulder and remove the safety.

I cautiously unlocked the door's latch. Every groan and creak of the metal were apart tearing my ears, so I immediately slipped out and surveyed the surrounding area while Cypher made his way up and secured the latch. As we were racing toward the truck we kept hidden in the bushes in case of emergencies such as this one, bullets started tearing through the bushes in our direction, and one of them found its way onto my shoulder.

It jolted me forward a bit, and although it hurt less than it surprised me, the burn was present. Cypher turned and began firing quickly in the direction they had come from, and I imitated his actions while still backing up toward our van.

"You alright?" I Cypher asked between the volley of shots.

"You know I'll be fine," I said through gritted teeth as I changed my magazine,

Cypher gave the impression that he was about to say something when the gunfire abruptly ceased, and it became very silent. His focus immediately swung back towards the trees, and his eyes narrowed as he put his rifle on the ground and pulled out his blades.

"They're coming."

In the dimly lit, abandoned warehouse, the air was heavy with the scent of damp wood and old machinery. Cypher's heart pounded in his chest as he stood amidst the shadows, the only light source was a flickering bulb hanging from the ceiling just as he uttered his defiance, a menacing figure materialized from the darkness, its features obscured by the shadows.

With a swift and deadly strike, the assailant lunged at Cypher. Reacting with agility, Cypher deftly reached for one of his razor-sharp knives, driving its hilt deep into the man's eye socket. A gut-wrenching cry filled the air as the man crumpled to the floor. As Cypher withdrew his weapon, he couldn't resist a shiver of revulsion. Without hesitation, he brought his foot down with brutal force, reducing the once formidable skull into a grotesque paste. The sickening crunch echoed in the grim surroundings, leaving an eerie silence.

"They are Vampires, open your senses and listen," Cypher remarked to me as he finished licking the blood off his blade, grinned at me, and then blinked into the darkness after he had finished.

"Fuck . . ."

I have a terrible habit of overlooking my skills. I need to get better at remembering them. I shut my eyes and opened my senses, allowing everything around me to flood in. As I did so, I could hear my environment becoming increasingly loud and distinct. When I opened my eyes, I noticed that everything was significantly brighter, and I could see faint shadow lines dancing around the trees.

"Ah... shit," I breathed as I spat some saliva.

I waited calmly while attentively listening to the sounds approaching from all directions around me. My reaction was perfectly timed, and I could snag two of the cretins straight out of the air and hold them by their throats as I brought them down. The man and the woman hissed at me as I used their momentum to swing them around and toward the ground.

I brought all my strength down into them, forcing my hands to crush their throats and the blood to ooze between my fingers. I watched as they both desperately grabbed at their necks as I dropped my heels down onto their skulls to finish the job. I hurriedly whirled around in the direction of a hiss that I heard coming from behind me.

As I did so, I saw a figure for a split-second approach towards me, but then another shadow shot passed it. The severed head of the vampire came tumbling down towards my feet when I severed it. I turned to look up as I was stepping on it, and I could make out the words 'You're welcome' coming from the shadows.

Before I heard footsteps approaching from behind me, I grinned and shook my head in response. I instinctively glanced around to discover a towering figure staring at me from below.

"I figured you'd be bigger," the man said to me with a confused scowl on his face.

I simply smirked and motioned for him to come at me with both hands. He did as I asked, and he was quick. I was unprepared to absorb such a blow from the man, but looking back, I realize I should have known better.

Oh well. After falling to the ground and rolling to my feet, I reached into the pocket on the back of my shirt, removed the knuckle guards, and put them on before driving my fist into the side of the man's chin, which caused him to lurch backward. I didn't back down and continued to press my attack by grabbing his shirt and repeatedly punching him.

I stepped forward to keep up the momentum until the man fell to the ground, and then I continued to pummel him until I heard clapping coming from behind me. I didn't stop until I heard the clapping. I removed my fist from the paste on the ground, turned around, and saw Cypher grinning and applauding me from high up in the tree.

"How long have you been sitting there?"

"Long enough, Psycho."

"That's rich coming from you." I laughed as he jumped down and made his way towards me.

"I saw many more of them up towards the house; I think it's in our best interests if we get out of here." He nodded back towards the house with concern on his face.

"I agree; we need to get out of here before more show up."

As we rounded the corner, got to the vehicle, and got inside, I could see Cypher struggling inside with the idea of leaving Rakai. I was having a pretty difficult time as well, but for some reason, I trusted her, and I had this strange feeling that she would be okay even though I was having a terrible time myself.

We began to make our way down the old dirt road in complete silence, neither knowing what steps to take next. On the one hand, we had to deal with a pack of werewolves because their attack resulted in our close friend's death; on the other hand, we had to deal with this vampire problem. At this pace, we would have far too many adversaries to monitor properly.

"What are we going to do?" Cypher's words snapped me out of my thoughts.

"Rakai wanted me to give this to you." I fished into my bag, pulled out the vial, and handed it over. "She said you'd know what to do?"

A big grin pulled across Cypher's face. "Oh yes, I know exactly what to do. But we will need to get back into the house."

I sharply looked over towards him. "Are you crazy!"

"It's debatable, but I don't want to go back to fighting; I just want to watch; I suspect they weren't there for us."

CHAPTER 21

RETALIATION

Cypher

The night skyline of the city started to poke its head on the horizon as we made it to the top of a hill, a place we hadn't stepped foot on for what felt like an eternity—familiar but felt like a faraway memory at the back of my mind. As we bent down our upper body and slid our feet to the ground, it created a toe-tall dusty tornado that slowly danced along with the breeze of night's wind scented with nothing pleasant but earthy, dreadful smell.

After turning around, I peered down to see the carnage that was taking place in the location where we had just come from. As Angel, who stood by my side, likewise stared down at the events that were taking place a few meters away, I could feel how tense he was. I knew that even though the area below us was already obscured by thick and tall trees, he was still able to sense the continuous rumble that was emanating from the ground beneath the bottoms of our shoes.

My jaws were clenched because of the relentless flashes of light that came from a specific location. Because I had no other option, I had no alternative but to clench my fist tightly. If I was feeling this way right now, I can't really begin to fathom how Angel must be experiencing everything right now.

"How hilarious . . . we gained powers, but we still can't protect ourselves without the help of other people. It's just like what happened to Chris. We're still useless . . ." Angel murmured through his gritted growing fangs.

I could sense the wrath that was building up in him. His eyes were crimson not because of the need to morph into something else but simply because he was fighting within himself to resist the urge to go back and sabotaging our earlier plan. This was why the urge to transform wasn't the cause of his red eyes.

His hands were similarly clenched into a ball. I had the exact same feeling, and it was very difficult for me to hold back from going down there and fighting.

"Isn't that the reason we train until we pass out? Maybe we're not there yet, but I can feel it. We are stronger than before." Our eyes met. It seemed like he was crying, and I couldn't help but feel bad for my buddy who was going through it.

This wasn't only a conflict with our adversaries; rather, for Angel and me, the stakes were much higher than anything else we could ever imagine. Due to the fact that we are kilometers away from the battle, our ability to detect sounds that are coming from a great distance was severely compromised. We were unable to take the chance that our adversaries might also hear us while monitoring a particular radar.

It was essential that we eliminate the possibility of either of us overhearing the Other. Even though it's hard to believe, Rakai had all of this planned out. Her strategy went into a lot of specifics.

Was it possible that the fact that she's been around for so many years and seen so many different conflicts gave her the ability to devise a strategy like this? At first, I was unsure what to do. Despite this, I was unable to place all of my confidence in her because all she did was instruct us and offer guidance.

I was at a loss to understand why Angel would always nod his head in agreement to whatever that lady said, yet I was unable to go more than a minute without frowning or bringing up an argument to doubt her capacity. She is good, and in my mind, she is head and shoulders above anyone else that comes to mind. Was it enough of a reason to put your faith in someone who is more powerful than you?

If Angel was able to trust someone so easily, then I just couldn't do it. To achieve it, I need something profound and significant. My everyday life consisted of much more than just handing out candy to kids.

It is only possible to acquire trust through virtuous actions. But just to be sure, up to this point, I still hadn't placed any of my faith in Rakai . . . well . . . fifty?

"Want one?" I asked him after lighting up the cigar I found in my back pocket.

Angel shook his head. "Why the hell do you have that?"

"I'm always prepared, dude. Would've been better if there's weed."

"Don't joke around, Cypher."

"You're just too tense, Angel. Shake it off."

"What if the plan turned? What if there's a failure and we have to actually go there? What if Rakai is in danger—"

"Oh, please." I rolled my eyes and puffed the smoke. "Stop your what-ifs. Are you a freaking girl?"

"Whatever. Just give me one," he said and extended his hand in front of me. I smirked at him and gave him one. He got my cigar and met the one with fire on the end of his to light his smoke.

After that, we sat there in complete quiet, listening to the fire that was going on around us while simultaneously attempting to soothe our fears by inhaling the smoke. No one had the courage to even voice a word or open their lips to speak. We sat in utter quietness, although our environment wasn't as quiet as ours.

Even the buzzing of nearby bugs and insects, such as crickets, wasn't enough to divert our attention from the monotonous rumble that was occurring. The moon's crescent began to become visible through the gap in the cloud cover that was shaped like nothing. The wind blew, and even though we were located a significant distance from the incident, the wind carried the odor of blood and gunpowder to us.

I wrinkled my nose and tried to look at my friend who was rustling next to me. I had the impression that we might continue to be silent for a longer period, but Angel suddenly jumped up.

"I can't stay here like this," he said with finality, dusting off the back of his pants, making some of it blew at my side. I waved my hand in front to wipe away the dust with a frown face at him.

I shook my head and looked in front. "Well, you don't have a choice. It's either you'll ruin Rakai's plan and die, or you'll sit here, wait and live. You can pick your choice, dude. But I'm telling you, Rakai can do it."

"Cypher, can you hear yourself? The fight had been going on for more than half an hour! The sun will soon set in the sky, and it will be difficult –"

"I thought you trust her?!" Suddenly, my loud voice made the nearby insects and animals fly and ran to the deepest part of the forest. I sighed and looked up at my dear friend whose face was distorted with his mixed feelings.

"You just have to stick with our plan and wait for the result. It might be hard since you're overly worried about your love prospect, but I assure you—"

"What the fuck, Cy?"

"What?" I slowly stood up, patted the back of my pants, and looked at Angel. His expression changed from being tense and worried to overly shocked and embarrassed. I smirked at his reaction.

"Don't fucking what me now. What did you just say?"

I laughed at him, trying to ease his worries. I turned my body to face him. My back faces the fight scene, blocking Angel's sight of the irregular lights.

"I just simply want you to believe in her, like what you always did. So, calm yourself and don't make me say it again. You'll just get worried more if you process what I've just said."

As soon as I turned my back on him, the corner of my mouth began to draw downward. I clenched my hands and clenched my teeth, wishing without hope that the power of my words would never be undermined. Putting up a brave front was just something I very seldom do.

The thing was, I believed in being truthful all the damn time, but in these kinds of situations, I couldn't help but mistrust my own statements. The thing was, I believed it to be true all the damn time. Something unsettling was going on in the back of my mind, but it was something I didn't want to believe or even accept.

After then, though, both the light and the rumbling ceased. Before we started perking up, I stole a glimpse at Angel, who was doing the same thing.

One more hill may be seen off in the distance. It is close enough for us to use our capacity to see things from a distance, and to the utter disbelief of my whole being, I saw a few men and a body that was recognizable to me.

"What's that? Is that . . ." I murmured under my silent, heavy breath.

"Rakai!" Angel exclaimed. He assumed the stance of someone who was about to leap from this location to that one at any moment.

As soon as I noticed him grabbing his chest, I swiftly moved my hand to interrupt him. But I couldn't hold it against him for being as fired up as he was. The lady who was supposed to be the most powerful and experienced of anybody was being carried out by a couple of men like a dead pig and placed at the feet of some ladies without any conscience on their part.

"Did she lose? What the hell happened? Cypher!"

"I don't know! We've been together ever since, why the hell are you asking me?!"

Keeping a keen gaze fixed on the assortment of foes up ahead. It was the woman who had been standing on the rooftop all those years ago. It appeared from the white van that was following them that they had driven up to that hill in that vehicle.

They went so far as to bind Rakai's hands behind her back, even though her body lacked the strength to move in any direction. They actually had a difficult time catching her, if you can believe it. However, getting apprehended wasn't part of our original strategy.

I pondered why we didn't obtain a backup plan. I was reminded of their obnoxious facial expressions and awful hairstyles. I didn't doubt that it was them!

I turned to face Angel with the intention of informing him about the identity of those women; nevertheless, his frown deepened as I did so. I thought that he was familiar with the same people as well.

"Fuck. The plan is ruined," he muttered with a heavy voice.

The idea was straightforward, but Rakai gave the impression of having lost. When she was being kicked by those ladies or raised by pulling her hair upwards, her body was lying on the ground without any evidence of any motions or signals of struggling. Her hair was being pulled upwards.

It was a mystery to me why she couldn't overcome the obstacle. Even though I couldn't equal her in terms of ability and power, I was aware that she was someone who those thugs wouldn't be able to take down. Besides, I didn't want my comments at Angel earlier to go in vain.

It was necessary for me to put my faith in both my intuition and Rakai's remarks. However, what about Angel? Since then, he's been tense and worrying about everything.

I'm willing to wager that Rakai was unable to keep it together once he realized that he was under the control of the adversaries. I clenched my hand into a ball and gazed intently.

"Should we go?" I inquired, wondering of the next steps we would take if he responded positively. Angel didn't respond right away; instead, he looked calmly at the stronghold of the enemy, all the while his fangs were inching their way out of the corner of his lips. I was aware from that very instant.

Angel did his best to ponder the implications of this situation. A whole minute passed before Angel responded to my inquiry by shaking his head in the negative. He presented his face to mine and gazed intently into my eyes while he did so. I was able to sense the internal conflict he was experiencing about his own decision.

"We need to trust that she knows what she's doing. I will trust your words."

I nodded my head at his words. "That's expected. My instinct is more accurate than your brain." Smirking behind my worried eyes, Angel ignored my joke. His focus was given fully in front.

"If we could see them at this distance, can they also see us?" he said.

"Yeah . . . that makes sense. Let's take shelter first and lay low our aura."

Angel only turned his back and didn't say anything. I could see how hard he was trying to merely clench his teeth and not do something reckless even though his fangs were slowly returning to their regular state. As I trailed behind him, I stole one last look back to see where Rakai was standing.

Angel proceeded to wander farther into the forest until she came to a large, thick stone, at which point she halted. He addressed me by looking at me and conveying his message to me through his eyes. I signaled to him with a nod, and he proceeded to walk straight up onto the stone.

In all honesty, it's large enough to function as a bed. In addition, the position was more than enough for the job. At this distance, we were able to make out every detail of them, while also masking our scent with the rotting animal remains and mud that covered the woodland floor. Again, we sat in complete silence and endeavored to follow their motions without drawing too much attention to ourselves by exerting too much energy or presence.

I could tell they were having a conversation down there by their body language. Rakai gradually recovered mobility, and I found myself wanting to applaud her fortitude at every step of the way. After spitting at the women's feet, Rakai was pushed into the back of a white vehicle in front of us as witnesses.

Once the van drove off, it gave the impression that everyone else was following suit, which I believe was an intriguing move.

"We should wait a bit longer to let them get out of there before we head back down." I looked over at Angel to see what he thought of the plan. He jumped off from the stone and stood upright.

"Are you sure we need to go back there?" He kept his gaze on the van with Rakai being forced to get in it.

I stood beside him after I copied his jump, put my hand on his shoulder, and followed his gaze.

"We will get her back," I turned back towards the direction of the house we were staying in.

"And no, we don't necessarily need to go back to the house, but I feel that if we want to save Rakai, we will need to get more weapons. I'm sure we can't fight them all with our bare power when they also used guns and powder, right?"

Angel indicated her agreement with a nod, and we continued to wait for a little more. Even after they had loaded Rakai into the van, the other men and women remained outside the vehicle. It appeared as though the one woman with her hair pulled back in a ponytail was giving orders to the other women.

When one of the men stared in our direction while using binoculars, my nerves began to fray. I had a terrible feeling that they were going to find us, but Angel was quick enough to pull my collar down so that we could hide behind the rock. Before we started making our way back home, we checked to be sure that they were no longer in sight and that their odors could no longer be detected.

We had to park quite a distance away from the home, and then we had to navigate our way through the bright darkness. The appearance of the house suggested that it had seen better days. If I were to come to this place without any prior knowledge of its history, my first guess would be that a tornado tore through it, turning the home on its side.

"Our insurance will be going to love us," was all I could say after kicking the hand of a dead body blocking my way.

"It will only get worse, the closer we get," Angel hushed his words and continued walking forward. I rolled my eyes at him and gave a repulsed expression as I gazed at the dead body before trailing behind Angel as he proceeded through the bodies of the dead people.

I had a strong suspicion that all of that was going through his thoughts because the only thing he was concerned about now was acquiring weapons and saving Rakai. There was some kind of explosive symbol that was used to open the front door. Considering that I was able to detect Angel's scent from quite a distance away, we ought to have known better than to try to sneak up on her, but I guess old habits die hard as the old adage goes.

I turned to look at Angel, and we talked about the plan that Rakai had for us to carry it out. After we were sure that everything had been clarified, I looked around the surrounding area. Rakai stated that she would place it near the tree trunk that was the largest, which was located four steps away from the entrance.

In my brain, I followed Rakai's directions, and I smiled when I discovered what I was looking for. I got down on my knees right away to confirm.

"Are you sure you can do it?" Angel asked while leaning his head down, watching what I was doing with the blood I'd found on the ground.

"Dude, if you're going to pressure me, just shut up." Angel raised his hands in the air and stepped backward. A little time ago, Rakai instructed me on how to locate someone by utilizing their blood.

I have a strong suspicion that this is the very reason she taught me that; specifically, so that we might locate their hideout and prevent them from doing whatever it was that had Rakai so concerned. I zeroed in on the blood that was on the ground and focused my concentration there. It had a more crimson hue and appeared to be smoldering as though it dissipated into the atmosphere.

Any delay in acting might lead to feelings of regret. I had to pick up my pace. When you said that, I could feel my fangs coming out. I let out a low growl and then dipped the tips of my fingers into the blood.

As soon as I placed some of my aura on my fingertips, fragments of footfall and a hazy path road began to play back in my mind like a broken recorder. I wasn't sure whose perspective this was because I could see the backs of a couple of people in the front row, both men and women. I had the impression that was all there was, but then I heard a whisper. Due to its low volume, I was unable to make out what was being said.

"What are you saying?" I spoke in a hushed tone while attempting to address that person. But at this point, all I could see was a gradual lifting of my sight, during which I was confronted with a pair of terrible and demonic red eyes that held my breath. Angel was hunched over and looking up at me as I abruptly opened my eyes.

"Are you okay? What happened? Did you find them?"

I felt my heart racing and clutched my hands to my chest, which was where I could feel it. Even though I couldn't breathe due to the pressure that was building up in my chest, I managed to nod my head. Angel assisted me in standing up, and I can't stop seeing those eyes . . . I really, truly believed that my time had come to pass.

We turned around and proceeded back toward the home to investigate the area. We finally made it over to the store and looked around. Aside from the fact that we would need a new door due to the explosion, there was nothing else wrong with it. Even the entrance hatch to the bunker couldn't be located.

"I wonder how Rakai is now . . ." Angel whispered to himself, but because we both had the capacity to hear five times as well as the normal person, I laughed at him. I was attempting to lighten the mood while we were walking through the chaotic store.

"Oho, you're being a worrywart, huh?"

"Oh, please, Cypher. I'm simply worried as someone who knows her. Aren't you worried?"

"Not as worried as you."

Angel rolled his eyes. The middle finger was raised, and I couldn't help but chuckle along with him despite myself. I could see where he was coming from with that explanation.

I started to have my doubts about Rakai's ability to take on those terrifying enemies all by himself when I saw how their eyes could kill. If she just didn't have any plan, I would make a beeline for them right away. When we went back to the house, we discovered the same, same thing that we had discovered when we were in the store.

It seemed as though Rakai had come from the bunker and begun fighting inside the home in order to give the appearance that this was where she was residing. However, she did forget to take one of her sandals with her as she exited the bunker, as well as the wrapper from the lunch that she had had earlier. In spite of the vamps' awareness of both me and Cypher, the entrance to our bunker remained undisturbed by their presence.

It is highly unlikely that they were aware of the existence of the bunker. Withered husks of people's dead bodies covered the ground, rapidly deteriorating in front of our eyes as clouds of dust swirled about them.

'Such a neat concept.' I had this thought in my head.

Angel's eyes shot up and looked around. His body alerted me that something was going on. "We are not alone here," he said as he pulled his gun up and scanned the area.

I did what she said and looked about in the dimly lit area as well. I didn't notice on anything much, but I did get a sensation of something I couldn't quite put my finger on. The weight and tension of the air increased.

The stench of blood that had been present before had become even worse, and if the situation hadn't been so dire, I might have really thrown up right now. The branches of the trees scraped against one another, and the full moon, which was relatively low in the sky, was obscured by the thick clouds. Even though there are just a few hours left 'till sunrise, the entire area leading up to the woodland was completely covered in darkness.

"Six . . ." was all I said, and Angel nodded.

"They are still far away. I don't think they are watching us," he said.

"No . . . I think they are just a couple of blocks away. Would it hurt to assume the worst?"

"What's with you, tonight? You seem to do better with your words. Did Rakai hit your head too much?"

"Funny, dude. Try again when we survive this one."

Angel grinned behind his rifle. I only had to catch his fleeting gaze to understand what he was trying to convey. While I was distracted by looking into the void in front of me, he cautiously but methodically moved backward.

There was nothing in there save from the eerie, drawn-out shadows cast by the trees and the prolonged darkness. But the hair on the back of my neck kept telling me that there was someone hiding in the very depths of that darkness. When I realized that he had arrived at the door, I proceeded with extreme caution in my own movements.

To my relief, I managed to get to the door without making a peep as I went. We dug our way out of the hole in the house and made our way back outside.

"We knew somebody would return." Not because of any magic, but simply because of their aura, the murderous aura, both Angel and I were unable to move or even take a breath when we heard a very low but imposing voice. It was as if the words were designed to render us unable to move or breathe.

Angel flashed me a glance in return, which I returned to him. My entire body went into a protective position as soon as we heard the sound of a twig breaking underfoot. I twisted my body to face whatever it was, and as soon as I did so, I raised the revolver from my side and pointed it toward the nothingness that was around me.

Angel carried out the activity at the exact same time as everyone else. When we heard the voice coming from beyond the tree line, I clenched my teeth and gritted my teeth. Again, the wind blew, and even though the doorless door was obstructing my whole field of vision and that we were now around the room without any light, I was still able to make out the growing silhouette of a person . . . which eventually increased in number.

"I see that you're with an unwanted creature," the same voice from earlier had shown its face.

Even though I didn't recognize him, I was able to deduce that he was the leader based on the pungent odor of blood and the more hostile expression in his eyes. As he moved slowly behind them with his hands behind his back, the other vampires were following closely behind him. His clothing brought to mind several classic vampire films that have always been among my favorites to watch.

After seeing them, I wasn't sure if I would enjoy viewing them at all.

"Who are you?" Angel asked.

Angel caught the boss's eye briefly. Before he lifted one of his fingers, he gave a wispy smile that revealed his paper-thin lips and colorless gums. Angel flew to the wall behind us in the blink of an eye when he flicked it into the air and into the air.

"Ugh!" he groaned loudly.

My eyes widened when I saw his body penetrate to the wall and almost a meter away from me. "Angel!"

In a state of terror, I looked forward and readied my weapon to fire, but to my utter disbelief, the boss was already within an inch of my weapon. He raised his hand, and just before I passed out, I saw a glimpse of his lips moving while they mouthed something.

"... you ...get ..."

"No! That ... can't ..."

My mind started to slowly regain its strength as distorted noises started playing in the background. However, every time I attempted to open my eyes, all I could see was the whirling of my surroundings, and I was forced to close my eyes once again before attempting to open them. After the third attempt, everything started to become more understandable.

"Once again, I will ask you. Where did you come from?" I was forced to shift my head to the side by the voice of the boss. To my utter surprise, he was only a few paces away from me as I turned around. I went to launch an assault on him while gritting my teeth, but at that very moment, I became aware that two other vampires had both of my hands held captive.

"Let me go, you bastards!" I muttered under my breath as I struggled to get my hands away from them. And of all, who was I, the one who passed out again after receiving one knock on the head, that could do something to stop these thugs?

"Cypher!" The sound of Angel's voice caused me to whip my head around to face him.

"What ..." My friend kneeled on the ground, and the right side of his face was stained with his own blood when I saw him. At that moment, the question that I was ready to ask became lodged deep within my throat. At that second, I realized that our situation is hopeless.

"Now that everyone's awake, shall we begin again?"

The boss spent a substantial amount of time interrogating us, enquiring about our whereabouts and the specifics of the activities we were engaged in at this site. They had no idea who we were, and they were under the impression that Rakai's house was situated in this area, that much is certain to me. In addition to this, I discovered the rationale behind why they chose to have me fight on their team rather than Angel's.

They were angered by the fact that Angel was shown to be a wolf, but my friend had some cutting words for them, which, even though I was aware that they would spark a fight, I chose to ignore anyhow.

After I concluded that I didn't concur with what they were saying, I noticed that things started moving at a more leisurely pace. Simultaneously, bullets started to emerge from the tree where they had been concealed. It appeared as though the amount of cover available was really limited.

When I turned around to meet Angel, he had already begun firing his weapon the minute the first round affected him. Since he had taken refuge behind the debris that had been left behind after an explosion that had taken place earlier, this man was still alive. The kinetic energy dragged me back, and at a certain time, a bullet impacted my shoulder. I didn't feel it.

I continued shooting, and then I sprang to my feet and ran down the side of the house, continuing to fire as I went. I was able to successfully take cover behind the house. After I had completed reloading my weapon while it was in the air, I threw it laterally across the yard from a window on the second floor of the building.

I was able to figure out the route of the bullets that had followed me as I had fallen to the ground and then rolled behind the vehicle that was coming closer to the tree line. I was able to do this because the bullets had followed me as I had fallen to the ground and then rolled behind the truck. As I went down to the ground, this trail of bullets continued to follow behind me.

Angel whispered the words "Show off" in my direction as she looked at me with open eyes. I humiliated him by berating him and pointing my finger at him as a kind of reprimand. After turning my head, I could see that they were carrying on with the firing.

Before they had even begun to focus their fire, Angel had already eliminated two of them with headshots. I looked over and watched a bullet come dangerously close to hitting him in the head as he stood up and hurled a wooden beam at them, which caused the entire group to be brought to the ground. It seemed as though he was permanently embroiled in a fit of irrational wrath.

He looked at me and nodded as he continued to charge forward while simultaneously hopping over the wreckage. As a response, I tossed down my rifle, retrieved my other weapons, and then shot one of the men in the head as he stood as I was climbing over the hood of the car.

A few seconds later, I was hit by a tree, which knocked my firearms out of my hands and prevented me from firing them. I was unable to fire them because they were no longer in my possession. Because my hands were already full with my weapons, I was unable to discharge them. When I turned around to confront my assailant, I saw that someone else had already been involved in a collision with him.

When I turned my attention back to Angel, I noticed that he appeared to have tossed the other person toward the first person. I came to this conclusion when I transferred my focus back to him.

I inquired with a grin. "Who's showing off?"

I took out my knife and flung it towards Angel, who immediately adopted a shocked expression as a result of my action. The final man was blinded when the dagger that had been flying past his head caught him in the eye socket. This caused him to lose his sight.

As a response to my inquiry, he narrowed his eyes at me and mumbled, "I knew he was there."

"You are absolutely right," I responded.

After we had just gotten out of a fight, he looked around and saw that we had taken care of everyone, so while we were disposing of the dead and setting fire to them, I bragged and boasted a little bit about how well we had handled the situation. After all, we had just gotten out of a fight. As the fires blazed, we concluded that the bunker would be the safest place for us to be.

Collect our stuff, and then make a hasty retreat in the direction of Rakai, preferably before the vamps' clan is aware that their warriors have disappeared. At the same time as Angel was gathering our belongings, I went back to the tracing I had been working on. The moment I took a whiff of it, I was acutely aware of the precise location at which I was supposed to be.

Before we headed off, we ensured that we prepared by taking every precaution possible. Because I wanted to take one more look at our house before we went, I turned the car around as we were pulling away from the curb. I have a suspicion that this could be the very last time we run across it for a substantial length of time; it's been a while since we've seen it.

CHAPTER 22
UNLEASHING INNER STRENGTH

Angel

While we drove across the city on our approach to Rakai's rescue, we continued thinking of different strategies to accomplish our mission.

"Shall we just go in and attack?" Cypher posed the question when he was attempting to appear cool by sitting on the passenger side of the car like a gangster and lifting his feet on the car's port. I gave him a quick glimpse at the deserted road before firmly tapping his feet to get them off the floor. As a result of this, he was so taken aback when his feet landed on the floor that he almost fell out of his seat.

"Dude! The hell?" he exclaimed to which I replied with a snort.

"Are you a pig?" After asking that, a pain inside my cheek made me grimace. I gurgled my saliva, trying to gather the blood I tasted before spitting it outside the window.

"No, you are."

I poked him in the eye with my middle finger, and he chuckled. However, we should give thanks to all the saints since he didn't put his feet back. I had no way of knowing what kind of spirit had entered him because of him putting on his full-blooded shoes.

I couldn't help but shake my head because he didn't appear to take anything seriously. I was aware it was his strategy for maintaining his composure, but in situations like this one, I truly wish he would take things as seriously as I do.

"Aren't you worried?" I asked, fixing my eyes on the empty, long road.

Along both sides of the road was a seemingly endless row of paddy fields, which gently swayed in the breeze of the celestial dusk. At the very end of the road, directly in front of us, and precisely in the midst of that, was the slender line that divided the dark side of the horizon from the modest peak of the dawn. It was so beautiful . . . that it just served to increase my anxiety.

"Worried? Why?"

"I mean . . . Chris died, and here we are again, risking our lives. What if Rakai also . . ."

"My dear friend." He patted my shoulder, exaggeratedly shaking his head. "Don't be a worrywart, okay? How many times do I have to tell you that I trust Rakai? I don't fully trust her, but I know this is not the end. We trained so hard, and we improved drastically. If there's a strong opponent, I'm sure you'll get stronger."

Although I was clenching my teeth together to prevent myself from morphing and speeding up the process, I was still impressed at how well I was able to maintain control of myself despite the impulse to engage in some risky behavior. Cypher, on the other hand, who always thought with his head rather than with his head in the air, wasn't the same man as me. I should have known that acting irresponsibly in this sort of situation would lead to the same result as it did for Chris.

And even though Cypher and I never brought it up again, I always had the impression that he was just as terrified as I was. Although Rakai wasn't our buddy in the same way that Chris was, our affection for her increased throughout our time together. Because of this, I arrived at the end of the road to find a deserted town after taking four turns and traveling for close to two hours.

I glanced at Cypher who sat up properly now. He was looking in front and would turn his head once in a while to follow something when I drove past. While I focused on what I could see, I knew this place wasn't the same in the city.

As soon as I removed my foot from the acceleration pedal and gently applied pressure to the brake pedal, the vehicle began to decelerate. I cocked my head to the side to see over the top of the car's roof. In front of us was a collection of deserted cottages with roofs constructed from bonded deep deck panel panels. It seems more like a storage facility than a residential building to me.

In addition, there wasn't a car parked in either of the vacant spaces on either side. There was no evidence of permanent occupants or inhabitants that could be seen wandering about, and no people could be seen roaming around. A large, dilapidated, and seemingly deserted three-story structure stood during the clearing.

Cypher hushed, "Park behind those trees," indicating to his side where an entrance to a woodland could be seen. "Park behind those trees." After giving it a few seconds of my attention, I then gave the steering wheel a little twirl.

I also moved the vehicle as slowly as I could while trying to avoid making any audible disturbances, even though I was aware that I had no control over the noise that was produced by the engines.

After parking my car hidden among the trees, I went for a walk around the nearby woods. Remarkably, I was able to stroll through this for a quarter of an hour and reach the conclusion. But it was more than enough to disguise us; in addition to the stench of the dead animals and the waste heap in the area, it may mask our scent as well.

"You check on the right and I'll go to the left. Once clear, we meet at the entrance of that building—"

I sneered at Cypher's idiotic orders. "Don't you think that we should check together?"

"Dude, I know you need me, but it will be just for a few sec. You'll never notice my disappearance," he teasingly said.

"Fuck you, Cy. Be serious here. Sticking together will lessen the chances of dying alone. What if you walk past with five of them? Then, you'll be dead in a minute. Two is better than one."

"Yeah, right, Mr. Right. Just bring a decaying head of an animal in your pocket to hide your smell. You stink, literally."

Rolling my eyes, I couldn't agree more with him. Vampires like him were very sensitive to my smell. We'll be busted after a second of stepping out in this forest.

I obeyed Cypher's order. Even though the decayed head of this squirrel looked gross and smelled like a canal, I still slid it into my pocket. I wanted to cover it with plastic to avoid the feeling of touching it bare, but what's the purpose of bringing it with me if I could hide its smell?

That's Cypher's way of thinking. We decided to examine the area more thoroughly before deciding whether or not to try to force our way through the door and save our comrade. Though I really wanted to go inside now and save Rakai, I knew I shouldn't let my emotions get better than my rational.

"Both sides of the building are clear. No signs of anyone."

"Where are they? Do you think they are in this building?" As if my question was the dumbest he ever heard, he made a disgusting face.

"Dude? Are you okay? Where else? This is the one in my vision. I know they are here." He pointed to the old, cracked cement walls we're using as a shield to prove what he was saying.

"Then why can't we track them with our nose, or ears, or aura?"

"As if I know the answer."

Sometimes, I really wanted to smack Cypher in his head to try fixing how his brain works. Especially when a serious matter like this happened, I couldn't take any joke from him. Maybe that's why I was hard on him during our sparring.

Those were the only times I could hit him hard and feel super good about it. I wasn't doubting his vision. I knew he could do it (he practiced it for three consecutive days without food or water or any drop of blood), but if we couldn't sense anything, then that meant that these people were on the highest level.

Cypher picked a finger-long-sized stick at the side and started to draw the plan he created on the ground. Although I admittedly agree with his plan, I knew I could still think of a better one, a plan where we both didn't need to engage in a suicide mission. But I knew I wasn't in the condition to do so.

If I did, I would have already thought of something while we're still on the way. And I knew Cypher felt it too. That's why he tried to come up with a plan on his own.

After suggesting a few things, we started to move as quietly as possible. Rakai taught us how to lower our aura to avoid any detection, and how to move quietly but quickly. Cypher was in front. His body was lowered a bit as he opened a door that was about to fall with a single kick.

It was opened and was only hanging with a single screw at the top. It created a creaking sound in slow motion. I glanced at Cypher who didn't care about the sound he created after pushing aside the hanging door.

Although he did it gently, I still couldn't bring myself to stop worrying. We got inside successfully. Without any signs of enemies noticing us or any signs of discomfort in the air.

I didn't know if the head of the squirrel was very effective in hiding my odor if we both had mastered the art of hiding, or if the enemies were playing with us. Neither of them, we still continued to walk – going to the second floor now. We followed the shadows that were created by the light from the moon which was now brightening three times more.

After reaching the third floor, we saw nothing. No signs of anything.

"I can't understand . . . my vision was very clear. This is the warehouse!" Cypher's frustrated voice echoed in the abandoned building like a whisper of a ghost. I tried to stop him, but he was too frustrated.

"I can't believe this! My vision can't be a failure."

"Stop it, Cy. Being frustrated will lead to nothing. Let's try one more time—"

"No. I know this is the right place, Angel."

I looked at him. His face was darkened with his own shadow, but his eyes were bright. It looked at me as if sending a message to my soul. And I knew at that moment, Cy was telling the truth.

"I believe you."

"Then why aren't they here? They should be here. I envisioned a scene where we would face them."

I looked around. From the ceiling, walls, and finally to the dusted floor where our footprints were imprinted. I kneeled and followed our tracks with my eyes. Cypher mumbled something on his own when I realized something.

"Cypher," I called, but he didn't answer, and instead, kept on mumbling under his breath. He's trying to trace Rakai once again, using the piece of cloth he's holding. I glanced at him and called him once again, this time, with a loud voice.

"What?!"

"I think they are still not here."

"Huh?"

"They are still not here. Look." I stood up, walked beside him, and pointed out the dusty floor with our footprints. "If they are here, I'm sure this floor shouldn't be full of dust. Even if they are bats, they will still need to step here, right?"

Cypher stopped. He stared at the floor for a while before nodding his head at me. "You're right. That must mean that . . . my vision was for the future?"

I smirked at him. Even though I didn't confirm or decline, he smirked back at me with his smug, and proud face. I shook my head because I was sure he was showing off now.

"We should go now. We might see them along the way."

Without any ado, we moved back to the car. I started the engine and just about a second after our car's muzzle was out of the forest, we immediately saw Rakai being dragged out of the van. Her image of being dragged down and kicked like some dead meat, I couldn't help but imagine myself murdering every one of them.

They just simply didn't have any conscience left. Whatever they were or whoever their names were, I would make sure to make them pay!

"Watch out!" Cypher cautioned me to move out of the road as he believed that we were going to collide with something.

It made perfect sense that we were in the old manufacturing sector of the city because there were no other occupants there but homeless people, and it was common for homeless people to vanish without a trace. I was able to notice the presence of a few vamps now unlike earlier, but not nearly as many as I would have anticipated based on the number of people in the vicinity that I saw dropping off the van.

Because of the loud screech and the obvious presence of our car, the bloodsuckers were now looking at us. Some of them growled and positioned their pale bodies to attack. I frowned when I saw five of them stay and the others started to get inside the building. I even met the eyes of those women we saw in the valley.

I murmured a curse and moved the stick shift, preparing to hit the gas pedal to its full power and run them with the car. But Cypher held my hand and shook his head.

"What's wrong?" I asked, irritated that he stopped me from flattening the vamps' heads.

The grin on Cypher's face said it all, "Hey, I've got an idea," he remarked.

"Well, what is it?" That's what I had to say in response.

While I was climbing the ladder to get down from the roof, he said, "Let's go for a drive."

Smiling as he got ready to drive away, he added, "You've taken it long enough, fatty."

Asked, "Are you going to tell me what we're going to do?" As he made his way down the alley, I repeated my question.

"You'll see," he said with a big grin.

We drove for a bit before I grasped what he had in store for me. Yes, if that's your intended course of action. As a result of this, I began to chuckle.

"Oh, have you figured it out?" he said, never stopping with his toothy smile.

Cypher instructed me to remain in the warehouse for a few moments after we had pulled up.

"Were you going?" I asked.

Quickly, he jumped out of the car and sped off. "I'm going to start some crap, just keep the car running."

Having climbed into the driver's seat, I sat back and started smoking. When

I first heard the gunfire, I was only about halfway through. Then I heard a bang on the roof, and Cypher cried, "Go! Go!" while I searched for him. "It's time to get going!"

I accelerated down the road as soon as I put my foot on the throttle. Cypher entered the house stealthily through one of the open windows. He had a grin that reached from ear to ear. Before I had the chance to react, a gunshot rang out from behind us.

"I suppose you grabbed their attention," I said.

After that, he extended his middle finger in their direction while leaning out the window. It seemed like an eternity as we made our way back to Factory Alley because the dogs were following us the entire time. There were only a few occasions in which we came perilously close to being attacked, but we were only able to shoot a couple of the dogs that got too close for comfort.

The journey back to Factory Alley felt like an eternity. When we were about halfway through our trek, Cypher said.

"Okay, let them go." It didn't take very long at all both to my outstanding driving talents and his precision shot accuracy, which both contributed to the short amount of time it took. After that, we went back to where we were and re-climbed to the vantage point that we had previously established on the roof so that we could carry on our observations.

When we first entered the old plant, there was a great deal of disruption, and I assumed that it was a result of the noise that we produced. From a distance of a few blocks away, we were able to witness wolves protecting us by patrolling the area for us. Even though they appeared to be concerned about where we were, I could see that they were already aware of our whereabouts.

A new structure had been constructed in front of the old factory, and there were people spotted roaming about the grounds of the old plant. We waited for a few more minutes until we heard the screams and saw the bullets begin to rain from the sky before continuing to wait. Men screamed in despair as wolves emerged from the shadows and began to attack them.

Cypher grinned and added, "That's our cue."

Having examined my gear, I responded, "I guess we should head to the back garage area."

On the other hand, he indicated his assent by nodding his head. The two of us sneaked up behind them, and while Cypher peered over and communicated with hand signs, we sliced their necks. We moved toward the back, where we knew there would be a bigger number of men because we were anticipating that this would be the case. The fact that they weren't vampires caught me off guard in a big way.

Low-pitched "I hate familiars," Cypher muttered.

"Okay, blade," I replied with a raised eyebrow.

Cypher noticed my curious gaze as he bent over and began drinking. Asked, "What?"

"Waste not," he ended.

"It's still disgusting," I said.

"I think you should do the same. We don't know what we're going to find," he added.

Although I was reluctant to comply with your request, I did so nevertheless because I could feel a surge of excitement building up inside of me at the prospect of doing so. There were certain advantages to drinking blood, even though I didn't particularly enjoy the flavor of blood. After we had done it, we noticed that the radio had been turned on, and in the background, we could hear extremely loud growls calling for extra support. The method that we chose was the right one.

As soon as we turned our backs on the plant and faced it head-on, we noticed that the neon signs were beginning to rock back and forth. As the clouds moved closer to the tall building, which was already quite windy, the wind kicked up considerably. Cypher has captured my attention at this time.

"That's not at all odd," he murmured, his gaze fixed on the sky.

"Let's do this," I said, walking towards the building.

Once we were inside the building, we began to navigate our way through its many halls and corridors to reach our destination. We encountered a very small number of issues despite the activity that was going on all around us. Before we were able to locate Rakai, we had to search through multiple piles of trash.

She participated in a gathering with several other individuals in a room at the time. We were only able to recognize one of them, and her name was Kasha. She was the woman who had been on the rooftop earlier.

The enormous ring, which was placed towards the back of the room and had a dark green sheen, was rotating quickly but gave off the appearance that it was flickering.

"Do you think we can take 'em?" My haze from staring at the light was broken by Cypher's words.

"I shouldn't even have to justify that with an answer," I said as I changed my mags.

"What the heck is that?" he asked.

As I watched Cypher's eyes light up, I said, "I'm not sure, but I'm getting a Stargate vibe from it."

"Wow!!!" he exclaimed.

"Don't even think about it," I said with a chuckle.

"Fine," he huffed and smashed through the pane of glass to get to the other side.

There were only three of them left when they made an impact on the surface of the earth, and they needed to be eliminated. I couldn't believe what I was seeing, so I made a hasty descent from where I was standing. Everyone else in the room, except for one man who was standing at the back, was taken aback by what had just happened.

We had already taken cover before the sudden appearance of five troops pointing their rifles in our way.

"Kill them!" Suddenly, a barrage of bullets was heading our way, and Kasha yelled.

"Stop!" The man in the rear yelled. "I could smell the dog for a little while now. It's truly odd to see you two together. I didn't want to believe my love when she told me, but yet here you are."

While Cypher was protecting Rakai, he signaled for me to take shelter by pointing in my direction and saying, "Cover fire."

I did as I was told. I fired the trigger, which resulted in all five of the men being shot in rapid succession, and ultimately one of the men being killed in the line of duty. Rakai snatched Cypher out of the air and threw him to the ground when he was in the middle of doing the blink technique.

When I saw it, I was so shocked that I couldn't believe what I was seeing. His adversary smirked at him and shoved him to the ground rather than engaging him in combat. From a great distance, I was able to make out the voice of the man yelling at me "Come out here."

As I got closer, I kept a close eye on the man and Kasha to make sure neither of them had any weapons, and then I took a few steps back before continuing to go forward. I told the man that Rakai was the only target we had while directing my crosshairs at the man's head and pointing out that Rakai was the only target we had.

When the man shifted his attention back to the object that was spinning, he uttered a phrase that was roughly equivalent to "Sorry, but he is mine."

After he had finished his statement, he snapped his fingers, and at that moment, the blood of the soldiers who had fallen started to trickle toward the disc. He stated, "But there is still a need for more."

As it disappeared into the light, it made the light brighter as it continued to spread. Cypher had now managed to stand on his own and was observing my situation from a vantage point above us both. Simply by looking at me, he was able to figure out what I was thinking because he was standing in front of me.

He was now facing me after turning around. When I ran into them, all three of them were being fired upon by the other side. After my first shot hit the man in the head, I began spraying, striking Kasha in the arm, and aiming my shots toward the robot.

My second shot hit the man in the chest. There was a whirlwind of activity that was happening at the same time. Rakai's scream was the most audible of any of the others that could be heard.

My eyes saw a fleeting sight of the discharge of Cypher's firearms as they were pointed toward the individual. To all appearances, he was merely striking a pose for the camera. As Kasha pounced at him, a confrontation between the two of them immediately broke out.

I turned around to confront the person who had been staring at me from the very beginning of our interaction. The torrent of evil that was emanating from him was symbolized by the steam that was flowing from his eyes. Red smoke was on the verge of being released into the atmosphere.

I gave it one more shot, but by that point, it was obviously too late for me to be successful. I was unable to answer when all of a sudden, he had me in his sight, and I was slammed against the back wall of the room as a result. I was taken aback since I didn't think that I'd ever been struck that hard in the past, thus the severity of the blow took me by surprise.

To have a better understanding of what was going on, I cast my gaze upward. I noticed that the man was looking away from me to keep an eye on what was going on between Kasha and Cyphers while they were arguing, and I concluded that he was monitoring their conflict.

Rakai, who was still tied up and looked intently at the incoming foe as I watched him make his way into the conflict, came into view as I watched him enter the fray. Rakai maintained this behavior the entire time I observed him from a distance. Rakai was released, and I informed her that her blades were in Cypher's bag, which was lying on the ground nearby.

The bag belonged to Cypher, who was standing nearby. It was clear that she was aware that they were present. She then turned around to face them once she had finished delivering that comment.

My focus was drawn to Cypher as the attacker moved in for a blow, but he dove and sidestepped the blow until Kasha struck him in the face with her boots. At that point, I turned my attention back to the attacker. At that point, he was rendered unconscious by a blow to the head.

I shot her in the kneecap with a revolver, and she immediately fell to the ground writhing in agony after she was hit. The man's features became further twisted with wrath as he made his way back to his house. Despite everything that had gone wrong, I found myself back on the ground, wailing in agony.

He had his hands on Cypher's neck and was holding up Cypher's throat with them at the same time. The man proceeded to pierce Cypher's flesh with his claws, and blood began to flow from both of his necks as a result. It is not the case anymore . . .

At one point, I used everything I had and crashed into him with all my strength, which caused him to fall to the ground and electrocute himself while simultaneously sending shockwaves throughout the room. He smiled broadly at me while giving me the thumbs-up sign and pointing to both of my hands at the same time. I couldn't believe my eyes when I saw that they had ballooned to monster sizes and that the length of my claws had also risen over time.

I couldn't help but break out in a grin as I watched them return to their former size after being shrunk down. Before regaining her composure, Kasha stood up and screamed out a series of expletives before regaining her composure. I couldn't help but laugh nervously while I was racing up and glancing at her at the same time.

Her pupils began to spread further apart as I got closer, and before she had a chance to scream, I put the palm of my hand around her entire head and held it there. This was before she realized what was happening. As I continued to press her onto the ground despite her struggles, plasma began to flow from my hands.

I continued to crush her. I persisted in doing so until she became limp, at which point I was unable to move her any further due to my inability to move her further.

"Who's showing off now?" Cypher looked up at me and said that.

I drew a deep breath and retreated to my own space. "That's pretty awesome," he finished.

Before I could react, the man got up from his electrotherapy treatment and left the room. You are a group of insular fools, that's for sure. As the man began to transform, he yelled at his attackers.

"How dare you come into my house and butcher my women!" as he began to alter his appearance.

When he finished, he said, "You will die here tonight." In the blink of an eye, his eyes became as black as night. His complexion went a dark red as he erupted, shredding his shirt in the process. Cypher's eyes were wide as I approached, and I said, "Fuck . . ." Cypher stated this, as well.

He turned to face me and remarked, "You don't become thin again."

In response to his reassurance, "I'm sure man that was a heat of the moment thing."

Taking a deep breath, he said, "Well dude, this situation just got pretty fucking heated."

Rakai launched a surprise attack on the man from behind, plunging both of his blades into his neck. He then held on to one of the blades while using the other to repeatedly stab the man in the neck. The man screamed out in agony just before seizing Rakai and kicking her to the ground.

In addition to going above his head and hitting him in the face with a punch. Cypher stamped his foot forward as the man yelled in wrath, hitting the man in the mouth, and causing him to bleed. The man continued to scream.

When I fired my gun at the individual, I couldn't believe my eyes when the bullets continued to deflect harmlessly off of him even though I was firing at him. As the man continued to approach me, he pulled a furious face and shoved Cypher out of the way with his hand as he got closer to me. The action slowed down, and a machine in the backdrop began to whir and create pulsating lights as the tempo changed.

As I was in a position where I had no other choices accessible to me at the time, I did the first thing that came to mind, which was to punch him in the face as hard as I could. I did this because I felt like I had no other choice. and it had absolutely no effect whatsoever on the situation.

My neck made a squeaky sound as a man smirked at me and held me in his arms, which caused my neck to make the sound. He made me cough and gasp for air in response to his actions. I tried to harm the man hat by kicking and punching it, but it seemed to be impenetrable to my assaults.

I finally gave up. I had just recently fallen and had just begun to take some breaths, when all of a sudden, the blackness that was all about me overwhelmed me. When I opened my eyes, I saw the man staggering backward in agony, with his sword partially embedded in his forearm.

I had been out for a while. Behind a bush was where I had been hiding. Cypher has come up to speak with me here. "Are you okay?"

"Yeah, I'll be fine," After I gave my response, the man swiftly grabbed Cypher and proceeded quickly through both him and the wall while cutting through the wall with the sword. Before I could even stand up, he did it. The sight of my best friend being stabbed through the chest after being slammed into the wall filled me with dread as I watched the scene unfold.

He had not moved an inch from that position at all. Because I was so enraged, I went and grabbed the thing that was in the most immediate vicinity to me and swung it at the man. I continued to deal heavy blows to him even as my skin peeled away, and I got larger.

Even while I did this, I was still able to overcome him. I lunged at the man with my teeth and claws extended menacingly, and I attacked him with great ferocity. I first observed the man's wide eyes and then proceeded to stab and hack him multiple times before forcing him to the ground.

Before biting down on his shoulder and sending him flying into his spinning machine, I tore chunks of his scarlet flesh off his body. The man who was lying on the ground had his flesh torn apart everywhere, and his skin was returning to its natural form when I grabbed a large console from the ground and slammed it into him before he could say anything.

The man was left lying on the ground with his flesh torn apart everywhere. The normal appearance of his skin was starting to emerge. As a direct result of this, sparks started falling from the sky onto the horrible scene.

It occurred to me that Cypher was still perched on the wall, so I decided to concentrate my efforts on him instead. As the machine grew increasingly dangerous, I moved closer to him in the direction that he was facing to get out of its way. The man had a grin on his face as he pressed the button on the control panel, and the pulses became significantly stronger as he did so.

I went as fast as I could over to Cypher, and while I was dragging him away, I sliced him with my sword. I started to run when I heard a laugh that sounded sinister; but, as soon as I did, everything around me turned white.

CHAPTER 23

INTO THE UNKNOWN REALM

Cypher

The people who believed in His words would always say that everything that was happening was according to His plans. He had set a whole plan for your life, and whatever His believers chose, they would never escape His plans.

"Don't you think that's absurd?" Angel, who had been cursing under his breath while driving his hands with the game controller.

I had to blink quite a few times. My eyesight was progressively improving as I continued to blink, and after a few seconds, I felt shocked to see my old room from a few years ago. I continued to blink, and my eyesight continued to improve.

I felt conscious of the fact I was seated on my bed while Angel sat in front of me with his back turned to me. I creased my brow and tried to ask a question by opening my mouth, but instead of retaining control of my own body, I shook my head at him. I made a face by furrowing my brow and trying to open my mouth to ask a question.

"That's what my mother always told me. I just grew up believing it."

What the hell . . . where was I?

"You know, Cy . . ." Angel mumbled something as he hurled yet another slur at the person who had recently gone away, and his voice grew softer as he did so. He pressed the buttons as if doing so would bring back his character, but after nearly bringing the whole thing to a halt, he threw it on the ground and turned his head to look at me. He appeared to be confused.

"Whether you believe in it or you grew up believing that, choosing the path you'll walk on is entirely up to you."

I was jolted awake by a booming thump, which caused my paralyzed body to jolt upwards by an inch before tumbling onto a hard and jagged surface below me. My previously blurry perspective of my surroundings suddenly became crystal clear as I moaned in pain and glanced around for whatever it was that had given me a small stab in the back.

As I looked around, I realized that the pain had been caused by something that had given me a small stab in the back. I tried to sit my body up when I suddenly felt a severe stabbing pain and an electric tingling all over my complete body at the same time. When I looked up, Angel stood above me with a sword pointed at my chest.

He was less than half an inch away from stabbing me, and the pain was so excruciating that I was on the verge of yelling out in agony. Despite this, I found that I was unable to clear my throat and my voice grew hoarse.

This bastard . . . Was he going to kill me?! "What the fuck are you doing?" I spoke.

Angel's face was a picture of complete bewilderment as he looked at the situation. As he moved away from me and pulled his sword to the side, his eyes began to bulge, and the point of the sword that he had been holding against me began to shake. After that, he responded with an odd grin.

"Dude, I thought you were dead. I pulled the sword out of you and your eyes shot open. How amazing was that, right?"

"Oh . . ." I stared at the cut on my chest, which was beginning to close and start the healing process. When I looked down, I saw a thin cloud of smoke being produced by it as my tissues began to rebuild themselves. After one minute, everything went back to normal, except for the totality of my clothing, which was preserved in its original state.

"Well, I guess that rules out the theory of my getting stabbed through the heart. I'm immortal then. Minus the sun." I couldn't help but break into a wide grin as I extended my hand in front of me. It was a dried-out stain of blood that ran all the way down my arm from my elbow to my underarm. The stain began on my elbow and ended at my underarm.

"Not funny, dude," was all he said as he stood properly and gave me his hand to help.

I let out a chuckle at his expense and then rubbed my butt to clean it off. When I turned around to gaze in front of me, I was genuinely anticipating a typical image consisting of a bloody battleground filled with smoking corpses. But as the thumping sound continued to spread from my soul, adding to the sound of waves crashing and the salty breeze of the night, I realized that we had moved quite away from where we had been before. And the questions were . . .

"Where are we? And where is Rakai? Why are you alone?" I rose up and looked about, making sure I wasn't still dreaming like I had been earlier. My face was painted with a look of complete bewilderment. When I saw the shimmering hollow of what appeared to be an unending darkness of the ocean which mirrored the bright starry sky, it caused me to gulp down my own dried saliva.

The line at the end revealed the limitation of my eyesight, and it made me realize that my vision was restricted.

"I don't know, man, that machine blew in the factory, and I woke up here alone. I planned to look around to search for her and just carry you, but I obviously can't do that with this sword on your chest," he said as he showed me the bloodless sword.

"That's so freaking funny, I could literally die."

Angel showed his disapproval by shrugging his shoulders. I took a close look at his outward looks. His garments, like mine, were in pieces, and the sleeve that should have been on his right arm was nowhere to be found. The inhumane way his pants were cut produced an irregular hemline that exposed his hairy, wolf-like feet.

"Dude, we're lucky enough—"

However, neither one of us moved until we became aware of a rustling sound that was coming from the branches and leaves surrounding us. The placid, unnoticed front of the woodland gave the impression of being a setting for the terrifying monster that is shown in horror shows. I repositioned myself so that my back was to the front line, which denoted the beginning of the dense, hollow forest. I did this so that I might turn around.

Angel came up to me and joined me in standing here, and we are both presently watching the trunks of the trees as they shift position in the wind. It was made spookier by the unusual aspect of the sky, which covered what had been a clear view of the heavens with large cloud forms, cutting the view of the full moon in half. The noise of the waves, in contrast to the eerie stillness of the forest that lay in front of them.

Everything made me anxious, and for some reason, my senses intensified, so I couldn't help but feel terrified . . . and rushed at the same time. My gaze wandered throughout the surrounding area. I was looking for something, in the hopes that it might provide answers to the questions that were running through my thoughts at this very moment. To put it another way, did I have the nerve to question everything?

Were the events that had transpired ever since that day that we got to that mountain a coincidence, or had they been planned out in advance? I turned to look at Angel, who had just handed me the sword.

"You use this, and I'll use this," he said, almost growling as he turned his arms to his wolf form.

I gave him a crooked smirk as he knew that this tactic was better suited to the way I battle, and I knew that he was aware of this fact. My intention was to give a humorous response, but the background noise continued to pick up in volume and speed. Angel indicated some distance ahead in the direction where it seemed as though someone had strung led light strips through the trees.

The moon in the sky was completely absent at this point. The light that gave humans the ability to see in the dark had turned against us and was no longer on our side. My improved vision was unable to keep up with whatever it was that was moving, and I wasn't sure if it was a beneficial development or not.

As we drew closer, I smelt something that brought back memories of a place that was decrepit and horrifying that I had been to previously, so we decided to travel over there to check the location. We moved slowly but made sure that every step was calculated and full of care. I looked over at Angel.

However, despite the knowing look he gave me, I had to ask him the question myself.

"Remember that smell?" I asked Angel, making sure that I wasn't hallucinating or imagining things.

"No way . . ." he said to me, his claws showing sharply.

"You smell that too?" I spoke.

"Yeah, it smells like blood," he said.

At that very instant, we were startled by the sound of a loud roar coming from a distance, and it appeared as though birds were fleeing from the nearby trees. I followed the birds as they flew, and while I'll admit that their loud twirling did distract me, I instantly raised the sword that I held in front of me and prepared to cut through anything that might stand in my way.

"I don't think we are in Kansas anymore," I said to Angel, without moving anything or giving him a glance.

"And what gave you that impression, genius?" I was nearly able to comprehend what he said since I was certain that his fangs were about the same size as my finger and as thick as a tube. He's not talking, but he is growling, and that much is certain.

"The glowing fucking trees, the weird fucking sky, or the T-Rex roar we just heard," he said, back clearly not amused. I heard his loud thump on my side, indicating that he started to walk.

"I don't think it was a T-Rex," was all I replied, trying to joke but in a serious tone and low voice.

We went into the woods and started hiking through the underbrush to get where we needed to go. We hastened our progress in the direction of the opening in the clouds as soon as we became aware of its existence up ahead. As we proceeded further into the cave, the air became increasingly tight and heavier.

Even though I wasn't running or doing anything particularly strenuous, I could sense that my chest was moving up and down, as if I were having difficulty breathing. And as we continued to make our way deeper into the forest, suddenly, the sound vanished. I turned my head to look at Angel, who dribbled saliva and got his whole head ready to morph at any moment.

"Where the hell is that now?" I whispered under my breath.

I looked to my side and in front of me while simultaneously doing the same thing for a whole fucking second. That's when I observed a man standing just beyond the tree line, and all the hair on my body stood on end. His entire form was composed of dark outlines. If it hadn't been for the putrid smell coming from that way, I would have had a hard time determining whether or not that was the body of a human or a tree.

As we inched closer, however, we saw that it was the same man that we had just fought. It was the same pair of bloodshot, deadly eyes, and there was a distinct odor of gloom all around him. As I readied my brand-new sword by putting my feet and hands in the appropriate positions, Angel grabbed a neighboring tree, let out a loud roar, and came dangerously close to uprooting the tree.

We walked up to talk with him in his place. I was so sure that this would be difficult, but after a few slashes of my sword and Angel's flung off his arms and feet, the man eventually went on his knees after trying to dodge our attacks. I was surprised because I was so sure that this would be difficult.

I licked my lips and stared at Angel, who was wiping his mouth with his human hand at that very moment. I only needed a wink from him to realize what was expected of me. I brought the point of my sword up to the man's neck and held it there.

"Where the fuck are we?" I addressed the question to the man who was knelt on the precipice.

"You truly know nothing, and it really doesn't matter what you do to me. I have opened the tear and soon, my siblings will know it as well," he chuckled a bit, weak from something, maybe he was full of wounds and coughed on some blood.

"What tear?" Angel said.

The man shot him an evil glare and I pushed harder on his neck with the sword.

"I will tell you nothing as you are meaningless in the whole plan and you will not last long here, I can assure you that. Just kill me and be done with it. the dark realm will consume you."

Before he could continue, I ripped his head from his shoulders, and Angel threw his body off the edge of the cliff. The head of the man smiled as it dropped down to the ground at my feet. "The dark realm," I said to Angel.

I looked out across the horizon while simultaneously raising my gaze to the heavens. The sky gradually took on a color that could only be described as emerald. His position was unlike anything we had ever seen before since it appeared to have a pillar of power that shot raw energy right into the sky.

His place was unlike anything we had ever seen before. I looked over at Angel. He turned his head to gaze at me and asked, "Did you bring your light? I need to have a smoke."

ACKNOWLEDGMENT

I would like to extend my heartfelt gratitude to everyone who contributed and became my motivation and inspiration throughout the years of the creation of this book, titled *"The Chronicles of the Dark Realm."*

ABOUT THE AUTHOR

Auron Asteroth, a talented writer hailing from Canada, was born in 1987. With an unwavering passion for the written word, Auron aspires to become a full-time writer, captivating readers with captivating tales and vivid worlds.

Despite the challenges that life throws his way, Auron remains steadfast in pursuing his dream, embracing every opportunity to let his imagination run wild and bring his stories to life.

Through his unique pen name, Auron Asteroth weaves enchanting narratives that leave a lasting impact, proving that dreams can be chased and accomplished while still relishing every moment of life's journey.

www.ingramcontent.com/pod-product-compliance
Lightning Source LLC
Chambersburg PA
CBHW070847280626
47161CB00017B/2794

* 9 7 8 1 7 3 8 0 6 0 6 0 3 *